THE WIDOW

The Widow

Aidan Phelan

Copyright © 2024 by Aidan Phelan

All rights reserved. No part of this book may be reproduced in any manner whatsoever without written permission except in the case of brief quotations embodied in critical articles and reviews.

First Printing, 2024

Many of the places featured in this novel are drawn directly from fact, but characters and events are completely fictionalised.

Cover design by Aidan Phelan

Front cover image: Pearson and Co's new pocket map of Victoria. 1865. [Source: National Library of Australia, 912.945, Libraries Australia ID 7496631.]

FICTION

Paperback: 978-0-6457001-6-9
eBook: 978-0-6457001-7-6

 A catalogue record for this book is available from the National Library of Australia

Dedicated to my wife, Georgina: my biggest supporter and most trusted advisor.

One

The warm breeze kicked up dust by the gate of the farm. It was a quiet little selection in Myers Flat with a slab hut situated on the bank of a rivulet. The droughts several years ago had hit the spot hard, and it was only just showing signs of recovery. Tiny yellow-green spears of grass jutted unconvincingly out of parched earth where a paddock would normally be. The rivulet flowed reasonably well, making the banks on either side far lusher than elsewhere.

The slow march of weary hooves crunched in the dirt outside the fence line and a tiny figure dismounted and opened the gate.

Ellen McReady's forehead was glistening with sweat, her broad-brimmed hat was damp with perspiration. The tail end of summer had proven to be no less relentless than the rest of the season despite the anticipation of a cool and wet autumn. She led her bay horse, Old Tom, to the only paddock with grass and removed the saddle and bridle. The horse slowly entered the paddock and headed straight for the trough and drank with great slurps.

As Ellen walked to the homestead, she disturbed an errant chicken that had been pecking at the dust. She stored the riding gear in a tiny dilapidated shed by the front door. An old dog barked weakly from within the house as she entered.

Ellen was a handsome woman in her early forties, whose once sweet, plump features had become more drawn and contoured with delicate lines from the strain of Australian farm life, but she remained pleasant to behold; her face was round-cheeked and friendly but her eyes seemed perpetually tinged with a deep and barely restrained sadness. Her hair was blonde and wavy, but every now and then the breeze would reveal a thin ashen streak hidden among the dun-coloured strands.

The homestead was not a large building. It was little more than one large room divided by a wooden partition covered in newspaper. The first room she entered was the kitchen, which featured a small window above a bench where bread would be prepared, a black pot-belly stove that filled the chimney alcove, and a large wooden dining table that was surrounded by individual wooden chairs instead of the standard bench seating. By the stove an old sheepdog named Little John rested with its head up and alert. It settled once it saw that the new arrival was not a foe.

"Oh, yes, yes, yes..." said Ellen as she sat at the table. She pulled an envelope from her pocket and withdrew a letter and the two *carte de visites* that accompanied it. She recognised the handwriting as her daughter Susie's. Susie had moved to Sydney after marrying and wrote to her mother every month, usually including a small sum of money or some kind of gift. Ellen looked at the first of the photographs, which showed two plump, curly-haired infants in smocks, sitting against a cloth backdrop. This was the first glimpse Ellen had gotten of her twin grandsons as she had not been able to leave the farm to visit the family in the neighbouring colony. The other photograph was of Susie and her husband, Thomas. Ellen studied her daughter's face. She was almost unrecognisable as the barefooted ragamuffin that would chase the dog around the hen house little more than a decade earlier. So much had changed in such a short time.

Ellen had two daughters and a son; all three fledglings had flown from the nest. The boy, Terence, was her youngest and had headed off to work the railroads around Melbourne. Susie, now twenty-one, had married at sixteen and moved to Sydney. Catherine, the eldest, had married a painter and moved to London. Ellen was a mother hen with an empty nest and no rooster to help her tend and protect it since her husband had died of a heart attack a year ago.

Wallace McReady had been a man of many skills. He began his working life as a seaman then upon rediscovering his land legs he took up work as a carpenter's apprentice and then as a miner before finally deciding to focus on farming and working the land to care for his family. The mining money had got them the farm and the farm kept the family fed and housed. For some time, he had been in failing health but one day it all caught up to him and while sitting at the dining table after a delightful repast prepared for him by Ellen he was suddenly gripped by intense pain in his chest and collapsed on the floor. There was no way that a doctor would have been able to reach them before he passed. It was supposed that the Australian summer heat had hastened his demise by putting even further strain on his already weakened heart. Regardless of the cause, Ellen had felt adrift ever since, especially since her boy Terry had been gone almost as long as Wallace had been dead and he had suddenly ceased contact. Her attempts to get the police to investigate had been fruitless and she found that not knowing what had happened was worse than any bad news that might have come her way. Life had fallen apart for her in dramatic fashion.

Little John heaved himself to his feet and shook out the stiffness in his muscles. Padding over to his owner, he nudged her knee with his nose. Ellen stopped and gave the dog an affectionate scratch behind the ear.

She sat at the table and picked up Susie's letter. Ellen's eyes flicked and dipped with each swoop and serif of the cursive text scrawled across the page.

Dear mother,

I pray you are well. It is still strange to think that father is no longer with us. I have included a carte de visite of the little terrors for you. Don't let their angelic smiles fool you, they're positively devilish in the mischief they get up to. Why, just this morning they went into the larder looking for jam and caused a frightful mess! I do hope you can see them soon.

Tom's health has been poor of late. The doctor says it's drinking that causes it, but Tom is always sober as a judge. He has been so yellow you would think he was turning into a Chinaman! He remains in good spirits and despite his illness he still works hard. Some nights he sweats terribly, and the bed is positively soaking. Our affection has not deteriorated one jot and when the mood takes him, he's positively a nuisance! I shall spare you the details but suffice it to say I suspect there will be another grandchild on the way soon. I wish you were here; I do so miss our conversations and a letter every now and then is hardly compensation.

I have also sent you a carte de visite of Tom and I just in case you were wondering how we look these days. I have not heard from brother or sister, but I presume all is well. No doubt Kate is far too busy being a society lady to worry about us and Terry has far more pressing things to concern himself with than writing letters, I'm sure.

Goodbye for now. I shall try to write to you more often. Give Little John a belly rub for me.

Much love,
Susie.

Ellen folded the letter up and tucked it back into the envelope. She looked across the table to the empty chair where her husband would always sit. She imagined him the way he would sit with his legs spread, hands tucked into his breeches, corncob pipe hanging lazily from his mouth. As much as it had surprised her, she found she even missed the way his snoring would interrupt her sleep. She felt like she had lost a limb and could not for the life of her figure out how to adapt to a life without him, yet she was too strong to fade away. Everything just seemed so much harder than it needed to be. She missed the way that he was so affectionate, even after a day of back-breaking labour. The way his rough hands felt on her soft skin when she performed her marital duties always reminded her of how hard he worked to keep everything going.

Suddenly she broke down. The loneliness of life on the colonial frontier was brutal and demoralising. Her belly ached from being underfed, her joints and muscles felt like they were burning, her chest felt tight as she heaved with bitter sobbing forcing its way out of her. Her body tried to purge the deeply rooted sadness and a lusty wail unfurled out of her from a place deep and dark, the kind of sound that only those in the deepest pits of misery and despair know.

Outside the house the dust kicked up again, tarnishing the drying washing hanging on a line near the hen house.

***

As dusk enveloped the selection Ellen rummaged through the pantry for food but only managed some flour and a jar of offal. She opted to go to bed and sleep through her hunger. She was thankful there was only one mouth to feed, but even more thankful that she didn't have to fret about her children starving anymore. There had been many times during the days when Wallace was away for work when she had gone without food to allow her children to eat. She tried to distract herself from the gnawing pain in her stomach but it was driving her mad.

The heat had not died down with nightfall and Ellen decided to sleep nude to try and cool off. She lay unable to relax, staring at the ceiling with the soft flesh of her body, pale and unblemished by the sun where her clothes kept it covered, vaguely luminous as it caught a few rogue beams of moonlight through the window. Her fingers lazily brushed over stretch marks on her belly that reminded her of the times when she was plump with growing babies. She had not relished the experience so much at the time but thinking of it took her back to simpler days.

Her lips pursed and she thrashed around in frustration at her circumstances as much as the pressing discomfort from the unrelenting heat. Unsurprisingly it didn't help.

The following morning Ellen got to work, watering the crops and tending the chickens. She fetched eggs from the hen house and cooked herself breakfast. Yet, despite the welcome food, it was still not enough and given the decreased yield from her kitchen garden her supplies ran low. She had considered finding a job in town, and she had even considered getting on the game and using her home as a shanty, but these ideas were deeply unappealing or impractical. In her desperation, she began to contemplate things that she had never entertained before — things a good, God-fearing woman should not ever consider.

***

Elliot McKenzie was positively furious when he discovered one of his sheep missing. He was bordering on the point of obsession when counting his animals and the fact that a single sheep was gone without a trace had made him apoplectic. He immediately mounted and rode into Ironbark to report it to the police.

"Mr. McKenzie," Senior-Constable Haigh responded with a sigh, "we are understaffed and overworked. The bushranging problem in this district is getting worse by the day, and crime in the town is on the rise too. We have not the manpower to go looking for a lone, bloody sheep. I recommend you get one of your boundary riders to go and look for it. Blasted thing probably just wandered off through a gap in the fence."

"I made sure that mah property was secure, there is *no* way that a sheep could escape. I am outraged! I pay mah taxes and what good has it gotten me? You should be ashamed of yourself," McKenzie ranted, his Glaswegian burr more pronounced in his rage.

"Good day, Mr. McKenzie. Please show yourself to the door," replied Senior-Constable Haigh as he slammed his hands on the reception desk. McKenzie swore under his breath and stormed out. Haigh retired to the office.

The police station was a small wooden slab building with a detached log cell. The office was comfortably secluded from the view of the townsfolk. Haigh sat at his desk and opened a decanter of brandy, pouring himself a decent sized drink. He was a man of thirty-two but felt as if he had lived a hundred lifetimes since joining the police force. The irregular hours and stressful work had seemingly made him age more rapidly than was reasonable for a man of his maturity. His hair was thinning, and his whiskers flecked with grey hairs. He was in charge of two other constables, Molloy and Martin, and charged with servicing a region where crime was rapidly growing out of control since the gold yields were decreasing. He stared at the huge map of Victoria mounted on the wall behind his desk. He wished he was anywhere else, preferably somewhere with a more hospitable climate.

***

Billy Buttons was a man that was best described as hapless. He had spent the past year and a half picking over the remnants of the goldfields along Bendigo Creek. Alas, there was precious little left since the rush had ended a few years earlier. He had followed the creek from Huntly to Kangaroo Flat without success but completely by chance he had made a major find just near the township of Bendigo while looking for a spot to camp.

He had heard the tall tales of men tripping over the nuggets sticking out of the ground, but in this case, it wasn't a tale but reality. He had been walking through the undergrowth and caught his toe on what he thought was just a rock. When he looked down, he realised he had lifted up a gold nugget the size and approximate shape of a ripe pear. He wasted no time in getting to the town and having his photograph taken with the find before he visited the bank. It was a decent nugget, and he was properly flush after cashing it in. He returned to the spot and managed to find a few smaller nuggets nearby that he stowed in his pocket. He felt like things were looking up for him.

It was as he was riding his horse after recovering these nuggets in the vicinity of Ironbark, through an area that was still heavily wooded with box-ironbark trees, that he heard the dreaded cry — "Bail up!"

Before him on the road were three men all mounted on powerful looking horses. They levelled pistols at him and wore grey ponchos, wide-brimmed hats and cloth masks that completely hid their faces.

"Empty your pockets and we won't empty your head of its brains," said the lead horseman in the unique accent of the young men born and raised in the Australian colonies.

Billy was not keen on handing over his wealth and decided to take a big risk. He simply turned and galloped away in the opposite direction. The bushrangers pursued him, closing on him with their superior mounts as Billy bolted through the bush. A shot was fired and went wide of him, but it was enough to make him snap to attention and glance over his shoulder. He darted between trees, dodging branches and crouching in the saddle in order to better stick to it. The bandits kept on his tail like cheetahs pursuing a gazelle. Billy panicked and tried to sham a right turn but only succeeded in confusing his horse and causing it to rear up. The bushrangers scattered to avoid a collision. The horse threw Billy to the ground and escaped. The discarded rider could only stare upwards and wheeze as the wind had been knocked out of his lungs.

The bushrangers dismounted and surrounded him.
"You're game, I'll give you that," said the leader, "foolish, but game."
They rifled Billy's pockets, finding the nuggets in a pouch made from a kangaroo's scrotum. The leader emptied the contents into his palm.
"I'll relieve you of these. You can keep the pouch."
With that the bushrangers mounted and left. Billy took a moment and suddenly remembered something important. He probed his boot and found the banknotes left over from his big find still in place. He sighed with relief, but as he sat up, he felt a burning sensation in his side. He looked down and saw a broken branch had pierced his body just below the ribs. He could see it was a flesh wound and nothing vital was hurt, but he wondered how far he would have to go to find his horse so he could ride to a surgeon. *Just my luck*, he thought.

***

Ellen washed blood from a large butcher's knife. Her dress was also stained with blood, despite her attempts to stay clean, and her hands were soaked in gore. She had remembered the lessons her father, a butcher by trade, had taught her about slaughtering animals and the cuts of meat and applied them to a most nefarious undertaking.

The night before, Ellen had gone to the McKenzie farm and stolen a single sheep. She had managed to get it off the property without raising an alarm and kept it in the barn overnight. The slaughter had been quick but far messier than anticipated. Ellen had no idea how she was going to cover up the evidence and as she had suspended the carcass from a beam in the barn to drain the blood. After the body had been suitably exsanguinated, she skinned and gutted it. She frantically tried to hide the tell-tale signs of what she had done.

As she scrubbed the cutting implements, Ellen chuckled at how easy she had found the process of stealing and butchering a sheep. There was a rush that had gone through her as she had successfully removed the sheep from the squatter's paddock. Something about the danger of being caught thrilled her in a way that made her feel more alive than she had felt in a long, long time. She was positively giddy.

That night, Ellen ate fried mutton and damper. The meat, cooked just so that the outside was brown and crispy, but the inside was tender and pink, was perhaps the freshest meat she could remember eating since her childhood. As she chewed on the fat, her mind was flooded with memories of her youth back in England.

Her father always had fresh, choice cuts of beef, pork or mutton to bring home from work for her mother to cook. Their Sunday roasts after were renowned; the fry-ups that accompanied the morning after a big celebration were absolutely mouth-watering with thick pork sausages, salty slices of ham off the bone and crumbly chunks of black pudding with a side of green peas and fresh bread. Ellen knew her childhood was one of considerable privilege. Her belly was always full, her clothes well kept and her home in a Yorkshire cottage was beautifully furnished and surrounded by idyllic farms and woodland. Her grandparents would always lavish her and her siblings with wonderful gifts. Her most precious possession was a wax doll that she named Tess. It had a sweet face framed with chestnut locks and garbed in a white smock.

When she married Wallace McReady and sailed to Australia, the drop in her quality of living was sudden and profound, but she loved Wallace so much that she was prepared to sacrifice the high standard of living she was used to in order to be with him. She was forced to learn very quickly how to work on a frontier farm and it was a dramatically different environment than the lush English countryside she had grown up in. Proficiency with a hoe and a plough were important skills she learned very quickly. Wallace taught her how to do maintenance work on the house when he was away.

Then she had to learn all about child rearing without the support of her family around her to help her through. She had become reliant on help from the wife of a neighbouring squatter, Mary Ryan, to get her through her last pregnancy, which was not an easy one by any stretch.

For Ellen, church had been a crucial part of her life, allowing her to make connections and build relationships within the community.

When Wallace died Ellen stopped attending church. It was not simply that the loss had dropped her into a state of depression that made her unmotivated to leave the house. The injustice of the death had made her question her faith and she withdrew from engaging with the church. The vicar had made a trip to the farm to coax Ellen back to attending services but had left with his tail between his legs after Ellen had exploded at him with rage and grief.

She stopped chewing momentarily to pluck a chunk of gristle out of her mouth. She looked down at the floor where Little John the sheepdog lay staring up at her, hoping for some food. She looked at what was left on her plate and decided she was no longer hungry. She placed the plate on the ground where the dog gulped down the food and gnawed at the bones. Ellen got up, picked up the hurricane lamp from the kitchen table and headed to bed. She had now had a larder filled with her ill-gotten meat that would keep her going for quite some time. Though she regretted having stolen the sheep, she was feeling quite relieved with the knowledge that she would not be starving any time soon.

Two

The following morning Ellen awoke and followed her usual routine: quick wash up from the basin; eggs for breakfast; get dressed; feed the dog. Everything was normal until she ventured outside where, waiting for her bold as brass, were three men. They were all dressed in threadbare clothes and sweat-stained felt hats. Their faces were smeared with what appeared to be soot or grime anywhere that wasn't covered in hair. Ellen assumed they were miners or stockmen. Rather that fright, the feeling that spread through her was annoyance.

Ellen grumbled under her breath, "That dog is useless!"

The shortest of the men had dark skin, a bushy beard and was dressed in a threadbare, red striped Crimean shirt, cinched with a wide belt around his waist, moleskin trousers and a faded felt hat that had been brown sometime in the past. His deep brown eyes were large and intelligent, his lips were plump behind his facial hair, and there were small scars on his brow and cheek.

The tallest had light brown hair, a wispy blonde beard and wore a blue Crimean shirt under a striped cutaway frock coat. His trousers were ripped but not mended, and held up with a rope. On his feet were kangaroo-skin moccasins, and he had a satchel slung across his chest. His features were thin and handsome in a bookish way. If he were better dressed he wouldn't have looked out of place in a library or as a banker.

However, the most striking and handsome of the three had a far more cultivated appearance, his hair was long, wavy and almost black in colour, his beard was thick and long, his moustache was waxed to curl up at the ends. His blue eyes were piercing and smouldered intensely. He covered up most of his outfit with a dark grey poncho, but around his throat was a blood red neckerchief.

"Ma'am," said the dark-haired man, "We are desperate men in need of food and shelter. I was told you could help," said the dark, handsome stranger.

"Is that so?" Ellen replied with great curiosity, "Are you miners?"

"No."

"Swaggies?"

"Not exactly."

"Well, I can't imagine who would have recommended me as I don't have a lot I can offer. As you might be able to imagine it is hard for a widow to work the land on her own — especially in these conditions. The dry weather has made growing things very difficult, but I have a little meat and some eggs that I can share with you. If it's accommodation you need, there's space in the barn where you can make beds."

The men looked at each other with uncertainty. A keen eye could spot a hint of guilt in their faces.

"Look, instead of standing out here in the sun, why don't you come inside and cool off?" Ellen said. The men nodded and followed her indoors.

Ellen directed the men to sit at the kitchen table. She poured water into cups from a jug on the bench and handed them out. She sat opposite them and interlocked her fingers as she rested her elbows on the table.

She wondered who could have suggested her as someone to seek out. She was not on good terms with her neighbours, whose farms were not exactly close to hers. *Still, when an opportunity presents itself,* she reasoned, *it's best to take full advantage.* Here was a poor widow suddenly presented with three fit, young men to potentially lighten her load around the place.

"My name is Ellen, but you can call me Mrs. McReady."

"Yes, ma'am," the men mumbled.

"What are your names?"

The handsome man was the first to speak.

"My name is John Cooper. The others call me Jack. The short chap in red is Dan Thatcher and the willowy chap is Owen Brady."

"Your name sounds familiar. Should I know you from somewhere?"

"Well," said Jack, "the blunt truth is we're wanted by the law."

Ellen grew nervous but retained a calm exterior.

"Look, missus, we just need somewhere to lie low for a while before we start for the border," said Dan.

"I see," replied Ellen, "and why should I not turn you all in for the price on your heads?"

The outlaws reached behind themselves, and each drew a pistol. They levelled them at the widow. Ellen rolled her eyes.

"Do me a favour and pull the trigger. Do you have any idea how hard it is living the way I have to? No, you're probably too busy out gallivanting about the highways depriving hard working farming folk like me of their hard-earned money and anything shiny they might be carrying. Go on then, fire away!"

Ellen's face took on a baleful expression with pursed lips and furrowed brow. It shocked the men to see such a gentle face take on such a hardened quality. They hesitated, then put their weapons away.

"Sorry, missus,"

"Damned right you are. You want my protection there's got to be something in it for me," Ellen said, pointing her finger at the men.

"What do you want?" Jack asked. "Money?"

"I need workers. There's fences that need mending, animals that need tending. I need someone to take care of the pests that eat up my crops too, scarce as they are. Show me your hands."

The men were confused. Ellen repeated the directive, and the trio extended their hands for inspection.

"Well, I can see that you're not strangers to a little graft. What do you think? I provide you with food, shelter and protection and you provide me with the labour I need to keep the place running. Fair?"

The men silently consulted. It was a better deal than any of them were likely to get from anywhere else. Besides, they could not help but be taken in by Ellen's assertiveness and her quick wit. She was, in a word, formidable. Jack nodded to her.

"So, we have an accord?" said Ellen.

"I suppose we do."

"Alright. Finish your drinks then I'll show you around. Trust me; a bit of honest labour will do you all a world of good. And put those bloody guns somewhere I don't have to look at them."

Jack smirked wryly as he ran his gaze over this firecracker of a widow who had the audacity to dictate terms to armed criminals.

***

Following the negotiation and tour the three men retrieved their horses from the scrub near the house. Jack had a black Arabian mare named Pathfinder. Owen's mount was a placid chestnut mare named Ruffy. Dan had a roan gelding named Kelpie — a tempestuous horse who would routinely lose its mind near water. The beasts were placed in the paddock with Ellen's bay, Old Tom.

As the bushrangers went about the selection doing chores, a great novelty for them after life on the run, Ellen remained in the house preparing dinner for everyone. As she gazed out of the window, she saw Jack and Owen mending the old fence to the cow yard. She remembered watching Wallace putting the same fence up years earlier. He had cut and split the logs and employed the assistance of their son to put everything into place. It was a proud moment, not least because it had meant they could start procuring some cattle for milk and meat. Fate soon played its hand, however, and Ellen had sold the last of her cattle to the butcher a year or so ago to spare them the indignity of starving, but she appreciated the gesture of the men repairing the fence. She had given a pair of Wallace's decent trousers to Owen to replace his raggedy ones, as well as a pair of her son's old boots to replace the well-worn self-made moccasins he had been wearing, which were not appropriate for farm labour by anyone's definition.

Suddenly she was overcome by the absurdity of her situation, and the gravity of harbouring outlaws. Who was she becoming? First the stolen sheep, now this! She sat at her table and held her head in her hands.

In the midst of her internal crisis, Dan entered the house. He saw the widow slumped over her table in distress.

"Everything alright, missus?"

Ellen looked up; her eyes possessed of the same panicked quality seen in the eyes of an animal chased by wolves.

"Here, missus, this'll do you a world of good," Dan said as he offered Ellen a drink from a flask.

"What is it?"

"The water of life. I take a nip before we bail people up. Trust me, it steadies the nerves."

Ellen hesitated. To demonstrate the safety of the drink, Dan took a swig then handed it to Ellen. Nervously she took a mouthful of what turned out to be neat whiskey. It tasted sour and smokey, and it burned her mouth, but she gulped it down.

"That's the way," said Dan.

"I hate whiskey," said Ellen.

"More for me then," Dan replied with a smirk.

"Your accent," said Ellen, "London?"

"Well, I'm from all around, but I started off in London. Got away from there as soon as I found a way. Wretched bloody city full of snobs and crooks."

Dan was of stout build with dark curly hair that was barely contained under his hat and a thick black beard that contrasted with his neat, white teeth when he smiled. There were old scars on his head indicating some violence in his past. His sleeves were rolled up to the elbow to show off muscular forearms and a tattoo of an anchor that, although faded, stood out against the dark brown of his skin and hinted at his past.

"You were a sailor?" Ellen asked.

"Oh, yeah. Before I came out here, I went around on a few cargo ships and the like. I tried my hand briefly in the Royal Navy. Wouldn't recommend it."

"Was it so bad?"

"Let's just say there's a reason I prefer to be a bushranger. Sleeping in a cave and living off salted beef and damper is a damn sight better than the festering ships and the mouldy, maggoty hardtack that passes for food in Her Majesty's Royal Navy. The floggings are not ideal, either."

"You must have had an interesting life?"

"Yeah. Mother was from the east end but she would tell me my father was a foreigner though, a 'blackamoor' she'd call him, not that I understood what that meant. She used to say that he worked on the sugar plantations in Jamaica and that's why he was so sweet. Never met him though. He died before I was born. There was a lot of different kinds of folk where I grew up. Gypsies, Jews, Irish, Chinese. All of us seemed to flock together because we'd been chased out of everywhere else."

Ellen frowned. "That sounds awful."

"I'd be lying if I told you otherwise, but it teaches you about the way the world works. You see, there's two sorts of people in the world: those who have property and those who have character. Those with property see owning things as being more important than character. They think that what they own gives them the right to treat others poorly because they can't imagine a world where they don't have what they own and they believe that those who are without must envy them. Those people with character see that owning something doesn't make you important, doing great things with what you have at your disposal does. And the best thing about character is that you can't lose it in a game of cards, it can't be stolen or ruined or bartered with. If a man with wealth loses his property he is destroyed, but a man with character is always rich no matter how many trinkets or fine clothes he possesses."

"That seems very wise," said Ellen, "maybe the whiskey is good for something..."

She reached across and Dan eagerly handed her the flask. She took a mouthful and winced.

"Ah, it's a better world you step into now, missus," Dan chuckled as he took another mouthful himself. "Being a rogue isn't about being cruel, missus. It's about taking what you need instead of begging and whining and hoping. Hope can't put food in your belly, but snatching the bread from a snob's table can."

Dan was soon back to work, but his open and easy demeanour had worked wonders on Ellen's anxiety. She began to ponder about his assertion that living as a criminal fugitive was preferable to the honest way of living. Reflecting on the recent turn of events in her life she began to entertain that there was some wisdom in the notion and eyed the mutton on the bench. *Yes*, she thought, *perhaps he is right*.

***

The following day there was a commotion as two riders made their way towards the selection. Jack and the others had been up early to get cracking on the chores before the day got too hot and had noticed the horsemen approaching around noon. Both riders were dressed in full mounted police uniforms – navy-coloured woollen jackets with brass buttons, skin tight white breeches, tall black boots with gleaming spurs, and leather shakos that looked like wonky top hats. From their waists hung sabres sheathed in low-hanging scabbards.

The bushrangers were not willing to wait and see where this would go and hid in the barn.

The troopers rode up to the homestead and dismounted. Ellen responded quickly to the knocking that followed. Before her as she opened the door were two constables from Ironbark — one of average height with a paunchy build and five o'clock shadow, the other tall and gangly with a beak-like nose.

"Yes, Constables?"

"I'm Constable Molloy and this is Constable Martin, we're checking in on the farms in the area due to a missing sheep," said the flabby policeman with barely contained disdain. Ellen's heart skipped a beat.

"Missing sheep?"

"Yes, one of the local squatters has lost a sheep and lodged a complaint with the district superintendent so we have to do the rounds and see if anyone has seen it," explained Constable Molloy.

"Mr. McKenzie?"

"That's the one."

"Oh, well, he's always grumbling about something," said Ellen, "unfortunately, there's been no sheep around here. Plenty of rabbits though."

"See? I told you there was a rabbit problem," Constable Martin said to his colleague. Molloy shushed him.

"That's alright, ma'am. If you see anything don't hesitate to let us know. Have a good day."

"Yes, you too, gentlemen."

The police returned to their horses and mounted. Ellen watched them ride away and allowed herself to relax once they were out of view.

When she noticed that the men were not at work, she began to look around for them. She found them in the barn hiding with their pistols drawn and ordered them back to work. While Dan and Owen were quick to get back to their jobs, Jack lingered. He approached Ellen with a stern look on his face.

"What did you tell those traps?"

"They weren't even looking for you. They were looking for a sheep," Ellen replied.

"Would that be the sheep that you pinched and butchered?"

Ellen studied Jack's face. His blue eyes seemed to shimmer like opals. He gave a wry smile.

"You're perceptive," said Ellen, "What are you going to do about it?"

"Oh, nothing. I just like knowing we're in good company," Jack said with a wink. Ellen felt flustered and unexpectedly began to blush. She watched Jack leave and then went into the barn. She was certain she had hidden the traces of the butchering properly and couldn't think of how he could have known. The only thing she could see was the remnants of the rope around the beam. She had cleaned up any spilled blood, and the instruments had all been thoroughly cleaned as well. Ellen furrowed her brow.

At lunch, the men ate quietly. They weren't fond of mutton for a second day in a row, but food was food. Ellen kept her eyes trained on Jack.

"Is there something wrong?" Jack asked.

"How did you know about the sheep?"

Jack chuckled. His smile showed off dimples and surprisingly straight and well-maintained teeth.

"I didn't."

Ellen placed her fork down and folded her arms.

"Look," Jack continued, "you've got no sheep, but we've been eating mutton for two days. Where else would the meat come from?"

"Maybe I bought it?"

"You told us you had no money. A glance around here attested to that."

Ellen's eyes bugged open.

"Excuse me!"

Jack threw his head back and gave out a great belly laugh. The others joined in. Ellen's indignation struck them as the height of comedy. Ellen began to go red in the face and averted her gaze.

"Aww, don't be upset. Just having a lark. Besides, money can't buy character."

Ellen looked up at Jack who returned a smouldering gaze that unsettled her.

After the meal the men returned to work. Dan and Owen tended the tiny patch where Ellen was attempting to grow corn and potatoes. It was not an impressive bit of agriculture, but it produced enough for one person to live off.

Jack, meanwhile, occupied himself with splitting logs for the stove. He took the logs and stood them on an old tree stump, then brought an axe down to split them lengthways with a grunt. He stripped down to his waist so he could lower his body temperature as he worked. With each swing of the axe his muscles flexed and strained, the sweat made his skin slick. His long, black hair clung to his wet brow, and he swept it back with his hand. Out of the corner of his eye he spotted Ellen watching him from the kitchen door. He smirked to himself and continued his work, but slower and more deliberate to give her something worth watching.

***

That evening over the dinner table discussion again turned to the stolen sheep.

"Hey," said Owen, "If the missus here was able to pinch a sheep on her own, what do you reckon we take a trip down to one of the squatters and have a crack at something bigger?"

"I don't know..." Ellen mumbled.

"Yeah, I could go for a bit of beef steak!" Dan said.

"You're not suggesting I steal a cow?" Ellen squawked.

"No," Owen replied, "I'm suggesting we all work together to steal one."

Ellen clapped a hand over her eyes and wondered what she was getting herself into.

Three

Ellen rummaged around in her dead husband's trunk and fished out some of his old clothes. They were far too big to be a proper fit on her, but they didn't need to be. This was a disguise. She pulled the smock-like shirt over her head and plunged her feet into the breeches. She pulled the suspenders onto her shoulders and adjusted them until they rested comfortably. She tied the collar closed with a neckerchief and slid her stockinged feet into Wallace's old boots. She plucked his coat from a peg behind the bedroom door and pushed her arms through the sleeves. With some adjustments everything was sitting roughly where it ought to. She put her hair up in a bun on top of her head and hid it under a floppy, high-crowned felt hat.

She examined herself in the mirror and sneered in disapproval. It would never work.

She berated herself for even considering doing something so stupid. It was one thing to steal a single sheep to keep herself fed, but this was totally different. *These men must gain some perverse joy out of convincing a poor widow to throw her good, lawful life aside to join them in stealing an animal to butcher.* But then she could always have said no. She *should* have said no. But she didn't, and now here she was dressing up as her dead husband to commit crime.

Her thoughts turned to the man who had previously occupied the outfit she was wearing. *What would Wallace have said?* She tenderly ran her fingers along the seams and over the folds and savoured the textures, hoping it would somehow connect her to him. She wanted to hear his voice in her ear telling her that she was being a fool or that it was all a bad dream but no voice came.

There was a knock at the door.

"How's it going in there?"

It was Jack. Ellen opened the curtain that blocked out prying eyes and presented herself to stifled laughter.

"Well, it's something," Jack said. He ran his gaze over her and pondered. He removed his neckerchief and tied it around the lower portion of Ellen's face as a mask. He seemed satisfied.

"You could fool me," he said.

"I think I know the perfect farm to hit. Not far from here, but far enough that we wouldn't be the first ones they come looking for," said Ellen.

"I'm all ears," said Jack.

***

It was a Sunday morning, and as usual the bulk of the locals ventured into town to go to church leaving their farms briefly unattended. This was the perfect time for Jack and the gang to make their move on Henry Neville's run. They approached the farm through the tree line, their sights set on the cow paddock.

A short distance away, near the roadside, Ellen waited dressed in her bizarre and rumpled disguise, checking that the area was clear. Once certain that the area was clear, Ellen signalled to the others.

The gang sprung into action. Dan ran to the fence and opened the gate delicately. Jack pushed through with his rope at the ready, followed by Owen who approached the cattle and dropped to one knee when he was a short distance away. He reached into his jacket and curled his fingers around steel. Carefully he drew back his hand and revealed the flute he had carried with him. Resting his fingers on the keys, he pressed them experimentally, the hollow clacking assuring him it was in working order. He pressed the mouthpiece to his lip and blew gently. The gentle tune of "Black Velvet Band" wafted towards the grazing cattle. At first, they did not respond, but as the song continued their furry ears twitched and they swung their ponderous heads towards the sound. Bewitched, they began to walk towards Owen who slowly stood up. Closer they came, a black and brown wall of cattle, some slow and shuddering with each step, some at a charging pace. When they were within a few paces of Owen he began to slowly back away towards the gate. The cattle followed quietly save for the odd rattle of a cowbell.

Suddenly, Jack slipped a loop of rope over the head of a cow. The caramel-coloured beast struggled as the rope was tightened but seemed strangely accepting as Jack stroked its hairy face. He led the cow out of the paddock, Jack maintaining his performance to keep the rest of the herd occupied. Once the cow had been removed, everyone left the paddock and Dan shut the gate.

Ellen could see the men returning with the cow and began to cross the road to where she had hitched Old Tom to a sapling. She mounted and began to ride back home with the others following behind.

It was afternoon when the cow was successfully deposited in the barn. Ellen had asserted that the paddock was too exposed given her own cow was long gone. In the house the men and Ellen toasted a job well done.

"So, what do we do now?" Dan asked.

"Well, we don't have the tools for butchering such a beast here. We should take it to a butcher and get the meat that way," Jack suggested.

"Where would we do that?" Ellen asked.

Jack threw back the last of his whiskey and licked his lips. "There's a bloke I know called McFeely. He specialises in beef of questionable origin. He can do the trick. We will have to do it soon because that beast will make a din once it realises the rest of the herd aren't nearby."

"I can change the brand if need be," Owen said, "I just need a pin or a needle and some iodine and I can take care of it."

"Sounds like you're old hands at this," said Ellen.

"You don't stay on the run long without knowing a few things," said Jack shooting her a knowing look and a smirk.

Ellen gazed at him misty-eyed and speculated on just what knowledge he had come upon living outside the law. There was a dangerous allure to Jack that she was finding difficult to resist.

It was decided that success in thievery was not adequate excuse for chores not getting done and whatever was necessary to complete for the day was done before dusk.

While the men worked, Ellen turned the last of the mutton and vegetables into a stew. She looked forward to something fresh to eat.

***

After everyone had eaten, Ellen cleared the plates and Dan and Owen headed out to the barn to bed down. Jack remained in the kitchen. He leaned back in his chair and fiddled with his pipe, filling it with tobacco in preparation for a smoke.

"You're a natural at this caper," he said.

"A natural?" Ellen replied.

"You knew the perfect place, the perfect time and you fit in with us like a finger in a glove. I wouldn't be surprised if you had some experience in roguery after all."

Ellen wiped down the plates in a tin basin filled with murky, cold water then wandered over to join Jack.

"When I was a little girl back in England, I would climb over the wall to our neighbour's garden and go scrumping. I would fill my pockets up with apples and go scrambling back over the wall quick as lightning. I got such a thrill. The fear of getting caught set my heart racing. But I knew that it wasn't a harmful thing to do and that made it easier for me to convince myself to keep doing it."

"So it's the thrill you seek?"

"No," said Ellen, "I don't seek the thrill. I never did anything more dastardly than scrumping until lately when I found myself struggling to keep food on the table. The drought pushed me into desperation. I tried to weather it and stay on the right side of the law, but every night I would sit here trying not to collapse from hunger and think about how I could pick off just one sheep or one pig. Maybe I could snatch a couple of hens and sprinkle some feathers about to make it look like a fox got them, that sort of thing."

"Did you get a thrill today?" Jack asked.

"Yes," Ellen replied after a pause. "I suppose I should feel guilty about that, but for some reason I don't. Is that how you feel? When you steal, I mean."

"I can only speak for myself but, yes, that's exactly how I feel."

Jack lit his pipe and puffed on it while seemingly in deep thought.

"Have you ever wondered about taking something other than livestock?"

"How do you mean?" Ellen said furrowing her brow.

"What if you could sneak into some rich bugger's place and lift some of their jewels or the silverware?"

"Oh," said Ellen, "I never even entertained the thought. I could never take someone's valuables. I know how many hard working families there are around here. It wouldn't sit well with me."

"Yet stealing fruit or livestock is fine?" Jack asked with an arched eyebrow.

"That's different. Stealing to eat is not the same as taking things because you think they are pretty."

"Are you sure? I doubt the farmer losing a cow or a sheep or some of their harvest is going to care much about whether you're hungry.

In fact, they are, in all likelihood, going to be at a much greater disadvantage than some old miser who lost a few shiny trinkets."

Ellen was subdued as she processed Jack's point. "You make it all seem so... logical," she said.

"Look, of course there are victims when we rob, but victimhood means different things for different people," Jack said as he removed his pipe from his mouth and leaned towards Ellen. "Let's say we rob a fellow whose estate is worth thousands and we take £20 from him. That money makes a big difference to us, but he still has enough money to be considered rich and he won't be missing any meals. Yet, if we robbed a poor man of his last £20, we would be just as well-off as if we had robbed the rich man of that money, but that gentleman is now destitute. He cannot afford the loss. This is why we are careful when we choose our targets. It would be wrong to push a man into desperation in pursuit of our own gain, but a rich man can afford to share his wealth. Let's be honest, the men with the most to spare are usually the ones who got what they have by pushing others into desperation."

Ellen let the ideas marinade before she seriously entertained them. Was there really an argument to be made for being free to rob certain people without feeling guilty?

"Tell you what," said Jack, "how about we take a crack at it?"
"At what?"
"We sneak into a house, help ourselves to some of the finer things they can afford to part with and then vanish."
Ellen wrung her hands. Everything was telling her it was a bad idea, but when she looked at Jack, and the way in which he justified these criminal acts, she couldn't help but feel inclined to drown out that niggling sensation in the back of her mind. After all, she had so little and there were squatters a stone's throw away that had more

wealth than they knew what to do with — why shouldn't she help redistribute that wealth a little?

***

It was the early hours of the morning at Amery's farm when Ellen found herself once more dressed as a man about to commit crime. Jack was with her and scoped out the surroundings before giving the signal to proceed. They moved carefully through the scrub towards the boundary fence, trying not to accidentally break sticks underfoot and alert others to their presence.

"When we get to the house we have to take our boots off. They'll be asleep in there and we don't want to wake them. Bare feet are quiet feet. I want you to tackle the bedroom and I will poke around the place for anything worth grabbing," said Jack.

Ellen pulled her mask up over her face, but Jack made no effort to conceal his identity. As they reached the house the wind kicked up. Despite being so early it was already warm and the wind seemed to spread the warmth rather than disperse it. However, both of the burglars knew that the noise would help cover their movements.

Having found the back door unlocked the pair entered the building cautiously. They quickly adjusted their eyes to the gloom and saw frames hung up everywhere on the walls. In the frames were portraits, some painted, others photographic, depicting relatives of the pair's unsuspecting victims. The Amery family was evidently a large one. Jack gestured to Ellen to search for the bedroom. He opened his sack and began to scan the room for valuables.

The wooden walls creaked and the rush of wind through the leaves outside disguised Ellen's delicate footsteps as she gingerly pressed her naked feet tiptoed against the floorboards. She gently turned a doorknob and peeked through the gap as she pushed the door open. She saw a bed with two people on it under blankets and snoring loudly in syncopation with each other — the farmer and his wife. She crept in and ran her eyes over everything before spotting the vanity table. She shoved a jewellery box into her sack and looked for more. A silver pocket watch on a golden fob chain, a handful of silk handkerchiefs and cravats, a cameo brooch and silver snuff box were all collected before Ellen headed back out. *Who would have thought farmers could have such nice things?*

Ellen breathed a sigh of relief and met up with Jack, who now had a sack full of trinkets of his own to show for his efforts. Both burglars made for the unlocked back door and left the house. They put their boots back on and took off to where their horses were hitched among the trees.

As they rode back to Ellen's selection, they allowed the adrenaline to wear off. Ellen was feeling a buzz from the hormones flooding her body. She had never contemplated breaking into a house and stealing valuables from right under people's noses, but it was something that made her feel energised and ready to take on anything. She felt untouchable and invincible. But mostly she felt guiltless, and she no longer cared about whether that made her a bad person.

***

The thrill of burglary was soon dulled by the return to farm life. The men tended to the stolen cow, doing their best to keep her happy and well-fed in preparation for her visit with the butcher.

In between tasks, Ellen sat at the table and fondled the stolen jewels. Shiny gems set in precious metals, beautiful pearls on a string, an intricate silver cameo brooch. Ellen held the brooch to the light and examined the silhouette on the oval base. It seemed to be a woman of a bygone decade — she couldn't quite place it, *maybe turn of the century.*

"I'm a thief," Ellen muttered. She returned the purloined goods to the sack in which she had transported them.

"Ellen, what are you doing?" she asked herself, "you're straying too far from the path."

She stood and looked out of the window at her dry and dusty selection, a fruitless place of toil that she expected would be taken away from her soon enough once people discovered her lawless behaviour. She had been lucky to have been granted some time to find money to cover the arrears on her rent just before the men had arrived. The little bit of money Susie would send once in a while was not enough to cover her payments, even if she supplemented it with money from selling eggs and doing odd jobs in town. Under the law she should have had the title to the land by now, but her inability to jump through the hoops the government held aloft had left her in this position. She frowned.

"All I do is struggle and work and I have nothing to show for it. No security, no safety, not even enough food to keep me alive to work unless I steal it," she said bitterly to nobody in particular. "Why should I worry about straying from the path when all the path brings me to is misery? I work harder than Amery and look at the precious things he had just lying around his bedroom. No more shame. This is me forging a new path. Jack is right. This country is made for those with wealth at the expense of those with nothing. I'm through with it."

***

"It's a fuckin' Jersey cow, Jack," said McFeely.
"What difference does that make?"
"It's a milking cow."

"It's got meat on it, doesn't it?"

"Barely," McFeely sighed, "You always were lousy when it came to livestock, Jacky boy. Alright, I'll sort it out. Come back in a bit and I should have her slaughtered and bled for you. You know the score by now."

Jack had taken the cow overland to a tiny village on the goldfields that was known as Quartz Hill, though some of the diggers had taken to calling it "El Dorado" after the mythical city of gold. As it turned out, it was little more than wishful thinking. It was here that Richard McFeely operated his dodgy butcher shop. He was a heavy-set man with a jowly face like a British bulldog. He was a frequenter of the brothel and of the opium den nearby. He was a man who seemed to think vices were meant to be collected as a full set. He knew Jack from years prior when the pair had worked an unsuccessful gold claim together. Both had reasoned that if they could not earn money from gold mining, they were better off taking money from those who could. The only difference between them was their methodology.

While obviously not happy about the task, McFeely took the stolen cow to the slaughter yard. The animal's watery black eyes bulged, and it strained at the lead as the unmistakable stench of death wafted up.

Jack decided to stroll through the village. Not much had changed except for everything seeming greyer. The ground was rock hard and the whole area stunk of horse manure, night soil and caged fires, all of which dotted the street. He saw two drunk Irishmen grappling with each other as he turned down an alleyway. He walked past the men as the larger of the two landed a blow to the other's temple and he dropped like a sack of manure.

The alley led Jack to the back of a farrier's shop where he saw a portly older man being fellated by a younger man behind some crates. The older man made a guttural noise and threw his head back against the wall, grabbing a handful of the younger man's strawberry blonde hair. Jack assumed it was the farrier and his apprentice but didn't linger long enough to think any deeper on it.

The goldfields had always been scarce on women and some men had needs that could not be satisfied with whiskey, fighting or gambling. Jack had seen it enough to barely even register it. Though he never spoke of it, he had succumbed to such an urge one drunken night after the seventh month without a substantial yield from the claim. He found that it had only served to make him yearn for women all the more and had played a large part in his decision to go bush rather than slave away on the goldfields without reward. This ugly place full of vice and misery had not been missed.

Jack's wandering took him to a hotel. It was a converted tearoom — as evidenced by the painted signs in the window advertising Devonshire Tea for a shilling. He went inside, where he was greeted by a woman whose features indicated she could have been anywhere between thirty to forty years old. She was mostly undressed, with only her chemise and stockings on, and her hair was worn loose. The sparsely populated liquor shelves behind the bar suggested that she probably did not get enough business to necessitate restocking, let alone getting properly dressed. Meanwhile, her demeanour suggested the nature of her business was more one that required her to wear less clothing and less one that constituted selling drinks.

"Awright thare," she began with a thick Scots accent, "whit kin ah git ye?"

"A little whiskey would hit the spot."

"Maist o' th' men in thae parts like a little gin," the woman replied gesturing to a young Aboriginal woman seated near the fire. She was nude under a possum-skin blanket and looked utterly miserable. Jack did not appreciate the pun. The hostess poured cheap liquor into a small glass and extended her palm. Jack placed some coins into it.

"The place is pretty quiet," Jack commented.

"Wance I realised diggers aren't tae keen oan tea and scones we started offering ither refreshments. Then, wance the yields stairted getting wee'er because the mining company pushed in, folk stairted goin' awa in search o' virgin country. Nawt virgin around 'ere anymair. We make jist enough tae bade afloat maist weeks, bit I suspect we'll be gaen afore lang."

Jack nodded solemnly and sipped his drink.

"Whit's yer name, laddie?"

"I'm Jack Cooper."

"I'm Elizabeth, bit the diggers call me Lang Liz, oan account o' mah height."

Jack scrutinised the woman and estimated she stood a touch over six feet tall. He had initially assumed the floor was slightly raised behind the bar. He took a mouthful of cheap whiskey and winced.

"Wid ye be interested in oor ither services th'day, mibbie?" Liz said.

"Hmm?"

Liz lifted the hem of her chemise high enough to show off her thick thighs and bushy pubic hair. Jack paused as he processed what he was looking at.

"Something tae soothe yer loins?"

Jack hesitated to respond.

"Or mibbie you prefer something mair native…" Liz said, gesturing for the Aboriginal woman to come to the bar. She did as she was directed, and shed her covering to expose her tiny frame and velvety black skin. She stared at the floor, but Jack could not tell if it was shame or bashfulness. It made him uncomfortable.

Jack looked at his pocket watch. He had plenty of time. He gulped down the remainder of his drink.

"You know, I'm not really in the mood for gin. I think some Scotch would go down much better."

Liz came around the bar and took Jack by the arm with a smile.

Liz guided Jack into a sparsely decorated room at the back of the hotel and directed him to a high-backed armchair. She began to undress him and draped the clothes over the chair. Her hands wandered over his body, tracing old scars and raking through his chest hair. She nuzzled his throat and moved her hands to his groin where she was met with the anticipated appendage twitching to life.

"You're a lot mair handsome than mah usual punters," she said.

"Do I get a discount for that?"

"We'll see."

Liz stood back and removed her chemise, exposing a taut physique and healthy complexion. She motioned for Jack to sit back in the chair, and as he did so she kneeled before him with a dish full of clean water and a cloth. She delicately washed his penis, gently pulling back the foreskin and examining the organ for tell-tale signs of the various scourges that the miners had inflicted upon her other working girls. He was as clean as a Sunday shirt.

She took his freshly cleaned member into her mouth, explored its textures and form with her tongue, and rubbed the swollen head against the soft, slick flesh inside her cheek just as she had done for so many of her patrons before. She felt like she had it down to a fine art by now. Jack began to stroke her hair and his mind wandered. He started to feel relaxed and thought about how nice it was to be in a padded armchair being pleasured, even if the woman administering the pleasure was not precisely to his tastes.

When he was ready, he motioned for Liz to head to the bed. She kept her eyes on him as she moved towards what was a positively luxurious piece of furniture — a four-poster bed with a red velvet curtain around it. It was certainly out of place in a dingy room behind a bar in a dying boom town. She sat on the edge of the bed and admired Jack's form as he approached: slim, muscular, and healthy. He walked with a self-assured swagger towards her. He was a far cry from the weedy boys who had barely scraped into adulthood and the lecherous old miners that usually frequented her business.

"Howfur wid ye like me?"

Jack motioned for her to turn around so he could enter her from behind. She climbed up on the bed on all fours and presented herself to him. Wordlessly, he glided his hands over her buttocks and then grabbed his tool, probing between the delicate folds of her lips for the desired opening. There was no tenderness in his actions, only his desire for release. He thrust in and out of her with desperation and Liz gasped as he roughly grabbed her shoulders for purchase. He squeezed his eyes shut and imagined who he would rather be with. Half-remembered faces of women he had seduced drifted through his mind's eye, but none quite sufficed. He paused thrusting and pulled out. Stimulating his body was nothing without stimulating his mind.

"On your back," he said almost as a grunt.

Liz did as she was told, and Jack gazed down at her. Somehow, he struggled to see a person, instead only being able to take inventory of the parts that made up the sum: ginger hair, green eyes, pretty mouth, small breasts, large pink nipples poking out, taut belly, uneven lips, strong thighs. He began to think about Ellen McReady. He fantasised about what she looked like under her clothes, how she might kiss him, how she might feel wrapped around him in the throes of lovemaking. He overlaid her features on Liz's and slid into her while lifting her legs up to rest on his shoulders. Suddenly there was passion in his movements. He guided his hands over Liz's body, exciting her. He thrust deeply into her with his eyes shut to maintain the illusion that this was really Ellen he was making love to. It did not take long for him to climax. He grunted and let out a sigh of relief as the feeling of electricity rushed through his body and exploded at the end of his member. For a few seconds the world spun around his head, and he dug his fingers into the bed covers to keep himself in place while the last spurts rippled through him. Liz grinned.

When Jack re-entered the bar room with Liz, he ordered her to grab some brandy and made a point of sitting across from the Aboriginal woman and gestured for Liz to join them.

"What's your name?" Jack asked. There was an awkward pause as the young lady looked to Liz.

"Gang oan, tell the Jimmy!" Liz snapped as she joined them.

"They call me Mary."

"Mary," Jack repeated, "what do you call yourself?"

"I am Walert, the possum. I am small, but I am fast and climb good so my mother would call me Walert, and so I call myself that too."

"Alright, do you like brandy, Walert?"

"Ah ne'er allow Mary tae dram liquor," Liz interjected.

"I don't like white man's drink. It poisoned my father, my uncles…"

"I understand," said Jack, cutting the young woman off, "my father was a devil for drink too. Drank himself to death because he got into the rum and couldn't stop. He drank to forget his worries but only found more at the bottom of the bottle."

"Whit are ye swallyin' fer?" asked Liz raising her glass.

"I'm in the company of two beautiful women. Is that not enough to drink to?" Jack replied before throwing back his drink.

He reached into his coat and pulled out a stack of bank notes. He laid a portion on the table.

"Whit's this?"

"Well, Liz, I see your situation and I feel like you deserve better. You and young Walert here. This is £100 so that you have a little something to help you find a way out of here and go where you can run a business without having to offer yourselves to bounders like me. I'm only sorry I can't afford to give you more."

Liz and Walert were silent. The offer was certainly generous, but not really enough to start fresh. Liz couldn't help but feel a little insulted by the condescending way in which the money was offered, but not enough to refuse it. She was keen to find greener pastures and this would do more to boost to those plans than hinder them.

"Thanks, Jack," was all she could muster.

***

That evening, when Jack returned to Ellen's selection with the freshly butchered beef, he appeared to be more reserved than usual and barely spoke.

"What's the matter?" Ellen asked him.

"Oh, don't worry about him," Dan interjected, "he's probably got the morbs over having the beast butchered is all. He'll come good in a day or so."

"I was thinking," said Owen, "d'you reckon we should take a crack at a coach soon? Pinching dinner is one thing, but we could use a bit of coin."

"Once we find somewhere to pawn off the stuff Nellie and I gathered the other night we will have plenty," said Jack. "Besides, we probably ought to let the dust settle a little bit first before we strike again. If we do too much at once the traps will be on us like Dan's head lice," said Jack.

Everyone looked at Dan who was absent-mindedly scratching his head. He didn't have head lice, but Jack knew it was something that even the thought of which made his skin crawl.

"You're a bastard, Cooper," he grumbled.

"I don't think I ought to be doing any robberies," said Ellen.

"If I can get Dan and Owen working efficiently as highwaymen, I reckon it should be no trouble whipping you into shape," said Jack.

"Keep up this talk of whipping and see where it goes," said Ellen facetiously.

"He likes a little flogging, our Jack," said Dan with a wink. He and Owen both burst out with mocking laughter as Jack blushed. Seeing Jack blush caused Ellen to grow bashful and hide her face.

"What precisely is your objection to robbing?" Jack asked pointedly.

"Well, I suppose it's the violence. I don't think I could bring myself to point a weapon at somebody and threaten their life."

Jack produced a pistol from his belt and showed it to Ellen.

"See this? It's what I use to convince people to hand over their money." He opened the weapon up to show Ellen the empty chambers where bullets should have been. "I keep it capped but unloaded. When I pull the trigger it goes bang, but there's no shot. It scares the life out of them, but nobody will get hurt because there are no bullets in the weapon to shoot. It's all about bluff. We know they won't get hurt but they don't."

"You're still terrorising people," said Ellen.

"The threat of violence is a powerful tool for persuasion when confronted with obstinate people," Owen interjected.

"They have what we want and they won't give it up just because we asked politely. I would say a scare is better than a wound — or worse — wouldn't you?" said Jack.

Ellen wrung her hands as she wrestled with her own wavering opinion. The men were right in that it was hard to part someone from something they didn't want to give up and violence could be a good motivator. However, up to now the crimes she had committed had not involved any threats. Indeed, she had not ever actually come face to face with her victims. Perhaps her objection was really to the guilt that she would have to carry after seeing the impact of her deviant behaviour on her victims? She couldn't accept the possibility that her objection solely rested upon a fairly selfish desire to do ill towards others and not have to face the consequences.

"Look," said Jack eventually, "I won't force you into it. Have a think and if you really can't bring yourself to follow through, then you can simply say so. If you decide you want to give it a go, we will show you the ropes and make sure nobody even has the slightest suspicion that you were involved. You'll get away scot-free."

He reached across the table and held Ellen's hand. His was warm and strong with powerful fingers and some slight callouses from holding reins and doing manual labour. Ellen felt her heart in her throat and her stomach doing flip-flops. She forgot about her moral quandary.

***

Later, after the men headed out to the barn to turn in, Ellen tidied up then headed to the bedroom. As she faced her bed, she imagined her late husband reclining naked under the possum skin blanket as he had done every night. A pang of loneliness struck her, and she cursed silently under her breath.

She undressed and lingered in front of her dressing table, watching the bobbing of the flame in the hurricane lamp. Her thoughts drifted to Jack. She wondered if he thought about her the same way she was finding herself thinking about him. Her mind was filled with adolescent fixations about his voice, his eyes, the way his hand felt curled around hers. She imagined herself embracing him, running her fingers through his long, black hair, squeezing his muscular buttocks and biting his throat as she breathed in his masculine musk. She imagined the feeling of their bodies pressing together and the feeling of him massaging her breasts with those strong hands that had clasped hers so reassuringly.

She slapped herself on the wrist to snap out of her fantasy. He was hardly older than her own children. Why would he be interested in her when there was the option of younger, prettier girls to woo? She scolded herself for allowing her mind to be polluted with such thinking.

She lay on the bed and stared at the ceiling. Without hesitation, the fantasies drifted back in front of her eyes more vivid than before. She imagined Jack standing before her as naked and anatomically perfect as a marble statue. She wondered how accurate her imagination was to the reality. Surely there was no harm in imagining? She wriggled around as her body began to feel hot and her heart began to race. Her stomach ached and she craved the touch of another human being, like her flesh was starving and the only thing that would halt the pangs of hunger was a caress, a kiss or just being pressed up against someone. She sat up on the edge of the bed and scolded herself.

"Enough of this nonsense, Ellen," she growled at herself, "you're a grown woman, not a girl. There are more important things to think about than some silly fantasy."

Despite knowing that she needed sleep, once she had calmed herself down Ellen lay awake contemplating the notion of being involved in a highway robbery. She was no Ben Hall, but she was sure that she would have no issue adapting to such depredations if the boys trained her as they had offered to. There was some strange allure in the outlaw lifestyle that she could not articulate. Why all of a sudden, after three law-abiding decades, had she begun to fall so far from grace? Was it this country? Had her husband been the only thing preventing her from succumbing to its corrupting influence? Was she really a rogue deep down and only now discovering her true self? How far down that path was too far?

She got up and walked outside. She gazed up at the ocean of shimmering flecks that were strewn across the night sky and suddenly she felt insignificant.

She heard the sound of footsteps behind her and spun around. It was Jack.

"Couldn't sleep?"

"No," Ellen replied.

"Worried?"

"Why would I be worried? I'm only straying down a path of moral deviancy."

Jack stood beside Ellen. He was in his underwear and a clay pipe hung lazily from his lips.

"It must be difficult having us here. Especially when we are roping you into our escapades."

"Oh," said Ellen, "no."

"No?"

"Well," Ellen paused, "before you came, I was in a strange place. I've followed the rules as much as I could. I went to church without fail, obeyed the law to the letter, was a loyal wife and devoted mother. Yet, even though I did all the things I've been told from as far back as I can remember that are supposed to make you a good person, all I have to show for it is this run-down farm that I am damned close to losing, and I'm barely surviving. I didn't steal that sheep because I was jealous, or because I didn't want to work hard. I stole it because no matter what I do, no matter how much I do the right things, I can never make ends meet, and I needed proper food. Can you tell me what kind of justice there is in a world where those who do the right thing suffer while those who do the wrong thing thrive?"

Jack nodded. He brushed back his hair and gazed down at Ellen with eyes bluer than lapis lazuli. They were hard eyes, but there was a kindness she could see in them, which seemed out of place given his occupation.

"I understand you," said Jack, "I too have asked that question. All of us bonded together over injustice. We didn't go bush because we were born criminals. We didn't do it because we enjoy taking from others; though I will admit that there are times when that is part of the appeal. All of us see the injustices around us and refuse to be a part of a way of life that rewards bullying, corruption, slavery and extortion. So, we decided to strike back at those who do wrong by others. Those who deprive others to benefit only themselves."

"So, you see bushranging as a political act of sorts?"

"I suppose so."

"I don't imagine you're the first."

"Nor the last. As long as there is a cause to fight for there will be soldiers to fight it, and defiance against unjust laws means living outside them."

Jack puffed on his pipe and folded his arms. He was not a large man. Ellen could tell he was strong, but his limbs and torso were sinewy rather than bulky. His lifestyle was not one of toil, but of scavenging and strategy. He was a hunter-gatherer in a time of agriculture.

"So, I don't suppose there's a Mrs. Cooper somewhere out there wondering where her roving husband has got to?"

Jack chuckled.

"Not enough women on the goldfields whose affection is earned rather than bought I'm afraid. No, I need a real woman by my side."

"A real woman?"

"Someone capable, loyal and strong. Someone who sees things the way I do. And if she was beautiful besides all that I wouldn't complain."

"Where does one find a woman like that?"

Jack turned to Ellen but did not speak. There was longing in his eyes and something primal. Ellen blushed.

"How old are you, Jack?"

"I was twenty-seven at last count."

"Oh, you're just a babe."

"Pardon?"

"Do you have any idea how old I am?" Ellen asked, placing her hands on her hips.

"I don't care about age. Besides, it would be impolite to assume, let alone ask."

"I'm forty-five years old, Jack. I'm an old woman compared to you."

Jack gave a chuckle. He never seemed to allow himself to laugh much, only enabling the smallest expression of joviality to escape as if he were rationing it.

"Ellen, you are not old. You are mature. And I am old enough to know that maturity has more advantages than youthful naivety in what makes for an ideal partnership."

Ellen could feel her heart beating fast, her skin grew prickly and warm. Jack reached out and planted a hand on Ellen's cheek. It felt soothing and she leaned her face into the open palm.

"You know I have children."

"I do."

"You know I have grandchildren."

"I do."

"What is it that you want, exactly?"

"Well, I'd like to start with a kiss, if that's alright."

Jack leaned in, planting his lips upon hers. She allowed it. His mouth tasted smoky, but the warmth and the intimacy of the moment made Ellen feel like she was fifteen years old and courting again. This time, however, she had experience on her side and knew what she wanted. As the kiss lingered Ellen began to caress Jack's hair and neck. His beard scrubbed against her chin, but it was a welcome abrasion. Jack ran a hand along Ellen's spine and nestled it in the small of her back, pulling her close to him. Her soft curves pressed against his tautness, and it thrilled her. For just a moment she pulled away to catch her breath.

"Like that?" Ellen gasped.

Jack smirked.

"It's a start."

Four

There were two types of organised transport that utilised the highway near Ellen's selection. There were mail coaches that transported bags of mail and quite often had wealthy passengers as well, and then there were the gold escorts that transported the gold from the goldfields to the banks. The latter was the ideal target for highwaymen looking for a big payday, but the escort of armed police that accompanied the wagon made it very dangerous. Mail coaches, by comparison, were usually easy targets as the only protection was a carbine held by the driver's assistant on the box seat, and when presented by a gang of armed bandits they weren't usually keen to try using it. However, mail coaches usually yielded very little treasure as the increasing number of robberies had deterred people from sending money and valuables by post, and cheques were useless to a bushranger who couldn't go into town to cash them.

These were the same points raised as the gang and Ellen discussed their next escapade. It had been decided that a highway robbery was the logical next step, but it had to be something substantial, and it had to be something that would not unfairly disadvantage those who were robbed.

"My vote is on the gold escort," said Owen.

"Why is that?" Ellen asked.

"Think about it. No civilian passengers means no civilian casualties. And not only is it a bigger payout, the diggers don't cop it because when they deposited their gold at the bank it became the bank's responsibility to look after it and they're insured. So, the only ones copping it really are the banks – and I can't say I'll be losing any sleep over that."

"Fair points," said Jack, "but how do we deal with the escort? Bloody dangerous."

"It's a bit of a numbers game," Dan said.

"How so?"

"Well, if there's more of us than them they'd be mad to open fire."

"But there's not more of us," said Owen.

"I'm getting to that part. You see, if we can convince them there's more than four of us then we stand a chance of bluffing them into surrender."

"How do we do that?" Jack asked.

"I think we need at least four or five scarecrows. Make them look as real as we can, give them weapons, put them in amongst the trees so that it looks like they've got the buggers covered from the bush."

The others looked at each other.

"It's novel, but I don't know if it would work," said Ellen.

"I have a thought," said Owen.

"Just one?" Dan asked facetiously.

"Does the escort need to stop at any point during the trip?"

"They usually do a changeover at the Purple Rose Tavern," said Ellen, "my Terry used to work the stables there before he went to Melbourne."

"There's a chance we could simply steal the strong box from the wagon during the changeover," said Owen.

The discussion continued for some time with the members eventually deciding on their strategy. When the escort arrived at the tavern on the way from the diggings at Sandhurst they would attempt to take the booty. Failing that, they would establish an ambush location in a wooded area along the road, and here they would set up an army of scarecrows to bluff the escort with. One way or another they would get the gold without casualties if at all possible.

***

Ellen stood in a corner of the selection practicing her body language and voice. She surreptitiously watched Dan and Owen chatting as they tended to the horses and she mimicked their poses: *square up the shoulders; rest the weight of the trunk on one leg – <u>but keep the back straight</u>; folding arms across the chest looks standoffish (and conceals the breasts.)*

She was dressed once more in Wallace's old clothes and had a pistol tucked into a thick leather belt that held the trousers up. While keeping one arm across her chest, she casually drew the pistol and bellowed, "Bail up!"

It did not sound manly. Something was off. She had it deep but there was just something to the voice that was unconvincing. She pondered and then fell upon the idea of disguising her accent as well. She settled on something that sounded vaguely like scouse and gave it another go.

"Behl opp!"

That just about did the trick. She could feel the voice at the back of her throat. She relaxed her throat as much as possible and tried again.

"BEHL OPP!"

There it was.

That afternoon Jack approached Ellen while the others finished their jobs.

"I was thinking, Nellie," he said, sliding his hand along her back to her buttocks, "I reckon it's a good idea to practice with a mail coach."

"Practice?"

"Well, you've never bailed anyone up before so this would be a good way to break you in. The local mail coach ought to be the one. What d'you think?"

Ellen sighed.

"Alright. I trust you've done this before?"

"You could say that," Jack replied. He kissed her tenderly on the forehead.

***

It was noon when the Sandhurst mail coach made its way along the highway. Up front were the driver and his assistant, who sat on guard with a Spencer repeating rifle. On the roof, the mail bags were tied down with the luggage. Inside were three passengers: David Transom, his wife Margaret, and their daughter Louisa. Transom was a flamboyant and slightly effeminate man, and employed as a bank manager. His wife was a socialite, insofar as it was possible this far away from the high society in Melbourne, and had a reputation for hanging around with actors and their ilk. There was often hushed discussion about the true paternity of Louisa as she bore no obvious resemblance to David Transom, yet had a striking likeness to a popular theatre actor named Fleming Bartholomew who Margaret swore black-and-blue had never known her intimately despite the many first-hand accounts from people in the theatre scene to the contrary. Though these were well-known local identities, they were complete unknowns to the gang, who had no interest in idle gossip about the socially mobile.

As the coach bounced along the road, a chorus of creaking wood, straining leather and squeaking bolts telegraphed its presence. Jack and Ellen took their positions at the roadside. They remained silent but communicated through eye contact.

Suddenly the coach came into view. The bushrangers blocked the road, brandishing revolvers. The coach slowed and Jack strode forwards.

"Bail up!" Jack bellowed. It was a far deeper, louder sound than his voice usually mustered.

The driver's assistant cocked the Spencer repeating rifle and aimed at Jack.

"Don't come no closer. I'll blow your bloody head off."

Jack arched an eyebrow quizzically.

"I don't think you'll shoot that thing."

"Try me."

Jack continued to move towards the coach. Ellen's eyes were wide, and her breathing grew strained. She adjusted the grip on her firearm.

"Last chance," said the trembling gunman on the box seat. Jack cocked his pistol.

"Who has the better aim I wonder? You or me? I'm guessing that you've never fired a shot in your life by the way you're holding that thing."

The assistant quickly took his eyes off Jack to look at his grip. As he did Jack fired into the air. The blast caused the two men up top and the occupants of the coach to duck and cover their heads.

"Stop wasting our time and get down," Jack shouted. Within moments the victims were standing on the side of the road, lined up and looking sheepish, and the mail bags were off the roof. Jack walked along the line with an open sack in hand. As he passed each person, they dropped valuables in. Behind him Ellen was rifling through mail bags with the repeating rifle slung on her back. She rooted around for anything that felt like it could be carrying something more substantial than a letter, but it was fruitless. She grabbed a square package and rattled it close to her ear and thought she could hear the sound of liquid inside. She snatched up a few more packages and added them to Jack's sack. Ellen eyed the men and singled out Transom. She pointed at him and gestured for him to go into the bushes. He looked confused but quickly decided that perhaps he did understand after all upon Ellen cocking her revolver close to his head.

They went into the bushes and in her most manly voice Ellen ordered Transom to strip.

"I beg your pardon…"

"Now!"

Transom knew better than to push his luck and began to disrobe. He soon stood before Ellen in his underwear with a pile of clothes at his feet. Behind her mask Ellen smirked. She picked up his bluchers from the pile and handed them back with his top hat. They were not needed.

"Go," she ordered, directing him to join the others. When Transom was out of sight Ellen gathered up the clothes and carried them under her arm as she followed.

With the robbery completed the victims were put back on the coach and the driver told to make way post haste. No further word was uttered as the driver flicked the reins and shouted at the horses to get moving.

The two robbers remounted and rode a short distance into the bush. Ellen removed her mask and grinned broadly at Jack who returned a sly grin.

"Planning on selling those fancy clothes?"

"Sell? They're for me to wear," Ellen replied.

***

That evening as Jack and the men sorted through the booty, Ellen retired to the bedroom where she tried on Transom's clothes. She had a curvy figure, but Transom's generous proportions and diminutive height meant that his clothing fit her reasonably well while not giving away too much of her feminine form. Her stolen outfit consisted of a white linen shirt, baggy plaid trousers, a brocade waistcoat with silver fob chain, purple cravat, yellow kid gloves, and a long green coat with velvet lapels. She felt satisfied that now she not only had the perfect disguise, but a more practical one to boot.

On the bed lay the Spencer repeater. It was a strange weapon compared to what Ellen was used to. It had a lever for the cartridges, which were fed into the weapon through the butt. She picked up the rifle and slid out the sprung loading tube. She gazed down the track into the weapon and got to grips with the loading mechanisms. Luckily the weapon had been unloaded first.

Owen had shown Ellen how it worked, having been intimately familiar with this form of weapon in his time working on the gold escorts. Owen was usually very quiet about his past, especially his experiences on the goldfields, and not even the other two men really knew what he had done before bushranging. Jack had surmised that he was somehow involved with law enforcement on the goldfields due to the odd comments he made at times, but had never been able to gather specifics. Owen was happy for his history to remain a mystery. He had proven himself and the others trusted him. That was all that mattered.

When Ellen joined the others that evening she was dressed in her chemise and had her hair down. The men had opened the parcels and among the spoils was a bottle of Hennessy cognac. Jack eagerly gestured for Ellen to join him.

"We've been waiting for you so we can crack into this," he said.

"That looks expensive."

"Absolutely. Probably the best of the spoils from our little excursion, but that's all the more reason to have a drink."

Jack poured four drinks eagerly. They toasted and drank. The cognac burned its way to their stomachs, leaving a sweet, fruity aftertaste and heat in their mouths.

Dan pointed to the bottle with a dirt-ingrained finger and declared, "that's the stuff Napoleon drank, y'know?"

"Why would Napoleon have drunk that?" Owen asked.

"It's the good stuff," Dan replied.

"But it's Irish," said Owen, "why would Napoleon drink Irish booze?"

"Where did you hear that it was Irish? It's bloody French," said Jack.

"Look at it," Dan insisted, tracing the logo on the bottle of a flexed arm with the fist clutching a halberd, "See this? It means it's strong."

Ellen arched an eyebrow as Dan slurred his way through his rambling explanation. Twice he lost track of his train of thought and started over again.

"Surely the stuff isn't strong enough to have gotten to his head that quickly," Ellen declared.

"He had a bottle of scotch whisky in his swag he hadn't told anyone about that he got into. Sucked it dry," replied Owen. Ellen shook her head.

"It's a good thing you're here with me. You wouldn't last out in the bush like this," said Ellen.

"That's very true," Jack said with a nod. Dan slowly slumped over the table and closed his eyes. He mumbled a sea chanty as he fell into a drunken slumber.

"I suppose I had better turn in as well," said Owen. He gestured for Jack to give him a hand carrying Dan to bed. Ellen returned to her room and proceeded to get ready for bed.

As Ellen was just about to climb into bed there was a knock on the door frame from the other side of the curtain. It was Jack.

"What's wrong?"

"Oh, nothing's wrong," said Jack, "I just wanted to congratulate you again for today. You took to this caper as natural as a duck to water."

"Thank you, Jack," replied Ellen.

Jack lingered. There was an awkward pause between the pair.

"Well, I should turn in I suppose," said Jack.

"Alright," said Ellen. She couldn't quite get a read on what was going on in Jack's head. She could tell that there was something he wanted to say or do but he obviously wasn't having any luck in getting it out. For herself, every time she looked into his eyes or glanced at his lips she imagined kissing him again.

Suddenly he moved in close. Ellen stepped backwards into the bedroom. Jack drew the curtain closed behind him and gazed deep into Ellen's eyes. It was almost hypnotic and the world around them seemed to melt away as she felt her heart racing.

Jack reached out and placed his hand on Ellen's neck and leaned in, planting his lips on hers. She could smell the liquor on his breath.

"That brandy giving you ideas?" Ellen whispered.

"No, just the courage to follow through."

He kissed her tenderly then planted a trail of kisses along her neck and throat. She sighed.

"What about the others?" Ellen said.

"You really want them in here too?"

"You know that's not what I meant."

Ellen's breathing became shallow and she trembled. She gently grasped his hand and placed it over her left breast. It was warm against his fingertips, and he felt the faint thumping of her heart.

"Do you feel that? It has been racing ever since I first saw you."

Jack smiled and shook his head in disbelief. "Poetic," he said as he gently cupped her breast and squeezed it.

Jack embraced Ellen with intense passion and his hands roved across her body, traversing the ranges along her spine, to the valley in the small of her back and settling upon the roundness of her buttocks. Ellen wrapped her arms around Jack's body and pulled him close to her, nuzzling his throat, breathing in the salty, musky scent of the bushranger.

She began to help Jack shed his layers, revealing the slim, sinewy body underneath. Ellen stood behind Jack and closed her eyes. Her fingertips ran over his chest and traced every bump and fold, eventually reaching the tangle of hair at his crotch. Her chest felt tight, and her breathing was shaky as if she had been plunged into a cold creek. She pressed her body into Jack's and took his member in hand. She remembered Wallace's being somewhat bigger, but it was still the most thrilling sensation she had experienced in quite some time. She had often been curious about what other men were like. The feeling of her fingers gripping him made Jack let out a soft gasp, which excited Ellen even more.

Jack turned and gently guided her onto the bed. He got onto his hands and knees over her, and took her nipple into his mouth, swirling his tongue around it to create pleasurable sensations. He ran his fingers over her belly tenderly, feeling the soft stretch marks embedded in her skin. He kissed his way down her belly and looked up with great lust as he reached the sweet spot. She returned the gaze with breathless anticipation.

Her lovemaking with Wallace had always been fairly brief, straightforward affairs with no experimentation and hardly any disrobing, just rudimentary coupling the way the Good Lord intended. What she was experiencing in this moment, on the other hand, was absolutely scandalous and Ellen loved every new sensation as Jack indulged his lust.

She began to quiver as Jack gently pried her legs apart, exposing the tender region between them. Ellen's mind was racing, she did not know what to expect. She stared at the ceiling and suddenly began to fret about what Jack would think of what was presented to him. After all, she was not a young girl anymore and had brought three people into the world, but she didn't have any point of reference to know if that made much of a difference compared to any of the other women this rogue had conquered and ravished.

Jack began to caress her with his tongue. Ellen gave little gasps. She wanted to shout out for him to stop, but when she looked down and saw Jack's head bobbing between her thighs and felt all sorts of wonderful sensations he was creating, she changed her mind. She began to stroke Jack's head, gently pressing his face just a bit harder into her crotch. She began to gyrate her pelvis so he could hit the most pleasurable places better. The sensations grew more and more intense as Jack began to use his fingers. The pleasure became overwhelming as and Ellen climaxed with a wail. Her eyes rolled back in her head, and she clawed at her blankets. Her legs clamped shut around Jack's ears like a vice, locking him in place to finish the job.

When Ellen finally relaxed, Jack bent over her and looked into her eyes. She seemed to be away with the fairies, half dazed.

"Are you alright?"

Ellen gave a stupefied grin and nodded. Jack kissed her tenderly.

Jack positioned himself between Ellen's legs and pushed himself into her. She gasped and gazed up at him. It had been quite some time since she had experienced this. It felt much the same as she remembered. Jack's brow was furrowed, and he locked eyes with Ellen in an almost animalistic manner. It was like something had flipped over behind his eyes.

Jack thrust deeply, gradually moving faster and more frenzied. He grunted and lifted Ellen's legs so he could rest her ankles on his shoulders. He gripped her thighs with his strong, reassuring hands for purchase as he felt the world blurring around him. There were no thoughts or emotions, only movement and the bursts of pleasure they created. When Jack climaxed, he threw his head back and let out a guttural sigh of relief. It was like all the pressure in his body and mind being released at once. He looked down, dazed, and Ellen smiled softly back at him. She saw the animalistic look in his eyes soften. The passionate encounter had been brief but wonderful for both of them.

Until Ellen fell asleep, the pair lay in bed holding each other. Ellen felt a peacefulness that she had not felt in a long time. Once she nodded off, Jack slipped away to join the men in the barn.

**

The next day as Jack was taking chaff to the horses, he thought he spied police riding nearby. Although they did not stop at the selection, in fact, they were riding in the opposite direction from it, it was enough to make him spooked.

He summoned everyone into the house for a conference. He was visibly tense, constantly shifting his weight as he stood at the head of the dining table with his hands on his hips.

"There's traps searching the area. I saw them riding past just a few moments ago. They know we're in the area and the longer we stay here the more likely it is they'll catch us. They wouldn't suspect you, Nellie, but *we* have to go."

The others exchanged worried glances.

"Where will you go?" Ellen asked.

"We'll need to return to the cave."

"*Fuck* the cave," Dan said as he slammed his hand on the table.

"We have no alternative. It's too dangerous to stay here," Jack replied.

"You don't have to stay holed up in a cave. You can come back for supplies or whatever you need. The police won't be around all the time," suggested Ellen. The men considered the proposition. Jack looked to the others to gauge their opinions.

"Makes sense to me," said Owen, "What do you think, Dan?"

Dan merely nodded.

The decision made, the men set off to gather their belongings and prepare to head for their cave hideout in the bush.

As the bushrangers sat mounted at the boundary to the selection Ellen stood by the gate with her hand on the latch.

"We'll be back in a couple of days. We'll move by night to avoid detection as much as possible," said Jack.

"How will I know it's you?"

Jack proceeded to mimic a kookaburra's call. In response, a small group of kookaburras in the trees nearby returned the call, cackling like maniacs.

"Won't that be on the nose in the middle of the night?" Ellen asked.

"Does it matter if you're the only one hearing it?"

Ellen nodded. She unlatched the gate and heaved it open for the men to leave. As they left, each man doffed his hat to the widow.

Ellen stood by the gate until they were completely out of sight. Her heart felt heavy.

As Ellen returned to the homestead the old sheepdog opened his eyes a crack and began to beat his tail against the floor. Ellen sighed.

***

As dusk approached Ellen heard a furious rapping on the front door. The dog began barking furiously at the door and whoever was on the opposite side. Ellen opened it and was greeted by Senior-Constable Haigh. Dressed in full uniform and carrying a riding crop with a brass horse head on the pommel, Haigh presented an intimidating figure. His features were broad and solid, his jaw especially. His eyes burned with a crystal blue intensity that instantly unsettled Ellen.

"You're Mrs. McReady I presume?"

"I am."

"I'm Senior-Constable Haigh of the Ironbark police station. I have come to ask you some questions."

Ellen directed the policeman inside and saw constables Martin and Molloy waiting outside. She waved to them.

"Don't wave. They have a duty to perform," said Haigh. The dog growled at Haigh as he sat but Ellen shooed the animal away. Ellen apologised and sat opposite the officer.

"What can I help you with?"

"Your neighbours tell me you've had some men here lately."

"Yes, itinerant workers. They helped me catch up on some of the upkeep on the selection that needed doing. I'm a widow so upkeep can be difficult."

"I see. Were these men paid?"

"Of course. What kind of employer would I be if I didn't pay?"

"Of course," Haigh echoed, "and where did you get the money if you don't mind my asking."

"Well," Ellen began, "they were mostly repaid for their work with accommodation. I gave them a place to stay, they helped me with the upkeep. Beyond that, I had some money saved up and my daughter sent me the rest. She lives in Sydney with her husband, and she wanted to help her old mum."

"Expensive, is it?"

"Not exactly cheap for someone like myself, but they were mostly looking for a bit of beer money and some place to stay out of the heat on their way to the next diggings."

Ellen felt something of a rush in being able to lie so freely to an officer of the law, but she found it hard to get a read on Haigh.

"I think you must be mistaken, ma'am."

"Mistaken?"

"Those were not itinerant workers."

"Of course they were. What else could they be?"

Haigh sat forward and rested his crop on the table. The brass pommel made a heavy thud on the wood.

"They were bushrangers. In fact, my men and I have spent the entire day roving the district looking for information on their whereabouts. They have been involved in a series of incidents over the past few weeks including stock theft, highway robbery and murder."

"Murder?"

"Yes. I'm surprised you were unaware, actually. It has been quite the talk of the town. They shot a woman on the other side of town while trying to rob her home. Left her children without a mother. Terrible business, and all over a few shillings. Where are they now?"

"I don't know."

"No?"

"No. They just left. Didn't tell me where they were going. They looked to be heading towards Axedale, but that's just a guess."

Haigh narrowed his eyes and flicked his gaze over to the kitchen bench where the bottle of Hennessy was sitting.

"That's a nice bottle of cognac there. Where did that come from?"

Ellen looked over her shoulder and kept a cool exterior as she calculated.

"Oh, that? It was a gift from my other daughter. Her husband makes good money, so she doesn't see anything wrong with buying something fancy for her mum to wash the dust down with."

"Your daughters must care a lot."

"They do what they can. The fledglings have left the nest and now they have to feather their own, but they never forget their mum. That's the way life is. Do you have children, Senior-Constable?"

Haigh shifted uncomfortably.

"My wife has two children."

"Young?"

"I suppose she is."

"The children, I mean."

"Oh, yes. Just babies really."

Ellen sat forward and locked eyes with the officer.

"You suspect something don't you?"

"Suspect...?"

"If you think I'm in league with a bunch of murderous bushrangers then you need to think again. I'm a widowed grandmother. I have no appetite for robbery under arms."

"Grandmother..."

"Yes. These crow's feet take time to settle in, you know. I'm not a fool, Senior-Constable. Those men never gave me any indication of being outlaws or brigands while they were under my roof. They told me they had come from the goldfields at Bendigo and were on the way to New South Wales. They needed food and shelter, and I needed strong hands to help carry my burden around this place."

Haigh nodded and stood up.

"Well, thank you for your refreshing frankness, Mrs. McReady. You have been most helpful."

Ellen stood and directed Haigh back to the door. Just as Haigh stepped through the threshold, he turned to ask one more question.

"By the way, when did your daughter send you the money – before or after the men arrived?"

Ellen suppressed a nervous gasp and steadied herself.

"Before. She had been telling me for months to get someone in. I simply kept the money aside until I found men that seemed trustworthy and affordable. Is that all?"

"I don't suppose you still have those letters?"

"Of course not. Do you keep every blessed note you get sent?"

"Indeed. It is a pity there's nothing to prove what you say to be true."

"I could easily say the same for what you have implied, Senior Constable. If you ask the postmaster if I had received any mail in the time preceding the arrival of those men, I am certain he will happily present you the ledger that records my receipt of said mail."

Haigh glared at Ellen who closed the door abruptly and attempted to calm herself. She had not noticed that her hands were trembling uncontrollably. She buried her face in her hands.

Outside the police mounted and rode away, headed straight for the Ironbark police station. Haigh remained unconvinced by Ellen, but without something more substantial than a hunch to go on he had decided discretion to be the better part of valour. After all, the community always got very funny when a woman was arrested, unless she was a prostitute, and he considered it unlikely that Mrs. McReady was on the game.

***

That night as Ellen lay in bed, the inside of her head was chaos. She could not stop thinking about the policeman's claim that Jack had been implicated in a murder. She could not reconcile the man she knew with the idea of a bloodthirsty brute.

Her ruminations were interrupted by the sound of a kookaburra's call and Little John barking. Ellen got out of bed and hushed the animal before opening the door.

There, alone, was Jack — as if summoned by her anxious mind. In the fading moonlight his eyes glistened despite the shadow cast over his face by his hat.

The first thing Ellen did was slap Jack as hard as possible across the face.

"Hold up! What was that?" Jack complained.

"You never told me about a murder."

"Murder? What murder?"

"That woman who was shot in a bungled robbery."

"We never bungled a robbery. Never shot a woman, neither. What is all this about?"

Ellen clasped her temples in frustration.

"The police came. They know you have been here. They told me you had killed a woman."

"It's a lie, Nellie. We aren't the killing sort. You know us. Those pigs are trying to rattle your cage to get you to sing. I'll bet you there was never even a murder to pin on us in the first place. These bluebottles are far more crooked than the people they spend all day chasing down like hounds after foxes."

Tears began to well up in Ellen's eyes.

"What's wrong?"

"I was so scared, Jack."

"Scared of what? That they'd take you in?"

"No, I was scared that you were a murderer. I don't think I could bear it if you were."

As Ellen began to sob, Jack curled his arms around her and held her tightly.

"Why did you come back so soon?" Ellen asked.

"Because I felt something at the back of my mind that told me you needed me here tonight. Was I wrong?"

"No, you weren't."

Ellen reached up and pulled Jack's face to hers and kissed him passionately. Her tears moistened his thick, black beard.

"Will you stay with me tonight?" Ellen asked.

"I shouldn't. The others don't even realise I'm here and I don't want you to be in any more danger. I just came to see if you were okay."

"Please stay," Ellen entreated, looking up into Jack's eyes with a piteous expression. Jack was conflicted, cautious about the consequences that would follow if he was to give in to his desire again. Ellen was desperate for his company and believed she knew the perfect way to convince him to stay with her.

Pulling back from his embrace, Ellen pushed her slip off her shoulders and allowed it to drop to the floor, revealing her body in all its natural glory. The moonlight made her white skin glow in the gloom. Jack stood before her wordless. His fingertips danced along the goosebumps that dotted Ellen's shoulder.

"It's a little cold out here. We should step inside to get warm."

Without further word they retreated to the bedroom. In the comfort of her quarters, Ellen adjusted the wick on her oil lamp, dulling its glow, and giving the room a cosier vibe. The couple lay on the bed kissing and fondling. Jack stripped off his clothing.

"I think I might know a way to convince you to stay here tonight," Ellen said as she slid her hand between Jack's thighs.

"Is that so?"

"Mmm hmm," Ellen replied as she began to kiss around Jack's groin. He flinched as the kisses tickled him. She hesitated with her lips poised over Jack's manhood. She had forgotten the smell of a man who had been in the saddle and the aroma gave her a strange sense of nostalgia despite it not exactly being pleasant. She proceeded to explore his groin with gentle kisses. It was far more adventurous than anything she had even considered before. She looked up and saw a smirk on Jack's face and took it to be a sign he was enjoying himself. She paid great attention to him, kissing and massaging and caressing all those sensitive parts that were never mentioned in polite company. She noted the peculiar bend in his organ and the way it twitched when she tickled it.

Jack told Ellen to get on all fours. She thought it a strange request, but complied. Jack moved behind her and stroked her back and buttocks. He entered her from behind and Ellen let out a surprised gasp. It was a different sensation to what she had experienced previously and she liked it, although she was worried it might not be great for her knees.

"You like this?" Jack asked.

Ellen nodded, "I do."

Jack grabbed her hips and began to pump. Again, Ellen felt some kind of animal within him was being unleashed. It felt amazing, but she wished she could see his face as in this position she felt disconnected. She clamped her eyes shut and imagined his features — the stern brow, the straight nose, the pursed lips. She felt his grip tighten and he let out something like a roar as he pressed his pelvis into her with great force. She felt warmth filling her up inside and Jack pulling out with a sigh. She looked back over her shoulder and could see the look of accomplishment on his face. She wanted him to keep going and give her the same ecstatic release as previously, but the main thing in her mind was ensuring he stayed.

As they lay together afterwards, Ellen thought about how much lighter she felt now that she was no longer alone. She also thought about how loved it made her feel that Jack, this gorgeous looking man, would ride through the night just to be with her because he could sense she needed him. She felt ready to ride away with him there and then. She looked up at his face as he lay dozing with her nestled into his side. She was glad that she could share her bed with him tonight and save him from a night in the wilderness. She was sure he would appreciate her having insisted on him staying, but for now she was content to let him sleep. Having him there made her fell safer. The confrontation with Haig had made her feel exposed and vulnerable, but now she had Jack there to protect her.

Once Jack had rested, he awoke, checked that Ellen was still sleeping, then slid out of bed, dressed, and wrote a note to let her know when he'd be back. He made sure to instruct her to burn the note after she had read it. He left it on the table and headed out to his horse.

Instead of galloping away into the dawn, Jack lingered. He was troubled by the news that the police had been interrogating Ellen. He feared they may have left spies to watch the farm. He patrolled the perimeter until he was satisfied that it was clear then left.

Assured that Ellen was safe and nobody was spying on her, Jack quietly returned to the cave hideout where he anticipated interrogation from the others. It was worth it to have spent the night such as he had.

***

When morning came, Ellen awoke alone. Yet somehow, she didn't feel lonely. She couldn't tell if it was just puppy love or something else, but she felt that with Jack she had found something remarkable. Her mind was dizzy with impractical thoughts of love and romance, which was something she had not experienced since she was a young woman who had not yet experienced marriage or child rearing.

She felt more comfortable in her own skin than she had been for a long time. The sex with Jack was invigorating. She realised that the last time she had felt like this was just after she married Wallace a quarter of a century earlier.

She stood in front of her long-neglected vanity mirror, an item of furniture she had received from her parents when she married, and studied her nude form in the gaps between the dust and dirt caked onto the glass. She just couldn't understand what Jack had seen in her to provoke such lust as on the previous couple of nights and began to examine herself. The more she looked, the more she lingered on the ways her body had changed since she last felt desirable.

When she had moved here, she had the plumpness of youth and her hair was much more golden and wavy. She poked and tugged at the soft skin of her belly and traced her stretch marks with her fingertip, war wounds from three full-term pregnancies. This had been taut and unblemished flesh once. She lifted her breasts, which lacked volume now compared to their heyday, and looked down at her darkened nipples – the after effects from three hungry mouths feeding from them. She lifted her chin and was thankful that she had not been afflicted by the saggy throat that ran on her mother's side, but the skin was beginning to look looser. She leaned in to get a close look at the reflection of her face. The grooves across her forehead and the crow's feet in the corners of her eyes were the scars left by hot summers spent working the land, bags underneath her eyes were from the weariness her labours inflicted. Deep smile lines were mementos of happy times long past. Her lips seemed thinner than she remembered. She had always liked how plump and pink her lips were. Wallace always said that they were made for kissing.

A lifetime of scars left by doing what was right and proper.

She remembered the way Wallace used to press the end of her nose affectionately and as she looked at her reflection, she lifted her own finger to touch it the same way. She had felt so lost without him and now it seemed like she had a chance to have something new with Jack, and maybe it would amount to nothing, and she questioned how in the blazes it could ever work, but she felt vigour when she was with him and he made her feel capable, clever and attractive.

As she pulled her undergarments back on, Ellen remembered that she now had a lot more work to do on the farm without the men on hand to put to work. She rolled her eyes.

Five

In almost any other context the cave would have been a pleasant location. Deep in the bush, it allowed the bushrangers to seek shelter while having decent access to a spot for the horses to graze and an elevation to keep a look out for unwanted visitors. On this occasion Jack occupied himself with cleaning his boots while Dan lay in a drunken stupor at the back of the cave and Owen sat at the mouth watching a fluffy grey butcherbird bouncing around on a branch flicking its black-feathered head around as if taking inventory on everything around it. There was a gentle breeze pushing through the bush and a sense of serenity.

While many often spoke with more than a hint of romance of the freedom that living outside the law offered, few understood the monotony. Despite Jack's nocturnal excursions to see Ellen over the previous few nights, there was little else to do every day except avoid the police patrols, which generally only required them to stay in one place. They knew that the police, however motivated to bring the bushrangers in, were also not dedicated enough nor properly trained to plunge deep into the bush looking for them, and their mounts were little better than broken down nags. This had resulted in a lot of sitting around with not a lot else to do for the trio.

"Do you think Ellen's got any books we could bring up here?" Owen asked Jack.

"She's a clever woman. I'm sure she reads."

"We should get some things to read up here. I can feel my brain withering away from boredom."

Jack nodded and turned to Dan. He threw a piece of gravel at him, but it had no effect.

"I suppose the alternative is to just drink until you can't feel or think anymore."

Owen frowned. "I'm not convinced that's any better than getting shot."

***

That night Ellen was again roused by the sound of a kookaburra and her dog barking. She greeted Jack with a kiss and the others filtered in behind.

"Where's *my* kiss?" Dan asked.

"You can get a kiss when you keep your lips away from a bottle for more than an hour," Ellen replied with an arched eyebrow.

Everyone sat around the dining table as Ellen put the dog outside in his kennel to keep guard. Dan eyed the bottle of Hennessy on the bench.

"She still hasn't finished that cognac," he said.

"Despite what you may think, it's not going to go on the turn from sitting there for longer than a couple of minutes. Alcohol will last for a while if you're not in a rush to see the bottom of the bottle," said Ellen.

"I'll have you know my drinking comes from an appreciation for the finer things. They call it a *refined palate*."

"Who calls it that?" Owen asked.

"Rich folk."

Jack scoffed, "What rich folk do you know?"

"When I was in the navy..."

"Again, with the *bloody* navy."

Ellen took her seat at the head of the table and interrupted the bickering, "Now, boys, shall we discuss business? Are we going to rob that gold escort we talked about?"

***

The plan was locked in, and now it was time to begin preparing. Owen and Jack went out to scout along the mail route, looking for the perfect place for an ambush. Ellen, still considered merely an eccentric widow by most of the townsfolk, had begun asking questions about the gold escort whenever she went into town on her errands under the guise of finding out how to get her valuables transported to the big bank for safekeeping. Meanwhile, Dan had been left to construct an army of dummies using old clothes and whatever else he could get his hands on. It was an efficient operation, and the gang soon had enough information to formulate their plan.

Again, they convened at Ellen's selection under cover of darkness. The discussion was serious and detailed.

"The escort leaves the diggings at eleven sharp," Ellen stated, "it always has with it a guard of three police – two mounted and following behind, another sitting next to the wagon driver. They will ride as hard as they can to reach Springhurst by noon. They will stop at the Purple Rose Tavern. This is where they change the horses. They will take it in turns to go into the pub there, two at a time so that there's always two guarding the gold."

"What do you know about the pub?" Jack asked.

"It looks like an old English coaching inn. It's run by a bloke called Gulliver Geraldton and his family. Pretty well-to-do. They seem to have connections."

The men nodded.

"Do you think it's feasible we can overpower the guards at the inn?" Owen asked.

"With four of us against two of them there's a chance, but it will be hard to sneak up on them. I'm led to believe they position the wagon so that it can be seen from the bar through the window. Although there's only two with the gold there's always eight eyes on the lookout."

"So, ambush it is then," Dan said.

"Based on our scouting trips, the ideal place is about two miles beyond the location of the tavern," said Jack.

"It's a cutting, so there's steep embankments where it would be easy to fire down on them," Owen elaborated. "I think if we position Dan's scarecrows along the ridge, it's high enough that it would be hard for them to tell they weren't real people — especially if they're more focused on us."

Dan grinned broadly. He got up and dashed outside. He returned carrying what looked at first to be an adult man with a bag over his head. He placed the dummy on the ground to allow it to stand at its full height. It was dressed in ragged clothing, a threadbare sack coat, corduroy trousers, a floppy felt hat and gloves. Under the hat, the head was covered by a flour sack with eye holes cut in it as if wearing a disguise. The fingers of the gloves had been stitched in such a way as to appear to be holding a makeshift rifle. The "rifle" was made from scrap wood and a broken broom handle that had been scavenged, then joined and carved into shape with a penknife. Overall, it was an impressive bit of work made even more impressive by the fact that it was made by a drunk fugitive hiding in a cave.

"Splendid work, Dan," said Ellen.

"Yes, now we just need three more," said Jack. Dan's face dropped.

"Three? It took me over a week to make this one and I struggled to get the materials for it!"

"Don't fret, we will sort it out," said Ellen giving Dan a reassuring pat on the shoulder. "There's no rush. In fact, it gives us time to really make sure we have it all planned out."

***

Over the next four weeks the gang gathered materials for the dummies and put the finishing touches on their plans.

Jack continued to visit Ellen at night for lovemaking and to collect books and supplies to take back to the cave.

Owen took great interest in reading Ellen's novels, particularly *The Count of Monte Cristo* and anything he could get that was written by Charles Dickens.

Constructing the dummies kept Dan focused and away from alcohol. He took great pride in each one, which Owen named after Dumas' musketeers: Athos, Porthos, Aramis and D'Artagnan. As Dan worked, Owen would read the novels aloud to him, keeping them both entertained.

By the time everything was ready to go, all four of the gang were well and truly primed.

***

The day arrived without any dramatic portents. It was another run of the mill day where the strongbox was prepared as per the routine and loaded onto the wagon. The driver, Edmonds, took his position next to a foot constable named Roach, who gripped his weapon nervously. It was his first time on the escort. On horseback were mounted constables Tremayne and Gordon. Both were strapping young men, fully uniformed and equipped with pistols and sabres. The horses were fidgeting as they anticipated the journey. With a nod from the driver, the escort began towards Springhurst.

The first leg of the journey was uneventful, but the heat of the day was starting to wear the horses down. As they approached the Purple Rose Tavern the driver motioned to Roach to take a look at a wedge-tailed eagle that was circling overhead. It was a majestic sight but one that was wasted on Roach who was far more concerned with keeping his eye on the road, even if he had been blessed with the ability to appreciate the simple beauty of such a sight. He gave a fleeting glance over his shoulder at the mounted troopers who were keeping pace admirably.

The tavern was just as Ellen described it. It was a whitewashed wattle-and-daub building with a steep-pitched gable roof, black timber cruck framing, and ornate windows. In the middle of the building was a low archway that allowed wagons into the courtyard. At the front was a wooden sign hanging from iron hinges on a steel rod. On the sign was a painting of an ornate rose with purple petals and the initials V. R. — just in case anyone had forgotten who the Queen of England was.

The escort went through the archway and came to a halt in the courtyard where stable boys took the police horses to be fed, watered and groomed while fresh horses were brought out and hitched to the wagon. Edmonds and Roach went inside for a meal while Tremayne and Gordon stood outside guarding the treasure. Neither knew exactly how much they were guarding. It was never less than a few hundred pounds but had never been more than a couple of thousand to their knowledge. In fact, the gold and cash in the strongbox was equal to £3,300, give or take a few pounds and shillings. That was nothing to sneeze at. Even half of that was more than what the entire escort team would have earned in a year.

Unbeknownst to them, things were in motion nearby to ruin their day. At the cutting, Ellen, Dan and Owen set about standing the dummies along the edge of the rock face. The four fake bandits all had the appearance of a disguised but strangely motionless individual ready for action. Some were armed with dummy rifles, others with fake pistols. Each one was designed to be loose enough in its limbs so that the breeze would allow it to sway slightly to create the illusion of movement but not so much that it was obvious they were not real people. Once they were in position, Ellen looked up from the road. With the sun in just the right spot anyone passing through would fall for the trick.

Ellen was dressed in David Transom's stolen clothes with Wallace's boots and hat. In order to obscure her feminine features, she wore a flour sack over head with a torn slit to look out of. The rest of the gang also made an effort to hide their faces, not only to conceal their identity but to sell the idea it was standard across the whole gang of eight to wear baggy, shapeless masks.

Meanwhile, Jack had gone ahead to the Purple Rose Tavern to check out the escort. He stood at the bar as Edmonds and Roach entered and ordered some stew and ale. To avoid suspicion, Jack had dressed himself in an old cabbage-tree hat and one of Wallace McReady's old coats. He smoked a corncob pipe and tried to examine the men surreptitiously.

Roach was clearly nervous, and Edmonds berated him as they sat. A quick gaze through the window showed Jack that the other men were standing near the strongbox, which had been removed from the wagon while the new horses were prepared. They were relaxed and smoking. To carry the box would be a two-person job. He left some coinage on the counter and went outside where he promptly mounted and took off to meet the others with the new information.

It was just before one in the afternoon when the escort reached the cutting. As they ventured into the valley, suddenly a huge log came crashing down across the road and blocked the way out. The wagon came to a halt and the troopers armed themselves. There was a commotion behind them.

"Bail up!"

Jack and Owen stood in the road brandishing rifles. On the ledges Dan and Ellen shimmied the dummies forward before joining their comrades.

Constable Gordon took aim with his Webley revolver and fired. The shot zipped past Owen's head and he returned the gesture; his shot cut across the horse's ear. The animal whinnied and threw the officer out of the saddle. Gordon landed hard on his outstretched left arm. He felt something snap and a sensation like a red-hot poker being shoved up the length of his forearm. He wanted to scream but the wind had been knocked out of him. Before the others could act, Jack fired into the air.

"Hold up!" Jack shouted, "We don't want bloodshed, we just want the gold. Look around you gentlemen, you're completely covered. If we wanted you dead we needn't have uttered a word."

Tremayne threw down his pistol, Roach followed suit with his rifle. The robbers moved in and directed the police to stand aside. Dan and Ellen kept them covered while Jack and Owen liberated the strongbox.

Ellen eyed the police and noticed Roach, who didn't look a day over nineteen, was trembling. Gordon cradled his broken left arm and was visibly in considerable pain. He was pale and shaking.

"What's your problem?" Dan asked, jabbing at Gordon with his rifle. Gordon moved enough to show the blood soaking through his sleeve. Dan's eyes flicked around wildly, there was a little flutter of panic in his chest. He told Gordon to keep quiet so they can get things over with quickly.

Jack and Owen carried the strongbox as fast as they could to the scrub where Ellen's cart was waiting. They heaved the box onto the back and covered it up with a burlap sheet before joining the others.

Jack picked up the police weapons and unloaded them before giving them to Owen to hand back. Jack stood before the men and kept his weapon levelled at them.

"We have what we wanted. We never intended any harm. Get out of here and don't even think about forming a posse to come back and find us. The next time we meet we won't be so friendly," Jack said.

"You're nothing but cowards and thieves," said Tremayne bitterly.

Jack shot the trooper a withering stare through his mask. "Be honest - do you really want your legacy to be that you were killed defending the property of a bank that would readily dispose of you? You were outgunned and outnumbered, sir. Be satisfied that you have your life if not your dignity." He began to walk towards the scrub on the side of the road. "You will remain here for one hour. My men on the ledge up there will make sure you comply. I wouldn't test their marksmanship if I were you."

The gang quickly withdrew to their conveyances. Ellen and Jack took the cart while Dan and Owen rode behind on horseback. It was a full five minutes before the police suspected the bushrangers on the ledge weren't real. Tremayne and Roach climbed the embankment to see if they could get closer. It didn't take long for them to confirm that they had been duped. They were ashamed to have been taken by such a ridiculous trick but realised that they now had the opportunity to leave and get Gordon to a surgeon.

***

The strongbox was not taken to the selection, but rather straight to the cave. It was the first time Ellen had seen their hideout. It was hardly the stronghold of Ali Baba and his forty thieves, or Robin Hood and his merry men. There was no time for a guided tour, however, and the men set to work removing the gold and burying it in a shallow pit in the rear of the cave, underneath where the swags were laid out.

The men heaved and sweated with effort, digging and hauling. Ellen stood by with her hands on her hips.

"You know I can help. I'm not weak or useless."

"We know," Jack replied.

"So why don't you let me help?"

"Because we've almost done. You can put the dirt on top after we've divvied everything up if you like."

Ellen crossed her arms and huffed. The strongbox sat in the open hole and with a well aimed shot from Jack's rifle the lock was blown off. Inside were several gold nuggets and bags of gold dust as well as a bag of money.

"That's a lot of gold," said Owen with a whistle.

The next hour was spent weighing and measuring the gold nuggets on Ellen's kitchen scales, then splitting them up and placing the shares into canvas bags. The intention was to melt it all down into unrecognisable ingots, but they lacked the necessary tools.

"There's nothing we can do now. Tomorrow we'll head to the goldfields. I know a smithy there who can smelt this for us if we give him a little incentive," said Owen rubbing his thumb against his fingertips.

"How do you know him?" Dan asked.

"Back in the day it was my job to know about these people."

"I think I should head home just to check in on things," said Ellen, "I'll be back in the morning."

Jack helped Ellen unhitch Old Tom from the cart to allow her to ride faster and kissed her tenderly.

"You should wear men's clothes more often. They suit you."

"Maybe if you're lucky you'll get to see what's underneath them again soon."

"Stay safe. Steer clear of the roads. I'll see you in the morning."

Ellen sat astride her horse and took off. Her flight through the bush was swift but Old Tom tired easily. It was dusk when she arrived home. Totally exhausted, she fed the dog and left him tethered to the kennel, then went to bed.

***

The following morning at dawn, Ellen awoke to the sound of a rooster crowing as usual, but it was hardly a usual day. She put on the bare minimum of clothing to avoid indecency and went outside where she saw the dog slumped motionless in the dirt. She initially assumed he was sleeping but there was no sign of breathing.

Closer inspection revealed foam around the dog's mouth and a half-eaten lamb hock that she had not the faintest idea of where it had come from. She immediately began to panic and scoped the area, looking for signs of any intruders. With nothing in view, she began briskly walking through the selection. Someone had poisoned Little John, and she was certain she knew who was responsible.

As she reached the boundary, she looked beyond the fence line where several thick red gums stood near a granite boulder. She could see what appeared to be a blanket on the far side of the boulder. As she moved closer, she could also see a booted foot sticking out. It was a police boot. This confirmed her suspicions about who had poisoned the dog and it filled her with rage. *How dare they?*

Without uttering a word, Ellen sprinted back to the house, tears streaming down her cheeks and her booted feet pounding against the dusty earth. As soon as she was in the door, she began gathering supplies and shoving them into sacks. She went to the bedroom and packed her bushranging gear and a spare dress; after all, she may need to blend in at some point. The rushing around caused her to break out in a sweat, beads of salty moisture dotting her furrowed brow. She sniffled and wiped tears from her cheeks with her palm. As much as she knew she had to clear out, she was devastated at the fate of her furry companion. The last thing she grabbed was her collection of family photographs. Jewellery, fancy clothes — none of that was as precious as those portraits.

She did not dress properly, opting instead to wear Wallace's old boots, one of his coats over her slip and drawers. There was no time to be fussing over dresses and the many layers that made up the fashion of the day.

Despite the pressure of time, Ellen paused to bury poor Little John. After all, it was the least she could do for the old dog that had kept her company in the quiet time before the bushrangers burst into her life. A quick hack at the dust with her old pick allowed her to dig a shallow grave in the parched earth. Gingerly she laid the dog in the grave and covered him with soil. She did not waste time paying respects, instead rushing off to grab her things.

Ellen carried her supplies to the barn where Old Tom was in his stall grunting for food. She put her gear on him, though her haste made the horse uneasy, and he refused to cooperate.

"Just you listen here," Ellen scolded the horse, "if you weren't already a gelding, I'd be threatening to make you one. Just stay still while I put these bloody things on you now!"

Old Tom knew what was good for him and settled enough for Ellen to finish gearing him up. The sacks containing Ellen's things were tied together and fastened to the saddle, then Ellen mounted. She plopped Wallace's old hat on and pulled the chinstrap down to secure it. Ellen jabbed her heels into Old Tom's flanks to get him going. The horse did his rider proud and took off like a rocket.

The sound of hooves roused Constable Molloy and he sat bolt upright. He saw Ellen on Old Tom riding at full tilt towards the bush at the rear of the selection. He belted Constable Martin until he was awake and headed for the horses that were hobbled a few feet away.

"Whazzit?"

"The old girl's bolting, you cretin. What happened to you 'staying awake all night like an owl'?"

"Well, it's not night now, is it?" Martin moaned in reply.

"Just get on your damned horse. Come on!"

The police left their belongings and pursued the widow into the bush. Having gotten such a head start on them, Ellen was blissfully unaware of the pursuers until she reached a creek. Old Tom had never quite gotten used to running water and it always took considerable coaxing to get him across.

"Get over it, you big oaf!"

Old Tom shook his head and shied away from the creek. The delay was brief, but enough that Ellen began to hear the rumbling of hooves approaching her from behind. She tried to see through the trees, but the bush was too dense. She elected to cut her losses and directed the horse to follow the path of the creek rather than push him to go through the water. When she saw a shallow point, she pushed Old Tom as hard as she could and managed to get him across. A glance back over her shoulder told her that she was still out of the view of her hunters, so she pushed on, weaving through the bush as much as possible to create an obscure path.

As clever as this seemed, it proved to be unwise and as Ellen took Old Tom around a boulder at high speed, the horse trod in loose soil that gave way and caused the animal to fall on its side. While this was hardly a good situation for Old Tom, it proved disastrous for Ellen who was thrown from the saddle and down an incline. Stones and roots made their presence known with each roll and tumble. At the bottom of the hill Ellen's head collided with a tree stump. Luckily it was merely a glancing blow and Ellen was able to recompose herself. Though she was shaky on her feet, she climbed back up to her horse. She was so dazed that she could barely feel the blood trickling from the fresh cut on her head over her face. In the fall the boots had flown off her feet and she now had the unenviable task of trudging uphill over jagged rocks barefoot. By the time she was at the top where Old Tom was waiting, her feet were covered in dirt and blood and every step was agony. The bags had miraculously remained in place, which amused Ellen slightly as she gingerly climbed into the saddle.

With much splashing and whinnying, the police horses crossed the creek. They paused briefly to look for tracks.

"Do you see anything?" Martin asked.

"Nothing. Maybe she crossed further up or down. We should split up. You go down the creek and see if you can find any tracks, I'll head up."

"On my own?"

"Yes, on your own. We can't split up and go together, can we?"

"It could put us at risk."

"I know. I hope you remember how to use that bulldog of yours."

The constables headed in opposite directions along the creek and looked for any sign of passage. It wasn't long before Molloy found tracks.

Sticking closely to the trail, he followed Ellen's path into the bush but as he reached a large boulder that Ellen appeared to have gone around, his horse was spooked by a tiger snake. The horse reared up and Molloy lost his seating. Tumbling out of the saddle, Molloy struck his head against a rock and fell unconscious. His horse bolted into the bush. As Constable Molloy lay on the ground, insensible and bleeding from the head, the snake slithered away as if only slightly inconvenienced by the sudden turn of events.

***

Jack had ventured out in the afternoon to do a scout. It was a standard procedure to move through the bush a decent distance from the cave to intercept any potential police or bounty hunters. It was while engaged in this patrol that he spotted Ellen leading her horse through the bush, hobbling on her badly lacerated feet.

She was filthy, her skirt was soaked and muddy and torn wide open; the shoulder of her coat was ripped open and the right sleeve barely attached; her face and shoulders were covered in lacerations from the branches that lashed her as she rode and the effects of her tumble, and dried blood caked the side of her face. Old Tom was panting heavily and foamy. Jack immediately rushed to her aid.

"What on earth happened?" Jack asked.

"The police were at my place. They killed the dog so he wouldn't let me know they were sneaking around. They know I'm involved with you. There's no going back now. I'm chucking in my lot with you boys."

Ellen was out of breath and shaking. Jack wrapped his arms around her and held her close. Her heart was racing too fast for her to enjoy the comfort.

"Is there somewhere I can lie down?"

Jack helped Ellen into the saddle and led the horse to the cave. He then guided Ellen to his swag, and she lay down with a groan. When she looked down, she saw her clothes were now little more than rags and her feet were a mess. She relaxed and stared up at the roof of the cave. She swore she could see the faint image of a handprint on the rock.

"We need to get you cleaned and patched up, missus," Dan slurred from the back of the cave.

"Are you volunteering?" said Ellen.

"I ain't a doctor!"

"Pity," Ellen smirked. She closed her eyes and felt darkness envelope her.

***

It was almost an hour before Constable Martin saw his colleague stumbling around in the bush covered in blood and vomit. He didn't even bother helping Molloy find his horse, knowing he was in no fit state to ride. They rinsed the vomit coated jacket in the creek and Molloy sat behind Martin on his horse as they headed back to the police station.

Molloy wrapped his arms tightly around Martin as they rode, fearing he would once again come off.

In the afternoon they made it back to Ironbark police station and made their report to Senior Constable Haigh.

"Did you see the robbers?"

"No, we did not."

"Not even one of them?"

"The woman was out late. She was probably with them. They may not have needed to come if she had visited them," Constable Martin reasoned.

Haigh locked his fingers and considered the situation. No doubt his men had spooked the woman, and this had cost them their best lead.

"Sir, if I may," said Constable Molloy, "the bushrangers are carrying a lot of gold and if they intend to use it, they will need to find a way to sell it without it being recognised."

"This is true."

"Well, would it be prudent to monitor any goldsmiths nearby to see if they come into contact with large sums of gold with a mysterious origin?"

Haigh was surprised that the one policeman of the two who had suffered a severe knock to the head was the one coming up with the useful ideas.

"Excellent thinking, Molloy. Perhaps that sturdy knock was exactly what you needed to get your brain working. Maybe a beating for Martin is in order..."

***

After a brief nap, Ellen awoke to the men sitting close by with serious expressions. For a fleeting moment she felt panic grip her.

"She's back," said Dan.

"Where did I go?" Ellen replied, somewhat disoriented.

"You were out cold for a while. You've had rather a bad knock to the head," said Owen.

Ellen instinctively reached for a lump on her scalp. Her hair was clumped together with dry blood.

"Where can I wash?"

The men exchanged glances. The creek nearby was hardly appropriate for cleaning wounds. They had a brief, hushed conference in which Jack delegated the others to fetch water so that it could be heated in the billy can.

The men were swift and soon the creek water was being boiled clean and Jack was preparing to treat Ellen's wounds. An old gold pan was used as a basin, with the sleeves from one of Jack's shirts torn into strips for bandages. Once everything was good to go Jack gestured for the others to leave. They stayed.

"What are you doing?"

"Well," said Owen, "it's clearly a big job."

"We don't want you to be doing it all yourself," Dan added. Jack glared at him. "Just trying to help."

Ellen raised her head and arched an eyebrow.

"Jack, I don't care. I just need help."

Begrudgingly, Jack gave in and the men began to strip Ellen gently, noting where her injuries were.

Much to Jack's surprise the others did not appear to be interested in leering over Ellen as he had anticipated. As she lay naked before them the extent of her injuries was clear. It seemed like there wasn't a part of her body without a bruise or a scratch on it.

"Well, I have to tell you, missus, you've done a good job of it," said Dan, pushing his hat back.

"Let's get going, boys. Dan, take that leg; Owen, you take the other. I'll go up top," said Jack.

Though the wounds were stinging and whatever didn't sting ached, Ellen found that having these three men looking after her to be a very pleasant experience. Owen was gentle as he dabbed at her lacerated foot. Dan was not quite so delicate, but he was thorough and seemed to be experienced in treating wounds. As Jack mopped up the dried blood from Ellen's face, she looked up at him adoringly. She was taken by the sadness in his eyes.

"What are you so sad for, Jack?"

"You just don't seem to get many wins on the tally board."

"That's life."

Soon the men had succeeded in cleaning Ellen's wounds, back to front, top to toe. Her feet were bandaged, and Ellen was allowed to rest with a blanket over her for modesty.

"Can you fetch me clothes from my bags?" Ellen asked.

"If there's one thing that I know about injuries like this missus, it's that you want those wounds to get some air," said Dan, "all you need to worry about now is rest."

Fortunately, it was advice Ellen was hardly in a state to refuse compliance with. She soon found herself drifting off to sleep to the sound of Dan humming a sea chanty as he built a small fire close to her bed to keep her warm as night approached.

***

That evening Ellen awoke in the cave to a lone lantern lighting the interior, a smokeless fire next to her, and Owen sitting across from her, nursing his rifle. She attempted to sit up, but it was extremely painful. Every muscle in her body ached and it felt like there was not a square inch of her skin that wasn't in pain. With considerable effort she made it into a sitting position. Seeing this, Owen got up and brought her a plate of food. It was meagre; nothing more than salted beef and a lump of damper that had been scorched on one side. They had not explored her supplies to find any food.

"Sorry we don't have anything more substantial for you, missus, but we're running low."

"Where are the others?" Ellen asked in a croaky voice.

"They've gone to work so we can replenish our supplies."

Ellen furrowed her brow.

"Why don't you look in my sacks. I did pack some things."

Owen got up and retrieved the sacks and sat next to Ellen to open them. He paused.

"You packed eggs in here, didn't you?"

"Yes," Ellen began. Then she realised what must have happened when Old Tom had fallen.

"I'm sure the others will bring back something," said Owen.

***

Meanwhile on a run several miles away Jack and Dan were hitching their horses to the veranda of a modest looking homestead. Dan snuck in a nip from his flask and pulled his sack mask down over his head. Jack had opted for a neckerchief over his nose and mouth. The pair strode to the front door and rapped upon it with ferocity.

There was a commotion from within and the sound of a latch being drawn. The door was opened a crack and a girl who looked no older than seventeen could be seen in the gap. She was dressed in a maid's uniform of black dress, white bonnet and pinafore.

"Yes?"

It took a moment for her to process that the men standing before her were wearing masks.

Jack leaned forward, "We'd like to speak to the lord of the manor."

Jack brushed open his coat to reveal a pistol tucked into his belt. He drew it and pointed it at the girl. She shrieked.

"I hate it when they do that," said Dan.

The servant stumbled backwards, allowing Jack to push the door open. He pressed a finger to her lips with a shush.

In the parlour, the man of the house, James Churchley, stood to attention and immediately snatched an antique duelling pistol from the mantle. He was a burly man of average height with dark brown hair grown long and oiled down, and a thick beard of the same colour. His clothes were neat and clean, but not ostentatious. He strode with authority out to where the commotion was and levelled the pistol at the intruders. Jack snapped to attention.

"Who are you?"

"I'm James Churchley. What are you doing in my house?"

Dan whipped out a burlap sack and a pistol and extended both towards the indignant squatter. "Alms for the poor?"

"Put it away, man," Jack ordered Churchley, gesturing to the pistol.

"I'll do no such thing. Get out of here before I riddle you both!"

"But that's a single-shot pistol and there's two of us," said Dan incredulously, "He hasn't even closed the frizzen!"

Churchley flicked his gaze to the pistol in his hand. It was enough of a distraction that Jack was able to snatch the weapon out of his hand. Churchley raised his hands in surrender.

"What do you want?" Churchley asked.

"We need supplies. Where's your wife?"

"I have none."

Jack looked over at the young woman who had answered the door and scrutinised her appearance. Her hair and clothing were in disarray, though she had tried to straighten herself out before greeting them.

"I suppose you wouldn't need one with a sweet young thing like that around to attend all of your needs," Jack said gesturing to the maid. "Alright," he continued, "Keep an eye on the lordly squatter. I'll take Little Miss here to show me where the things we need are," said Jack.

With Dan keeping Churchley covered, Jack went to the storeroom with the maid. As she walked, she adjusted herself to look more respectable.

"I'm sorry for giving you a fright," said Jack.

"I don't know what you were expecting," the maid replied, "do people not get frightened of masked men carrying guns in whatever swamp you crawled out of?"

"Do you have a name?"

"I do."

"Would you care to tell me?"

The maid looked over her shoulder and gave Jack a dirty look.

"No, I would not."

Jack shook his head and chuckled.

"There's no need for that."

The maid halted and turned to Jack with a look of fury.

"No need? Jim works hard for everything he has. He built this place up from nothing. What gives you the right to come in and wave guns around and steal from him? Jim is a good man!"

The tirade wiped the smirk off Jack's face behind his mask.

"Miss, if I believed for one second that this kind of wealth came from anything other than stealing land and exploiting others I wouldn't be here right now. I'd be living in my own manor house in the country. I've done the graft. Trust me, hard work gets you nowhere in this stinking colony. Only the scum rises to the top."

Without warning the maid slapped Jack across the face. For such a tiny girl it was quite a wallop.

"He must have done a number on you," Jack said, eyeing the girl up and down. He finally noticed the way her pinafore clung tighter around her belly than it ought to. He sighed.

"I'm sorry," he said. The maid looked at him puzzled. Jack motioned to her belly and the maid drew her hands together in front of her.

"Please, tell me your name," Jack requested calmly.

"Lillian."

"Alright. Lillian. Would you like to know why we came here?"

Lillian gave Jack a look that said that she did not but knew he was going to tell her anyway.

"I have a very sick woman who needs food, blankets, bandages and clothes. I can't get them any other way because I'm a wanted man. I get what I need by taking from those who have enough to spare. Tell me, Lillian, does Jim have anything to spare for this poorly woman?"

Lillian averted her gaze. She turned and gestured for Jack to follow.

Lillian opened the storeroom and led Jack inside. On the shelves were blankets and sheets, preserves, bottles of liquor and ale, flour and all the other staples one would need, and all in copious amounts.

"Well, that's a lot of supplies for a man and his maid," said Jack.

"Not just the two of us. Come."

Lillian led Jack back into the house and upstairs into a bedroom. Inside was an ornate bed with carved ends and surrounded by fine furniture. Lillian went to a wardrobe and opened it wide to reveal a collection of dresses and other feminine attire.

"Is there something about Jim Churchley that I should know?"

"These are his wife's," Lillian replied.

"I thought he said he didn't have one."

"They're married under the law, but they live very separate lives. She is currently away with her lover, so Jim is not exactly in a mood to acknowledge her. Frankly, she's a fucking cow. Help yourself to whatever you need. She keeps her jewellery in her top drawer."

It was almost an hour later when Jack and Dan rode away from the house carrying all the goods their horses could manage. As they rode through the night Jack couldn't help but wonder about Lillian. He had heard rumours about what squatters did to the servants they knocked up. He hoped that it wouldn't come to that. *Who knows*, he thought, *maybe something will happen to Churchley's wife, and he'll make an honest woman of Lillian?* But he knew that would never happen. Men like James Churchley did not care about honesty.

Six

The robbery of Churchley's homestead had proven to be a very fruitful endeavour. The gang now had most of the provisions they had needed, as well as new clothes for Ellen and a few additional items that would be useful to sell or barter with.

Ellen awoke to the smell of Johnny cakes frying in a pan over the campfire. With effort she raised herself up and saw the men huddling around the flames preparing food. Dan plonked a lump of dough into an iron pot in preparation for baking that day's bread, and Jack, noticing she had awoken, plated up two Johnny cakes and smothered them in plum jam that he immediately handed to Ellen with a tin spoon. Though her arms ached terribly, Ellen eagerly wolfed down her breakfast.

"How are you feeling this morning?" Jack asked.

"I don't think I've ever felt this sore in my life," Ellen answered. Jack responded by offering her some rum. *In for a penny, in for a pound*, she thought and drank a mouthful of the sweet liquor. The warmth in her belly was most welcome and soon it would radiate outwards and soothe her wounds. She wrapped the blanket around her and hunched over.

"You slept well, I gather," said Jack.

"I slept *heavily*. Whose bedroll was I on?"

"Mine. So, you remembered where to find us..."

Ellen touched the swollen lump on her head gingerly. "After I came off the saddle, I managed to find a path that seemed about right, so I just kept going until I found something that looked familiar and eventually it led here."

Jack nodded. "When your injuries have healed, you'll be added to the roster."

Ellen shivered. There was a chill on her naked shoulders that she found particularly unpleasant.

"I don't suppose I could have my clothes now?"

Jack gestured to a pile of clothes he had pilfered the night before from Mrs. Churchley's wardrobe.

"I found you some things to wear. I wasn't sure of your size, but I reckon there's probably something in there that you can put on for now."

"I did pack some clothes, you know?"

Jack paused and gave a sly grin.

"Well, if I had known that I could have saved myself some work."

Once Ellen was dressed in the loosest of the dresses, there was one inconvenience that made itself known.

"Jack," Ellen said, "I need help with something."

"What is it?"

"I have to..." Ellen gestured a spraying motion at crotch level. Jack's eyes widened with the realisation of what she meant.

"There's a spot near where the horses are grazing. I'll take you down."

Jack helped Ellen to a cluster of bushes on the edge of a clearing. He took a branch and rustled the undergrowth, hoping to get any snakes hiding within to wriggle out.

"You're clear."

Ellen hobbled over to the bushes and with a look of great discomfort hitched up her skirt and squatted in such a way as to position the split in her drawers in just the right spot. The whole process was agonising and mortifying. Her back muscles felt like steel coils that had been pulled straight and were trying to curl up again.

The sound of liquid on dirt soon stopped and Ellen attempted to stand up. She steadied herself on a tree but the movement left her sucking in breath and grimacing.

"Let's get you back up top," said Jack.

As Jack struggled up the incline to the cave with Ellen, he attempted to make small talk to try and relieve the embarrassment of the situation.

"Not a glamorous life, is it?"

"Well, I'm not in it for the lifestyle," Ellen replied.

"Next time we do a house visit we'll have to fetch you a chamber pot — or maybe I'll just pinch Dan's hat when he's not looking."

***

Several days passed with the gang sticking to the cave. They knew that they needed the dust to settle to keep the traps guessing what their next move would be. The cave was still undiscovered, so to emerge while eyes were still on the forest would have been as good as writing an invitation. They occupied themselves with card games and re-reading the books they had taken from Ellen's house.

Ellen recovered admirably in a short space of time, and was soon able to move around, albeit not without considerable pain from her lacerated feet and what she suspected was possibly a broken rib. Her head continued to give her discomfort and she occasionally found herself dazed and confused for no good reason or struggling to remember things. As frustrating as this was, Jack had been very attentive to her needs and was usually found at her side.

***

Weeks passed and one morning, after a breakfast of oats and black tea, it was time to talk business. Jack naturally took control of proceedings.

"We can't stay here much longer. We're in a tricky position now: if we continue to stay here, we will be found, but while we lay low the police are still unsure if we really are here. So, before we get moving, we need to hit another station for supplies that will keep us going while we are moving. The supplies from our last job have stretched well, but we need to restock before we can move on."

"I know a place worth hitting," said Ellen, "McKenzie's run on Eaglehawk Creek. That grouchy bastard has been giving me and any other selectors around him grief for years."

"Is he the cove you swiped the jumbuck from, missus?" Owen asked. Ellen grinned in reply.

***

The afternoon sun was unrelenting on McKenzie's grazing land. Though his grass was lusher than that of most of his neighbours, his stockmen were struggling in the heat and the dust that caught the wind caked their faces and powdered their clothing. McKenzie always detested the days at the tail end of summer when the heat would flare up out of nowhere as if to remind everyone that the season wasn't over yet.

Through the clouds of dust that swirled on the edges of the property emerged three horsemen with their neckerchiefs over the lower half of their faces and revolvers in their belts.

"You right there, Number Two?" Jack asked Owen.
"Yes, Number One."
"And you, Number Three?"

"Right as rain, Number One."

They rode past the sheep that milled about mindlessly in the field, and up to the stockmen, of which there were seven.

"Bail up, gentlemen. Do as instructed and nobody will be hurt," said Jack calmly, "You'll accompany us to the woolshed."

"Fark orff," said a particularly grizzled looking boundary rider with a dismissive wave.
"What's your name, fella?" Dan enquired.
"Nahnya farkin biznez!"
"What do you think, Number Two, drunk or just stupid?" Dan asked Owen.
"Stupid, I reckon, Number Three."

The other men became agitated as Jack half-cocked his revolver.
"I'll give you until the count of three to start moving. One…"
The men reluctantly began to shuffle towards a large, open wooden structure where the shearing was conducted. Only the belligerent boundary rider stood firm.
"Two."
Dan ushered the men along with urgency, gazing over his shoulder at his colleague.
"Three."
Jack fully cocked the pistol and aimed it in the direction of the immoveable man and pulled the trigger. The blast spooked Dan's horse, Kelpie, which threw its head back wildly and attempted to bolt but Dan kept her under control. As the smoke cleared the boundary rider could be seen on the ground. Jack remained cool as he stared at the fallen man. The boundary rider promptly sat up, completely unharmed.
"Whadda ya farkin doin'?"

"Get moving or the next one won't miss."

The shot had seemingly been fired over the man's head just close enough to frighten him into hitting the deck. In fact Jack's revolver was capped but unloaded, just as he had shown Ellen, and it had worked perfectly. The stockman sheepishly joined the others in the woolshed.

Over the next fifteen minutes, more staff were rounded up and taken to the woolshed where Dan was on guard with two pistols in his belt and holding a loaded shotgun, taken from its mounting over the woolshed doors. In all there was a baker's dozen, and none were physically restrained.

"Gentlemen, it is time to make ourselves known to the master," said Jack. "Number Two, come with me. Number Three you stay here."

Dan held out his hand to halt Jack as he began to walk away.

"There's thirteen men here — How do you expect I can keep them under control on my own?"

"You did alright at Gowringalong when we stuck the place up. This shouldn't be any worse than that."

"That was five people, and one of them was a fourteen-year-old boy with a club foot. I need someone here with me."

"You have the guns, not them. Anyone steps out of line, you shoot them."

"I'm no killer," said Dan.

"They don't know that," Jack replied flippantly as he walked away. Owen shot Dan an apologetic expression as he followed Jack.

With Dan on guard at the woolshed, Jack and Owen headed to the homestead. They burst in to find Elliot McKenzie in the parlour sharpening a hunting knife, and his wife and daughter with the servants in the dining room.

McKenzie jumped up and lunged at Owen with the knife. Owen grappled with the enraged Scotsman, putting all of his strength into keeping the blade away. After only a short wrestle, Owen succeeded in disarming the old man by throwing him on his back and clubbing him in the head with the grip of his pistol, stunning him. He stood on McKenzie's wrist and put weight on it until he loosened his grip on the knife.

"You good, Number Two?" Jack asked from the doorway with minimal interest.

"Yeah, fine," Owen puffed, tucking the knife into his own belt. McKenzie groaned and rolled on the floor, bleeding freely from a cut on his scalp.

Jack held a pistol in each hand as he rounded the house's occupants up and ushered them to the parlour.

"Take the men to the woolshed while I get to work, then hurry back and give me a hand. The women can stay here," Jack said quietly to Owen as he segregated McKenzie and his sons from his wife and daughters before heading back outside to grab his saddlebags.

He rushed into the house and proceeded to rifle through drawers and cabinets looking for anything precious enough to be worth something, but not that could be easily recognised. He knew from experience how hard it was to pawn off a one-of-a-kind necklace or a bespoke silk-lined cutaway frock coat. Unique items were too easy to trace, so unremarkable pocket watches, rings, silverware and firearms were always the go-to items, and the McKenzies seemed to have plenty to spare.

In the parlour, Mrs. Yvonne McKenzie wept bitterly as she watched Jack darting from room to room taking anything he liked.

"Don't worry mother," said her youngest daughter, a girl of fifteen, "no harm will come to us from this bushranger, I'm sure."

"Stupid girl," Yvonne snapped, "it's not him I worry about."

Having been deposited in the woolshed, Elliot McKenzie was absolutely furious at his workers who were seemingly complicit in their own detention by a single man, and not a physically intimidating one at that. It made him sick to his stomach that not one of his staff would have fought to defend his property from these brigands – especially when they outnumbered them so greatly.

He stood and glowered at the men who were all seated on the ground smoking pipes or playing cards.

"Ye useless ne'er-do-wells! Don't just sit there like yer laying eggs, stop these thieves!"

A few of the men looked up with disinterest. After all, it wasn't their property being robbed, and between McKenzie's miserly wages and his unpleasant personality there was not much incentive to do him a favour. McKenzie's sons, aged eighteen and thirteen, knew about the way McKenzie treated his wife and this alone was incentive for them to sit idly as their father was brought down a peg.

McKenzie strode over to Dan who raised his shotgun.
"Get back!"
"Git that weapon *oot of mah face*," McKenzie snapped, his accent growing thicker in his rage.
"Last warning!" Dan said nervously.

Dan's threat went unheeded, and McKenzie was soon upon him. Wrenching the gun from Dan's grip, McKenzie grabbed him by the throat and threw him to the ground where they continued to wrestle. In the struggle, Dan tried to draw his pistols but they were dropped as McKenzie pummelled him around the head and body. The aggressor knocked Dan down and pressed his foot to his throat. Dan lashed out at the offending leg without effect. His face was stinging and throbbing, his chest ached, and he was struggling to breathe with the squatter's foot crushing his windpipe. He passed out for just a moment.

"Fetch me rope!"

The startled stockmen got up and gathered whatever ropes they could find. McKenzie ordered the men to tie Dan's hands. Five stockmen pinned Dan down while his wrists were bound, and the remaining length of the rope was flung over a beam so that his arms could be drawn up above his head. The end of the rope was tied to a support column.

"You lot, fetch whatever weapons you've got and get up to the house," McKenzie barked at the men.

At that, all of the men scattered in search of whatever dangerous implement they could find to attack the bushrangers with. As they began to approach the house, Owen and Jack were already putting the saddlebags on their horses.

It was Owen that first noticed the angry mob headed towards them, equipped with pitchforks, scythes, and a myriad of tools.

"Watch out, looks like we're in trouble!"

The pair sprang into action, mounting their horses and brandishing their pistols.

"Go on, shoot us you cowards," one of the stockmen boldly declared — a considerable change from his passive demeanour only a matter of minutes before.

The bushrangers decided to try dividing the mob and dug their spurs in, riding around and through them at speed, creating much confusion.

Back in the woolshed, McKenzie was beating Dan with the butt of the shotgun. A sick grin spread across his face with each blow. Suddenly, the rope slipped off Dan's wrists and he fell to the ground. He kicked out at McKenzie's leg, striking him in the shin. It was enough of a distraction to give Dan space to get to his feet.

Dan slammed into McKenzie, who returned a heavy haymaker to his jaw. He stumbled backwards and looked up in time to see McKenzie aiming the shotgun at him. Dan spotted one of his pistols on the floor. In a flash he dropped to his belly and reached for the grip. McKenzie whipped the shotgun around and pulled the trigger. The blast was not well-aimed, but it was enough to blow off the two outermost fingers of Dan's left hand. Dan howled in pain and unleashed a tirade of horrendous language at the trigger-happy Scot.

Outside, Owen heard the blast and Dan screaming. He immediately rode to the woolshed, leaving Jack behind to make a mess of the attempt to capture them with farm tools.

He dismounted and ran to Dan with McKenzie's knife out. Barely acknowledging the horrific wound, which pulsed blood copiously, he grabbed Dan and dragged him out. As he did so, McKenzie took aim again, but the gun misfired — the cartridge was a dud.

"Quick," Owen said with more than a little panic in his voice. He could hear the rumble of Jack riding Pathfinder around the men nearby.

They emerged from the woolshed and looked for their horses. In the excitement, Kelpie had gotten loose and was nowhere to be seen. Owen managed to spot Ruffy eating a bush and mounted. He hauled Dan up onto the horse behind him.

Jack looked over his shoulder at the others, then back at the angry mob. He fired at the ground just in front of them to hold them back as he rode towards Owen and Dan. This time he used the second pistol he kept tucked into his belt — a loaded one.

McKenzie ran out of the woolshed brandishing Dan's dropped pistol and fired it at the retreating duo. The ball cut across the back of Dan's head.

"Aargh! Leave me alone, you relentless whore-pipe!"

The trio spurred off just as one man threw a broken fence paling at Jack's head like a javelin, missing woefully.

Much to McKenzie's chagrin the bushrangers got away, but he took some comfort in knowing that he had gotten his own back. He returned to the woolshed and stooped to collect his trophy — two severed phalanges.

***

At the cave things were tense. Dan whimpered as Ellen stroked his head. At the fire, Owen heated the blade of the hunting knife until it was steaming. Once he was satisfied it was the right temperature he pressed the blade to the wound, searing it. Jack had placed a girthy stick between Dan's teeth, which he clamped down on heavily as he let out a muffled scream. The pinky finger had been completely taken off and a small nub of the ring finger remained near the knuckle. The back of the hand was peppered with shot and it presented a gruesome visual.

"Searing the wound will help stop an infection. At least you still have most of the hand left," said Owen in the most sympathetic tone he could muster. Dan failed to see the bright side.

Once Owen was finished attending to the wounds, he bandaged the hand and gave Dan a bottle of whiskey. He looked away, fighting back tears for his friend while Dan swigged lustily from the bottle.

The whole ride back Jack had not spoken, and even as Owen and Ellen looked after Dan's injuries, he could not look bring himself to even look at him. He felt furious that Dan had allowed McKenzie to overpower him and set the stockmen loose on him and Owen.

Dan retreated to a nook at the back of the cave and drank the whiskey until he fell asleep. He felt embarrassed at his impotence during the attack, and the severity of his injury had been too much to process on top of that. In fact, the entire group was in a considerable state of shock, and nobody felt like they wanted to be the first to speak. Any level of success that was to be measured by the haul was undercut by the way in which things had gone wrong.

It wasn't until evening had fallen over the valley that Ellen approached Jack, who had put himself on solitary guard duty. Her walking was tentative and laboured, but she refused to stay prone because of her own injuries.

Even when her children had been born, she was up and moving within a couple of days, despite the midwife's recommendations. Her strong constitution was almost a source of amusement for her doctor on the rare occasions that she had been visited by him. She often joked that even if you chopped off her legs, she'd still use her arms to drag herself around because she had so much work to do.

"What's the matter?" Ellen asked Jack as she planted a hand reassuringly on his shoulder.

"What happened today shouldn't have."

"Of course," said Ellen, "but that's the risk you take in this line of work. At least it was just fingers and not worse."

"Hmmm," Jack replied, "I can't allow things like this to happen."

"Brooding over it won't do anyone any good. How about tomorrow we do something less dangerous? Why don't we take some of that gold down to your smithy friend and get it melted down?"

"Alright."

"Dan will come good. We just need to help him while he recovers," Ellen said. Jack nodded and caressed her hand.

***

In the wake of the robbery, the Churchley house had become a very unpleasant place to be. The following day Wilhelmina Churchley, the squatter's estranged wife, had returned from a week's visit in Bendigo to discover her wardrobe had been raided and many fine imported garments were missing. Wilhelmina was German and severe. She was quick to anger and loved to take it out on anyone subordinate to her. Her wedding to Jim Churchley had been arranged when her father, Gustav Hahn, and Jim's, James Churchley senior, had agreed to merge their businesses – Churchley wool supplies and Hahn textiles. Jim had found it exceedingly difficult to get along with his wife, let alone consummate the marriage and produce heirs. Try as he might, Jim just could not suppress his distaste for Wilhelmina's plump body, permanent scowl and directive to "move appropriately, but do not make utterances."

For her part, Wilhelmina had no attraction to Jim either, or indeed to any men. Moving about in higher society allowed her to engage in her Sapphic desires without anyone making anything of it. Her affair with a local heiress, a frail-looking girl named Marie Fanshaw, was well-known amongst the party-going set but never discussed, lest the scandalous behaviour of everyone else be brought into the light as well. Wilhelmina wore a locket around her neck at all times that contained a lock of Marie's hair.

She had long suspected that her husband was getting a little too friendly with their maid and, in her own mind, required no evidence to justify treating the girl cruelly. Her first response to discovering her missing dresses was to accuse the poor girl of having stolen them.

"No, Mrs. Churchley, I did not."

"Impudent! How dare you talk back — and with lies no less," Wilhelmina growled gutturally. She swung her arm with full force and her knuckles collided with Lillian's cheek. It was a strong enough blow to drop the girl to the floor. Wilhelmina was not finished. She grabbed a lace parasol from her dresser and wielded it like a mighty weapon, thrashing the girl as she cowered and begged on the floor. So heavy were the blows that the fragile skeleton of the parasol snapped audibly. Wilhelmina paused to examine the damage.

"Stupid girl; do you see what you have done? You must be punished!"

The enraged woman hauled Lillian to her feet and began ripping at her clothing. Lillian attempted to fend her off, but it was like slapping a starving wolf to stop it biting. Wilhelmina grabbed Lillian by the throat and snatched up a letter opener from the dresser. She began slashing at the clothes to make it easier to tear them away. By now the girl was screaming hysterically in terror and pain, doubled over to protect the precious life growing inside her belly. Wilhelmina threw her to the floor and glowered down at her. She felt adrenaline coursing through her body, and the sight of Lillian, bare-breasted and bedecked in shredded fabric from the waist down, her soft flesh lacerated and bleeding, aroused her in no small degree, much to her own surprise.

Lillian cradled her belly.
"Why do you hold your stomach?" Wilhelmina interrogated. Lillian was so terrified that all she could do was sob uncontrollably.
"My husband has given you his seed! You seduced my husband, you whore!"
Wilhelmina screamed like some unholy creature as she paced around the room clawing at her own face. Her eyes took on a frightening intensity as she grabbed Lillian by the hair and began to drag

her out of the master bedroom. Lillian screamed for help but there was nobody in earshot.

"This is what whores deserve," Wilhelmina said in a low voice as she threw Lillian down the staircase. Truthfully, it was less a throw than a vigorous drop, and Lillian slid down the stairs on her side while curled in the foetal position. Her head bounced on each step and the stiff carpet that covered each step rubbed her naked back and shoulders raw. When she reached the bottom, her head struck the stone floor. It hurt, but it wasn't enough to knock her out. Hoping to stop the attacks, Lillian played possum at the foot of the stairs and remained motionless. It seemed to work.

She kept her eyes closed as she listened to Wilhelmina return to her bedroom cursing to herself in German. When she heard the door slam shut, she opened one eye to see if it was a bluff. It was not – the coast was clear.

With effort, she got up and headed outside. She looked across the property and could see Jim in the distance riding a chestnut horse towards the homestead. He was dressed in a frock coat and top hat, hardly practical attire for farm work, but it wasn't his job to do the labour, only to order others to do it.

Lillian ran towards him and waved. Her hair was loose, her breasts exposed, her dress no more than a few black scraps scattered around her waist. Her skirt was shredded, and her skin covered in cuts, punctures and streams of blood.

Jim rode to her side. "What has happened?"
"Your wife has gone mad and attacked me. She tried to kill me!"
"Kill you? Whatever for?"
"She thinks I stole her dresses and broke her parasol and that I seduced you."
Jim frowned.
"We all know you didn't steal the dresses. How absurd."
"Please, help me! Protect me; protect our child!"

Lillian grabbed Jim's knee with a pleading expression. He gazed down at her then up to the house. He considered the scandal that he had put himself in by satiating his carnal desires with his servant.

"Alright. Go to your quarters and prepare your things. I will sort everything out."

Lillian thanked her employer and planted kisses on his leg, the only part of him that she could reach. Churchley brushed her aside and rode off.

***

The trip to the Quartz Hill was surprisingly easy for Jack and Owen. Dressed in clothes pilfered from McKenzie's house, they were only distinguished from typical squatters by their long hair and beards.

Not far from McFeely's butcher shop was Jeremiah Goldsmith. As his name suggested, he was a jeweller and goldsmith by trade, but this was a family trade that had been handed down as far back as records went. Jeremiah, or Jerry the Jew as he was more commonly known, was not the best smithy in his family but he was the best one on the goldfields. He was not actually Jewish, but his curly hair and beard had convinced some of the miners he was of Semitic origins and the name stuck. When the diggings had begun to yield less of the yellow stuff he had fallen on hard times and began fraternising with some shady characters. He was desperate to keep the business afloat, and if that meant providing a place for thieves and bushrangers to smelt stolen metals then that's what it took. It was not as lucrative as he was used to, but it covered the bills.

Jack and Owen entered and doffed their hats to Goldsmith who replied with a cheerful, "Good morning."

"We've got some gold we would like melted down into ingots," said Jack as he placed a bag on the counter. Goldsmith looked at the bag, then up at the men.

"No questions asked, right?"

"No questions asked. No questions answered."

Jack and Owen waited at the front of the shop while Goldsmith tinkered around in his workshop. As he heated the mangled nuggets and gold dust in his crucible he prepared the ingot mould. Flames danced in the furnace as he hummed *The Pride of Petravore* to himself.

When it came time to pour, Goldsmith steadied himself. He knew one slip would mean very bad news. Carefully he lifted the crucible out with tongs. It glowed brilliantly in the dingy workshop, casting a golden hue on Goldsmith's broad features. As he poured the liquid metal into the ingot mould it was white hot and sparkling. Knowing his customers were short on time, he quenched the metal in a bath of water rather than allowing it to cool naturally.

At that moment two foot constables strolled past the building. The appearance of the men in their navy blue uniforms and black leather shako helmets caught the attention of the men in the shop who made an effort to hide their faces.

"Jack," Owen whispered.

"Yeah?"

"Why are we hiding when nobody we've robbed has seen our faces?"

Jack went to speak but hesitated. He observed the police pass by without stopping and relaxed.

"We're good."

"What's the point of wearing those bloody masks if we still hide even when we aren't wearing them?"

"No harm in caution."

When the ingots were ready Jack took them to the bank nearby, leaving Owen at Jerry Goldsmith's shop as insurance until he returned with payment.

The gold was exchanged for cash without inquiry; after all, banks only cared about the wealth, not where it came from.

Jack returned to the shop where Goldsmith was paid, and the two faux gentlemen took their newfound wealth and mounted up. As they left, they let Goldsmith know that they would return soon with more gold.

***

Lillian had done exactly as her employer had instructed, shedding her rags in favour of a brown dress with printed periwinkles. The dress was painful against the fresh wounds, but it was a pain that had to be endured. She collected her things, meagre though they were, and waited in the courtyard for her lover.

Twenty minutes elapsed and Churchley appeared. He was impassive and walked as if in haste. Lillian moved to kiss him but was rebuffed. Churchley handed her an envelope.

"What's this?"

"It's your pay, plus enough to cover any expenses in getting home."

"What?"

"You can't stay here. My wife is greatly upset by what you have done. You are being turned loose before you can cause any more trouble."

Lillian was aghast. Her face went pale and her whole body felt cold.

"You can't abandon me. You can't abandon our child."

"I have no child."

"What's this then?" Lillian screamed as she pointed to her belly. Churchley turned away.

"You may think you can extort me, but nobody would ever believe such a wild claim. I shan't provide a reference. I suggest looking for another line of work if you intend to reside in these parts."

With that Churchley returned coolly to his house, leaving Lillian to sob in the courtyard.

***

Jack and Owen decided to take the highway up to the point where they could turn off the road into the bush and make a bee line up to the cave without being seen. As they rode along the road, they saw a small figure clad in brown hauling a large carpet bag on the side of the road. Jack nosed ahead to catch up to her. When he did, he immediately recognised Lillian.

"Hello, miss, what are you doing out here?"

Lillian looked up and though she tried to speak, all she managed was to break out in tears and make a strange whining sound.

"I'm sorry, miss, I was only going to ask if you needed a ride..."

Lillian still could not form words so merely nodded. Her eyes were red and bleary from crying, her cheeks slick with tears. She was swiftly hoisted up behind Jack and as they rode down the road, she kept her arms wrapped tightly around him to stop herself falling off.

"Where are you headed?" Jack asked after a while.

"Where are you going?"

"Uh, nowhere that you want to go. Are you headed to your folks or something?"

"No, I have nowhere to go. If my family found out what happened they'd disown me. There's no way to explain that my employer got me pregnant then discarded me without being cast out."

"Religious, are they?"

"They're stricter Catholics than the Pope."

"So, I suppose that makes you something of a rover then."

"I suppose. Your voice is familiar. I know you, don't I?"

"Hmm, I don't know what you mean, miss," said Jack cautiously.

Lillian slid one hand down to Jack's waist and fingered his belt where she located the grip of his revolver. She froze.

"You have wandering hands, miss."

"It's you, you're that bushranger!"

"You got me. Still championing your boss?"

"No! If I ever see him again, I'll shoot his cock off and feed it to his bitch wife."

"You know, you're more than a little vulgar, missy."

"Not in front of polite company."

"I'm not polite?"

"I'm not in front of you."

Jack allowed himself to let out a proper laugh.

"Hey, Owen, remember I told you about the peppery servant girl?"

"Yeah," Owen replied.

"Guess who's riding tandem…"

"Lucky us," said Owen.

"Still want to go where I'm going?" Jack asked Lillian.

"Anywhere is better than on that farm," said Lillian, "but I reckon it would be interesting to be a bushranger for a while."

"Right you are, miss."

The riders turned off the highway into the bush upon spotting a large boulder with a broad arrow chiselled into it. This was a relic from the days when convicts worked in the area, clearing the path for the highway.

The riders moved smoothly through rugged terrain, their horses well adjusted to the conditions. Suddenly Lillian began to tug on Jack's jacket.

"What's wrong?"

"I need to stop. I have to relieve myself."
"Relieve yourself? You can't hold on a bit longer?"
"Have you ever been pregnant, Mr. Bushranger?"
"Can't say I have."
"When you have to go, you have to go."

Jack, not wanting to press the point gestured to Owen to halt and they stopped near a large stringybark tree. He dismounted and helped Lillian down. She dashed to the tree and immediately hitched up her skirts.

"Don't you be watching me!"
"It doesn't prick my fancy," Jack replied.
"What about your mate?"
"You're not into watching ladies pass water, are you Owen?"
Owen shook his head.
"He says he's not into that."

There was an awkward lull with the only sound, apart from the swaying of leaves and the twittering of birds, being the sound of urine on dirt.

"You're taking a while down there, are you alright?" Jack asked.
"I'm alright. Just you keep looking the other way."

When Lillian had finally finished, she allowed herself a moment to dry off and then straightened herself out. Without a further word they were back on their way to the gang's stronghold.

The arrival at the cave was met with a quiet reception. Dan was stupid with drink and Ellen was reading quietly. She looked up to note the new arrival.

"I didn't realise the bank had started giving out people when you cash in your gold," Ellen said.

"Lillian, this is Ellen, you already know Dan but he's in much worse shape now than when you last saw him."

"What happened?"

"Scotchman with an itchy trigger finger," Owen replied.

Ellen scooted across and made room for Lillian on the bedroll. The pregnant girl was happy to acquiesce. Ellen took a quick glance over the girl.

"How far along are you?"

"Pardon me?"

"You know what I meant."

"Um," Lillian hesitated, "I think about two months. I don't know exactly. It took a while to notice, and I wasn't allowed to see the doctor."

"I'm sure you realised straight away what was going on."

Lillian blushed.

"Don't be embarrassed. I've been there. Three times over. The burning in my chest was the worst for my boy. Hairy like a bottle brush when he came out. Got that from his Daddy."

Ellen got lost in thought and gazed out to the bush. She wondered what her children were up to and why it had been so long since she had heard from them, apart from Susan. *Surely Terence at least could have written home at some point?* Something had always troubled her about how after a few months on the railroads in the city she stopped hearing from her boy altogether without any notice. Her daughters had apparently lost contact with him too. She had corresponded with police in Melbourne in pursuit of information but received no reply. He simply vanished.

"I hope mine isn't like his daddy," Lillian said.

"Oh?"

"He needs a good man to show him how to be, not a rotten, deceitful scurf."

Ellen let the air settle a little before moving the conversation on.

"Are you sure it's a boy?"

"Well… I mean, mothers are supposed to know these things, aren't they?"

"We're mothers. We may be many things, but we're not superhuman. It's alright not to know things like that, they'll let you know soon enough themselves. Why are you here?"

Lillian pointed to Jack, "They picked me up from the road. My employer fired me after his wife tried to murder me. I have no place to go so here I am with you."

Ellen frowned.

"This is no place for a pregnant girl."

"I can decide what's right for me. I'm of age."

"How old are you?"

Lillian lifted her chin defiantly.

"I'm seventeen and soon I'll be eighteen. I'm a proper woman, and I can even marry if I want to. Younger girls than me have been married and had babies by now."

Ellen smirked.

"Alright then. Just let me know if you need any help. I've enough experience to give you a hand."

Ellen moved to lay down and read but noticed blood seeping through Lillian's sleeve.

"Lillian," Ellen began, "did you say your boss's wife tried to murder you?"

"Yes," Lillian mumbled as she gazed at her toes. "Just this morning. She was hungry for blood, and she would have surely sent me to meet my maker only I feigned that I was out cold after she threw me down the stairs and she left me to my fate. I swear, as God is my witness, if I ever see her again, I will make her wish she had never laid eyes on me."

Ellen reached out and held Lillian's hand tenderly. Nothing more needed to be said.

Seven

With the news of the audacious robberies on McKenzie's and Churchley's properties so soon after the gold escort robbery, Senior-Constable Haigh was feeling intense pressure to bring the bushrangers to heel. A telegram to Melbourne had requested the deployment of reinforcements and "black trackers" to help take care of the issue. The initial response from the Chief Commissioner, a man whose interest in the problems of country people was fleeting at best, was affirmative but non-committal. After a week of persistent letters and telegrams from Haigh, he had arranged the transfer of two constables from nearby stations named Herbert Wilson and Patrick Mainwaring, as well as a Wurundjeri man to be their tracker. The man sent was an older gentleman affectionately named by his people as "Bullen Bullen", the lyrebird, because of his remarkable ability to mimic bird calls. However, he was known by the name Billy when in the presence of white men, because he was not allowed to speak his people's *woi wurrung* language.

***

It was a mild day on the cusp of Autumn when the police headed into the bush in pursuit of the bushrangers. It had been almost over a month since Haigh had confronted Ellen about the strange men on her property. With Bullen Bullen ahead of the police, they plunged deep into the territory Haigh had set his sights on as bushranging country.

"Why have you chosen to go through here, sir?" Mainwaring asked.

"The bushrangers wouldn't want it to be too obvious where they were camped so would be striking out far from their base of operations when they were committing robberies. So, based on the information from constables Martin and Molloy, who chased the widow McReady on her way to meet the bushrangers, and using maps of the area to note where they have been active, I estimated that this section of forest must be where they are concealing themselves. It is reasonable to surmise they have a camp somewhere in here, don't you think?"

"If they're in here I'll find them, boss," said Bullen Bullen. He scrutinised the ground for signs of horses or human activity. The best he could come up with was signs that wombats had recently been burrowing nearby, but nothing to indicate any bushrangers had been through that way. The news was not well received.

"We'll go deeper. They have to be here somewhere," Haig snarled.

The entire day was spent bumbling through the bush with no result. The police, untrained and unprepared for bush work, headed home that night with damaged uniforms and bruised egos.

Bullen Bullen approached Haigh upon their return to the station.

"I was wondering, boss, where I was meant to stay," he said, "nobody has told me where I'm meant to sleep."

Haigh turned to face the man and looked down his nose imperiously.

"Well, I suppose you can sleep in the stables. I don't suppose you have any food, do you?"

"Only what's in my kit, boss."

"That will have to do for now. I was unaware that it was going to be my responsibility to have you fed and kennelled. See that you don't spook the horses."

Bullen Bullen bowed slightly and made his way to the stables with a lantern. He laid the blanket from his swag out on the floor in an unoccupied stall so that he had somewhere to lay down and opened a tin of corned beef he had been given. As he ate the salty mush that passed for meat, he wondered what the cow had ever done to white men to deserve such treatment.

***

Morning came and with it a cool breeze filtered through the cave and roused its five occupants. Lillian was first to awake. She had only slept lightly, and her back was tremendously sore and bruised. She gently shook Ellen awake.

"Ellen," she whispered.

"Hmm?"

"How do I have a bath?"

"...with water, dear."

"No, I mean, how do I have a proper bath here in the bush?"

Ellen sucked in a deep lungful of air and rubbed her eyes until they focused.

"That's a question that I do not know the answer to. We usually just fetch water from nearby and have a go at the sweaty spots and our faces with a rag."

Ellen stood and shuffled to Jack who was guarding the cave entrance.

"Jack, where can Lilly and I have a bath?"

"Bath?"

"You know, to get clean all over."

Jack looked over his shoulder at the pregnant teen and back up at Ellen.

"Maybe just take a dip in the creek with a block of soap and a rag. Do you want me to take you down?"

"Do we look like we're suited to go wandering near the creek unescorted?"

Jack rose to his feet with a groan.

"Tread carefully and bring a big stick. You'll want to bash the bushes around to flush out the snakes."

With Owen left guarding the stronghold and Dan still asleep, Jack escorted the ladies to a secluded spot at the creek. Here water flowed serenely over smooth stones, some of which were infused with quartz and sparkled in the sunlight. The trees bobbed lazily and created enough shade and seclusion to shield Ellen and Lillian from prying eyes.

"This spot should do the job," Jack said, his gaze lingering on Ellen as the women walked to the water's edge.

They assisted each other in disrobing and waded cautiously into the chilled waters with a gasp. Goosebumps erupted over their bare skin and their wounds stung. Although she was healing admirably, Ellen's body was still covered in scratches and fading bruises that ranged from purple and grey splodges to a sickly yellow colour. Both ladies carefully cleaned their bodies with carbolic soap where they could, gingerly wiping around their healing wounds.

Lillian washed her belly gently, wiping a soapy cloth over it in a circular motion, admiring the roundness. She noticed the way that faint pink stripes were beginning to appear on her belly where the growth was starting to stretch her out.

"It must be strange for you seeing those changes for the first time," said Ellen.

"I don't know. I don't care much about me. All I care about is the person growing inside. I just want them to be safe. I'm scared that something will go wrong because of what happened yesterday."

Ellen placed her hand on Lillian's back reassuringly.

"I'm sure you'll be alright. Our bodies are designed to protect our little ones as they grow in us. You've copped it pretty rough, but you are stronger than you realise. The little one is pretty lucky."

"Do you really believe so?"

"I think can recognise a tough old bird when I see one."

Lillian impulsively reached out and hugged Ellen. Tears were pooling in her eyes. Ellen was stunned but returned the embrace carefully. She could tell that what the girl needed more than anything right now was the kindness that she had been denied by those she had trusted with her wellbeing.

Ellen looked over Lillian's shoulder and saw Jack peeking out from behind a tree.

"Are you alright?" Jack mouthed.

Ellen nodded before gesturing for him to get back behind cover.

"Thank you," Lillian said, "it's so hard to get through this on my own."

Ellen smiled politely and nodded. Lillian returned to her bathing; her mood now much lighter.

"So, are you and he a thing?"

"Me and Jack?"

"Yeah."

"What makes you say that?"

"I may not have been here long, but it has been long enough to see the way he looks at you."

"And how is that?"

"Well, last night when he was meant to be guarding the cave he was just watching you sleep most of the time. Like you were more important than anything else. I don't know the right way to describe it."

"And that leads you to believe we're a *'thing'*, as you put it?"

"Well, I've seen how your eyes light up when you look at him too. The way I see it, two people that feel like that about each other should be paired off. It's the right thing, you know."

"Oh, I see."

"Don't be like that."

"Like what?"

"I'm young, but I'm not stupid."

Ellen frowned.

"I never said you were. Nor is it my place to judge. To be perfectly honest, I wish I was still optimistic enough to have such a strong conviction as you do. You and I are probably very similar though in many ways, I think."

"I don't think we are," Lillian replied sullenly.

"Well, yes, in some respects we're very different. You have a lot more anger in you than I ever did."

"If you lived my life, you'd be angry too."

"I'm sure I would. Every one of us here has a good reason to be angry with the world. Just remember to direct that anger where it's *deserved*."

Lillian looked sheepish for a moment.

"I'm sorry."

"Apology accepted. Now let's get out of the water before we go all wrinkly."

As the ladies dried themselves off and relaxed on the shore, Lillian's attention was grabbed by something in the water. She positioned herself by a tree and peered through the branches with a cheeky grin.

"What's caught your eye?" Ellen asked.

"Oh, I think you'll want to come and see for yourself."

Ellen got up and joined Lillian. Peering through the branches she could see Jack up to his knees in the water, naked as the day he was born and scrubbing himself clean. Ellen immediately placed a hand over her mouth.

"He's a big boy. I can see why your eyes light up."

"I've had bigger," Ellen replied. A second later with the realisation of what she had let slip she clapped a hand over her mouth. Lillian's mouth hung open with shock.

"Don't you dare tell him I said that!"

"Your secret is safe with me," Lillian replied with a smirk.

For a few moments more they watched Jack before Lillian got bored and whistled at him. Jack, unable to see where the sound had come from, paused and frowned.

"I'm eating for two and neither of us have had breakfast," said Lillian sliding her chemise on painfully.

"I'll whip something up for us all," said Ellen, "but I'll give you a hand to get dressed first. You really should get those cuts bandaged up."

"I'll be fine," Lillian groaned.

***

After a filling breakfast of porridge and steaming hot cups of black tea, the gang started talking business. The discussion centred around what the next move should be.

"I think we need to look at finding a new hideaway altogether," said Owen, "If we stay put, we make ourselves too easy to find. I reckon the police will be intensifying their search for us after the last few robberies."

"We should be fine for a few more days, I think," said Ellen.

"We can't move too fast with a pregnant girl," said Dan. Lillian gave him a death glare. "Besides, we're short on horses now."

"We don't have to move much, Dan. Just enough to stay out of reach of the traps," Owen replied.

"Without harbourers it's hard," Jack said. The others nodded.

"Now that the goldfields have stopped being profitable for anyone other than the big mining companies, maybe we can find an old miner's hut we can use?" Ellen suggested.

"I reckon I know where we might be able to find one," said Jack.

"That's a start," said Dan. He looked across at Lillian, "I assume you're coming with us?"

"Well, it's either that or I go home in disgrace. I'm not sure which is the better option, though."

Jack smirked. He wasn't sure what the saner choice was either. All he knew was that in the brief time he'd known her, this pregnant teen had proven to be peppery, capable in a stressful situation and, most importantly, fiercely loyal. The apple never falls far from the tree, he reasoned, so she must have had a good reason to fear facing her family.

***

So that they might travel without being instantly recognised, the men made sure to clean up their appearance. Ellen and Lillian derived much amusement from watching the men crowding around a single tiny shaving mirror, stolen from Elliot McKenzie's house, as they attempted to cut away their manly face fur with straight razors.

"Can someone get at my right side? I can't hold the razor," Dan complained.

"Look here, I'll sort it out," Owen said as he rubbed the blade's edge along a razor strop. He lifted Dan's chin and began gently shaving away the thick black beard.

"Don't you slip," said Dan.

"Keep your mouth shut then," Owen replied.

"Just shut up and shave. I want to get there before it's dark," Jack snapped. He was much aggrieved at having to get rid of his beard, which he took great pride in.

When they were shaved and dressed in their best clothes, they looked like respectable gentlemen of status, or at the least more like sons of a rich squatter, not hardened bushmen. Jack, however, wore a sour expression. He was uncomfortable and did not like how he looked one bit.

While Ellen helped load up the horses, Lillian occupied herself with dressing. She took one of Wilhelmina Churchley's pale blue pleated dresses and, realising she was too sore to dress herself, sought assistance. She could not find Ellen nearby and became frustrated.

"What's the matter?" asked Owen as he came up the slope to the cave entrance.

"I... I need help getting changed and I can't find Ellen."

"She's busy at the moment. Can I help?"

Lillian went quiet and averted her gaze.

"You can say no, I won't be offended," said Owen.

"Alright, alright. Just don't get any ideas."

The pair went into the cave and Lillian gestured for Owen to gather up her clothing. She unbuttoned her brown dress and attempted to unhook the top from the skirt to slide it off but could not reach around the back.

"Help me with this," she ordered. Owen followed her instructions to undo the hooks along the waistline, then Lillian gingerly raised her arms so he could gently tug the sleeves away from her. He could see that her wounds had opened up from the movement as there was fresh blood seeping through her shirtsleeves. He helped her remove the shirt and he examined the gashes on her upper arms.

"You've been in the wars. Let me fetch some bandages."

Owen rushed off to his horse to grab fresh bandages from his saddlebag. He had made a point of grabbing them from McKenzie's place after seeing how Jack had to tear up a shirt to make bandages for Ellen. He returned at a jogging pace. He dressed the wounds and continued to help Lillian undress. She wore no corset to allow her belly to grow comfortably.

"This chemise is bloodied as well," said Owen, "Shall we take it off and get you a clean one?"

"There aren't any. Your man there only stole dresses and shirts, not undergarments. If you men had any idea what we women have to go through just to look presentable for you…"

"Whoa, now. I just want to help. I thought you had some in that big carpet bag of yours."

Lillian froze and gazed over towards the dying fire where she had left her belongings. She had forgotten it as if there was a London fog in her brain that had hidden the memory from her. She felt confused and frustrated and began to cry. Owen was baffled and reached out to rest a hand reassuringly on her shoulder, but she batted his hand away. She pointed to the bag and bawled something incoherent at Owen. He assumed she was telling him to fetch the bag. He did so and rifled through it for a clean chemise.

"I'm sorry," Lillian sniffed, "I don't know what came over me."

"You've been through a lot, my girl…"

"I'm not a girl. I'm a woman."

"Well, obviously. It's just an expression. Just let me undo these skirts so we can get this chemise off, alright?"

"You promise you won't look?"

"Look at what?"

"At… *me*."

"Well, I'll do my best, but I need to be able to see what I'm doing."

"I don't want you looking at my private parts."

"I have no intention of doing anything like that. I just want to help you get changed so we can get moving. The sun won't stay up forever."

"Well, alright then. Get a move on," said Lillian impetuously.

"Jack was right. You are a bit of a boss."

"Maybe you need bossing? Did you ever consider that?"

Once Lillian was changed, she grabbed a large stick and used it to scoop up her old clothes and drop them in the fire. She watched as flames consumed the dress that she had worn to introduce herself to Jim Churchley and beg for a job — the same clothes she wore when he turned her out like a mongrel dog after he had used her for his own gratification. Tears rolled down her cheeks, but she forced them away with the back of her hand.

As Jack loaded his possessions onto his horse, Ellen beckoned him to join her by a blue gum. He dusted his hands off on his frock coat and joined her. She smiled broadly.

"You know, I think you look very handsome."

Jack grunted.

"Oh, come on, it's just hair. It grows back. At least give me a kiss so I know how your chin feels before it disappears again."

Nervously, Jack looked over his shoulder to see if anyone was looking then gave Ellen a lingering kiss.

"That was nice," said Ellen, "Maybe with a bit of luck we can see what it feels like when you kiss me elsewhere a bit later on."

Jack smiled and planted a top hat on his head.

While everyone prepared to leave, Dan went into the back of the cave and carved their initials on the wall with a knife. He felt it had been their home long enough that they needed to leave some kind of mark behind.

As the gang left their hideout, Ellen and Lillian rode on Old Tom, Jack rode Pathfinder, Owen on Ruffy, and Dan rode their packhorse, Tombstone. The procession was slow.

Lillian watched a bird with grey plumage, a black head and a straight beak, dart through the canopy. She knew nothing about birds and could not recognise it.

"Do you know what that bird is called," she said pointing to it. The bird gazed down at the passing riders and tilted its head. It let out a twittering, warbling call.

"It's a butcher bird. They're very common here," said Ellen.

"It has a pretty song."

Hanging from a fork in the branch upon which the bird was perched, like a carcass on a butcher's hook, was the remains of a lizard that the bird ripped at with its beak. Lillian scrunched her nose up.

"I don't think I like them so much now."

"We all have to eat, sweetheart. Unfortunately, even the sweetest looking things in nature can be ugly at times."

***

After a long ride, with frequent rest stops, the gang arrived at Jack's old miner's hut. It was a small structure made from wattle and daub with a bark roof, and enough cleared space around it for a horse paddock. There was a creek flowing close by that would provide an ample water supply, although the water was not clean, and it was far enough away from the road that they were not likely to be seen by too many travellers.

The hut itself was small but would allow enough room for the five occupants and their possessions if they were all happy to get intimately acquainted with each other. It was now in a state of near dilapidation, as it had clearly been unoccupied for some time.

"Here she is," said Jack.

"What's the story about this place again?" Owen asked.

"When I was prospecting this was where I lived with McFeely."

"Richard McFeely?"

"Yes, we worked a claim together."

"Did you build the hut?"

"We did."

"If your mining was anything like your building, I can see why you gave up on it," said Dan with a sneer.

"We gave up on it," Jack said with a half-lidded gaze, "because the mining company set up its operations upstream. There was no way we could get anything from the creek once they moved in. As usual the big fellas squeezed out the little ones."

The men unloaded the belongings and set up inside the hut. The walls were papered with old newspaper, creating an unintended time capsule into when the hut was created. Dan noticed some of the newspapers on the walls had pictures.

"Which of you read the illustrated papers?"

"That was Dick's thing. He didn't much care for newspapers with too many words."

Dan lingered over a pair of pages that had been stuck down next to each other, both with large etchings printed on them. On one page was a dramatic seascape with heaving waves assaulting a ship that reminded him of his days as a sailor. Underneath, a quiet pastoral scene with cows grazing under a tree in a paddock, a jumble of buildings on a rise overlooking them as two portly gentlemen conversed by a fence. Nothing particularly remarkable. The page parallel to it was a different story. More than half a dozen men carrying weapons crowded around a prone figure, a bearded man. His hat and a revolver lay beside him. Clearly this was the aftermath of some violent interaction. In the distance a man carrying a rifle ran waving as if to summon reinforcements. He read the caption:

CAPTURE AND DEATH OF MORGAN, THE BUSHRANGER.

"Any of you chaps know about this Morgan the bushranger?"

"Daniel Morgan? How could you fail to remember him?" Jack replied.

"Only been in Australia for a short while. What happened?"

"Wild man. Robbed coaches, killed police, burned the farms of anyone that opposed him. Was on the loose for years until a bunch of police and civilians surrounded a house he had bailed up, waited all night for him to come out, and one bugger who was out for blood and glory shot him while his back was turned."

"Never stood a chance, eh?" Dan said, scratching his chin.

"That's why we need to look out for each other," Jack said. He paused and joined Dan, placing his hand on his shoulder.

"I'm sorry about what happened at the McKenzie farm. I promise I won't let it happen again."

Dan smiled broadly.

"I can still hold a gun, I can grab a bottle, I can ride a horse and I can make a lover happy if I get lucky. Don't be losing sleep on account of me. You're too serious, Jack Cooper."

As the women settled in, Jack and Owen cut bark from the trees nearby and patched up the roof and the chimney. It was rudimentary, but it would keep them dry in a downpour and keep the sun off them in the heat of the day.

***

Another day, another fruitless search. Haigh had become almost obsessed with the idea that the bushrangers were in this section of bushland. Fortunately for him, Bullen Bullen was a good enough tracker that he was able to pinpoint likely hiding places on the slopes of the mountain that the forest sat at the foot of, which gave him hope.

"Boss, if bushrangers gonna be hiding anywhere, they'll be in the mountains. Plenty caves there. Easy to hide," he said. Haigh considered the suggestion, and assuring himself it would have been his logical next step anyway, ordered the party to proceed towards the slopes.

As they moved closer, the old tracker found old hoof imprints in the mud leading up to the mountain. He showed Haigh who directed him to follow the tracks by gesturing with his riding crop.

Gradually the party saw a cave come into view as they passed the tree line. Haigh's eyes lit up when he saw the remnants of a fire at the mouth of the cave.

"Martin, Molloy, take the nigger up to the cave and see if there's anyone in there. Make him go in first, just in case."

The constables did as they were told, gesturing for Bullen Bullen to join them.

"What did Boss call me?" Bullen Bullen asked the constables.

"He called you a nigger," Molloy explained.

"What's that?"

"It's an ugly word the snobs use to describe blacks," said Martin.

"Boss is a snob?"

"Yeah, a big snob," Molloy answered with a chuckle, "spends so much time looking down his nose at everyone he can't remember what his cock looks like. Don't tell him that, though, or he'll hit you with his crop."

"Is that why he tell us come up here and him sit on the horse down there?"

"Exactly right. He's an Englishman. We Irish are the same as you blacks in his eyes. He doesn't like us. If anyone is in the cave, we'll all get shot first and then he can run away and hide under his wife's petticoat."

"Nobody is in the cave," replied Bullen Bullen, slightly confused.

Molloy and Martin glanced at each other. They drew their pistols and carefully peered inside as they reached the mouth of the cave. Sure enough, it was empty. The tracker poked the ashes of the fire with his finger.

"Been gone coupla days I reckon. Maybe more. Looks like maybe they leave quickly."

"Did they leave anything behind?" Molloy asked.

"Someone been burning clothes," Bullen Bullen replied holding up a scrap from Lillian's brown dress.

The constables ventured inside and looked for signs of occupation. In a far corner of the cave was a pile of bloodied bandages, empty food tins and bottles. Carved nearby were the initials DT, OB, JC, EM, LB.

When the trio returned to the others, they explained what they had found. Haigh was conflicted. On the one hand he had his first tangible proof that his theory was correct and wanted to celebrate his vindication, but the bushrangers were gone, and this made him as furious as much as embarrassed. He gazed up and noticed dark clouds moving in. If they didn't head back, they would either get caught in the oncoming storm or be stuck in the bush come nightfall.

"Men, let's head back to the station. Tomorrow we will try and pick up their trail from here. I will arrange tents if necessary for us to stay out longer."

The group began to trek back to Ironbark, Bullen Bullen on foot at the front. He knew how to ride a horse; he had done so many times as a boundary rider and jockey on various stations over the years. It was Haigh's decision that he be made to go on foot rather than ride, so that he was closer to the ground. Billy knew better than to argue. He also knew there was no point trying to follow the tracks tomorrow after the rain, but the snob would learn that well enough come the morning.

***

That night a storm did indeed break. Fortunately for the bushrangers the roof was assembled well enough to shield them from the pelting rain

Owen had gotten a fire going in the fireplace and the ladies sat close by it with blankets over them. Occasionally raindrops shot down the flue and hissed as they landed in the burning wood.

The men sat on the ground at the other end of the hut playing cards by candlelight until a gust of wind that slipped under the bark window shutters sent the cards flying and snuffed the candles.

It had gotten dark very quickly and the it took hold fast. Jack had made sure the door and the shutters were closed as the wind kicked up, but the latches were rotten. He went outside and nailed the shutters down to keep them closed. White flashes of lightning were visible through the cracks.

As the lightning cracked and tumbled through the clouds, Lillian became visibly shaken. She had never been in a storm so severe in shelter so flimsy. She curled herself up, hugging her knees and drawing her blanket over her head.

A huge thunderclap shook the walls. The men cheered. And the women screamed

"She's a biggun," chuckled Dan.

"Must be because of all that dry heat we've had," said Owen.

Ellen was very conscious of Lillian's nervousness and tried to think of ways to soothe her.

"Any of you boys know a good song?"

"What kind of song?" Dan asked.

"Not the sort you normally sing. I don't care to hear about lecherous old sailors deflowering young maids."

"I might know something," said Jack. After a moment of thinking he seemed to decide. He sang:

> 'Tis the last rose of summer,
>   Left blooming alone;
> All her lovely companions
>   Are faded and gone;
> No flower of her kindred,
>   No rose-bud is nigh,
> To reflect back her blushes
>   Or give sigh for sigh!
>
> I'll not leave thee, thou lone one.
>   To pine on the stem;
> Since the lovely are sleeping,
>   Go, sleep thou with them;
> Thus, kindly I scatter
>   Thy leaves o'er the bed,
> Where thy mates of the garden
>   Lie scentless and dead.
>
> So soon may I follow,
>   When friendships decay,
> And from love's shining circle
>   The gems drop away!
> When true hearts lie wither'd,
>   And fond ones are flown,
> Oh! who would inhabit
>   This bleak world alone?

The rushing of the wind and the rolling of thunder heckled his performance, but shaky though his voice was it seemed to shift the mood in the hut considerably. Ellen gazed upon him with glistening eyes. The words spoke to her in a way that felt almost too personal, as if they were written by someone who could read her mind and feel her heart's pain. As Jack finished singing Ellen felt tears streaking down her cheeks.

***

Eventually everyone had to turn in. The storm provided, oddly enough, a sense of security. The fugitives were unanimous in their belief that nobody in their right mind would be out looking for them in such a storm. Owen had been consumed with guilt over the fact that there was no adequate stabling for the horses to protect them from the elements, although he and Jack had attempted to craft a temporary shelter for them out of the leftover bark slabs and hewn branches that afternoon. Several times during the height of the storm Owen went out into the tempest to check on the animals and returned drenched to report that they were accounted for.

With the occupants sleeping in close quarters on the floor, their combined body heat proved useful as the wild weather sucked the warmth out of the environment. After such a relentless summer the drought had broken with what felt like overcompensation.

Ellen made a point of being close to Jack, who had his back to her. As everyone else had seemingly drifted off to sleep, she wriggled in close to him.

She placed her mouth close to his ear and whispered, "hold me."

Jack rolled over and pulled Ellen in close, holding her to his chest. The gesture soothed her. No more words were uttered, and they soon joined the others in slumber.

***

At first light the troopers set out again. This time they knew where to go first and made a beeline for the cave. The bush was fragrant with the smell of damp eucalypt and soft earth as they moved through. As they approached the cave Bullen Bullen knew that he would have to deliver bad news to Haigh, and he expected that it would not be well-received. Not even the world's greatest tracker could find a way to track the movements of bushrangers after such a ferocious downpour as that which had struck the area overnight.

Sure enough, when they reached the cave, the slope was rippled with sludge that had been washed down in the deluge and any signs of human occupation outside the cave were destroyed.

"Bad news, boss. Rain washed everything away. Been a lotta rain. Hard to find tracks."

Haigh scowled and pointed the brass horse head on his crop at the tracker.

"Then you had better bloody well look hard."

Bullen Bullen was unfazed by the implied threat. He had been beaten, flogged, starved and degraded by white men as long as he could remember. As a child he was employed as a stable boy by a fat Glaswegian man at a pub. "Employed" was the polite word and inaccurately suggested that he had some say in the matter and received wages. Rather, he was kept there to cover his grandfather's debt to the Glaswegian. His grandfather was an alcoholic and the Glaswegian had taken great amusement in the man's lack of tolerance for liquor. He would keep him around and ply him with booze for his own amusement until one day the old man had enough. In a rare moment of sobriety, he listened to his daughters and decided to give up the drink. Of course, the Glaswegian did not take kindly to this and tracked the old man down and demanded he pay his tab. The old man had no money to cover the debt so the Glaswegian stated that the old man's grandson would work for him until the debt was paid off.

So it was that Bullen Bullen at the ripe old age of seven was snatched from his mother to live in the Glaswegian's stables. Night after night men would stable their horses while they went inside to get drunk. Some paid a shilling to the boy, others paid nothing, some kicked him and spat at him. In the end it had taken the Glaswegian's speedy demise from a sudden heart attack to release him from his bondage and he could not get out of there quicker if he had tried.

He often thought back to the smile on his mother's face as he returned home. It was always enough to get him through the dark days when the cruelty that he was subjected to made him question why he should continue. He pictured her as he paced around the cave looking for a sign of the bushrangers. He had never had a family of his own and he was too old now. His memories were all he had.

***

Lillian stood in the creek up to her ankles, which were swollen and sore. From the banks of the creek Dan watched her soothing her feet and swigged from a ceramic bottle of ale.

"Are you right there watching me?" Lillian snapped.
"Why are you soaking your feet?"
"Because they're sore. Carrying a baby does things to your body. My feet are all swollen up and this makes them hurt less. Do you object?"
"Why don't you try some of my drink? That'll help with the pain."
"I'd rather not imbibe any of that poison. Neither should you. It'll make you fat and smelly."
Dan laughed and shook his head. "I don't think it will."

"You don't? Your face is already getting puffy. Your nose will go all lumpy like porridge too."

Dan's smile faded. "You're a mean girl, you know that?"

"Then don't stare at me and ask stupid questions."

Dan had enough of the tongue lashing and decided to find something else to stare at while he polished off his booze. Lillian continued to bathe her feet in peace.

On the other side of the hut in a clearing, Jack and Ellen were grooming the horses. During the night the shelter had fallen over, though it wasn't clear if it had blown over or if one of the horses had knocked it down in a moment of brainless terror.

"So, what's the plan with Lilly?"

"Lillian? Well, I suppose she'll be with us for a little while. Maybe until she has the baby. I hope not. It would be a bad idea for her to be traipsing around with us in her condition."

"The bush is no place for a girl carrying a baby."

"It's just…" Jack paused, "She's got nothing to go back to and nothing to look forward to. Her boss put her in the pudding club and kicked her out and her folks will probably send her off to a nunnery or workhouse or something. I don't know what they do to girls these days."

"I understand, Jack, but you need to be realistic. If we have more nights like last night she's not going to cope, never mind when the baby comes."

Jack looked over his horse at Ellen.

"Be honest with me, Nellie. Have I done something foolish?"

"You've done many foolish things in the time I've known you," Ellen replied, "but this isn't one of them. It's sweet. You mean well and she seems to respond to that. I suspect it's just what she needed."

"I'm a bushranger. I'm not supposed to be sweet. What will the papers call me? 'Sweet Jack' Cooper?"

"Let's see what happens. Maybe the girl will get sick of life on the run and seek comfort in town. I'm sure it won't be hard to find her work."

With the horses groomed and hobbled to stop them wandering, there was business to attend to and Jack took Dan with him to get the rest of the gold melted down, leaving Owen with the two ladies at the hut.

Without much in the way of chores left to do Owen took some time to sit and play his flute to the remaining horses. As he did so, Ellen and Lillian watched him from the hut.

"He's not like the others really, is he?" said Lillian.
"How so?"
"Well, he's much quieter. He's gentle. Dan's a drunk and Jack has a bit of flashness about him, but Owen just likes being with his horse and playing music. He's gentle and thoughtful. There's something special in that, I think."
Ellen saw the smitten look on Lillian's face and stayed quiet.

***

Having failed to gain any useful clues from the cave, Haigh was forced to either concede defeat or create a new plan. In the meantime, the troopers had decided to take a break and enjoy the natural surroundings.

Bullen Bullen continued to examine the area around the cave for signs. After only a few moments of leaving Haigh's field of view, Bullen Bullen heard him yelling at his subordinates.

"Where's the black? Who was watching him?"

Bullen Bullen imagined the joy he would feel if he could take a club to Haigh's head and give him his just desserts. He giggled and at that moment he spotted something useful — signs of damage to the vegetation where horses had been through. He returned to the others with a toothy smile.

"Hey, boss, I found the trail. Went down this way with horses. Reckon we can follow through the bush."

Haigh stormed over to Bullen Bullen with a look of thunder on his face. The tracker refused to allow himself to appear intimidated.
"You ever step one foot without my saying so and I will chop it off and make you wear it! You do as I say."
Bullen Bullen smirked, "Gonna be slow getting around with one foot, boss."
Haigh slapped the tracker across the face with the back of his hand. It didn't draw blood, but it stung.
"Good hit there, boss. Makes me think of my aunty. You want me to show you where them bushrangers go?"
Haigh tightened his grip on his brass-pommelled riding crop and raised it in preparation to strike the tracker when he was stopped by Constable Martin.
"Sir, we should check it out," said the constable as he stepped in front of Haigh.
Haigh growled and lowered his arm. Realising he had lost his cool he straightened his tunic and returned to his horse.

***

It was in the early afternoon when the five troopers and their tracker finally emerged from the bush at the road. It took barely any time at all for them to discover the miner's hut a short distance away.

By that time Ellen had stoked a fire in the fireplace and smoke wafted from the bark flue lazily. Haigh gestured for his men to follow him to the hut. The police dismounted and Haigh summoned them close.

"Mainwaring, Molloy, I want you to go around the back as quietly as you can and see if anyone is there," Haigh instructed. The men did as ordered. Haigh then directed the others to keep an eye out at the sides of the building as he went to the door. He knocked at the door with his crop handle. After a short wait the door was opened by Lillian.

"Yes?"

"I am Senior-Constable Haigh. I'm searching through the area, and I wondered if you might answer some questions, Miss…?"

"Brook. Questions about what?"

"Well, for starters, who is here with you?"

"It's me, my brother and my aunt."

"How long have you been here?"

"I've been here for a few days. I'm not staying long. Brother is working a claim here. I'm just visiting."

Haigh narrowed his eyes.

"I don't suppose you've seen three rough looking gentlemen come past with an older woman, Mrs. Brook?"

"That's *Miss* Brook. I'm sorry, you'll have to be more specific than that."

"I'm looking for three men. A tall, dark-haired man with a long beard; a thin man with long brown hair and beard; and a short, swarthy man, missing two fingers on his left hand. They are travelling with a middle-aged woman with blonde hair."

Lillian maintained an expression of disinterest.

"Sorry, I can't say I've seen anyone like that around here."

Haigh was determined to make progress and kept up the pressure.

"Think — have you seen any people matching those descriptions?"

"Honestly, that could be a hundred people I know. I think maybe you are going to have trouble finding these people without more information."

Haigh was beginning to fume. He felt sure the girl was hiding something.

"Whose horses are those in the yard?"

"My aunt's and my brother's."

"Where is yours?"

"I don't ride in my condition. I came on the back of my aunt's horse."

Lillian could sense Haigh's growing frustration and wanted to laugh in his face.

"Where are your brother and aunt now?"

"They've gone down to the creek somewhere to fetch water."

"Alright, well I might just see if I can find them to corroborate your story."

"Do you think I am lying, Constable Hay?" Lillian asked, cocking her head and folding her arms.

"*Senior-Constable Haigh.* I should hope not, Miss Brook, but it would not be the first time I have been lied to about these individuals lately. I must bring these men in, they are outlaws, and I am in no mood to be going around in circles following bad leads or being misled by ladies of questionable virtue," Haigh snarled as he gestured to Lillian's belly. Lillian glared at him with the fury of a thousand suns, resisting the urge to spit in his face.

"I'm afraid I have more important things to do than stand around having aspersions cast about my virtue by the likes of you. You might care to reconsider how effective harassing pregnant women is as a technique for hunting outlaws and instead focus on doing something useful," Lillian stated forcefully and slammed the door in the officer's face.

Haigh sneered and returned to his men.

"Anything?"

"Nobody else here by the looks," Mainwaring replied.

"The girl stated her brother and aunt were down the creek. Let's head down and test the legitimacy of her story."

Mounting up, the police headed upstream in pursuit of two people who they had no description of beyond their genders.

Lillian opened the door enough to watch them leave without being spotted. Once they were out of view she went to where Ellen and Owen were hiding beneath a tarpaulin.

"It's alright, they're gone now."

The pair emerged from their hiding place and relaxed.

"Did they go upstream or downstream?" Owen asked. Lillian wasn't sure how to respond and simply pointed in the direction they went. Owen furrowed his brow.

"What is it?" Ellen asked.

"That's the way Jack and Dan will be coming back, but I doubt they'll cross paths."

**

At that very moment, Jack and Dan were on their way back with a purse full of money from cashing in more of the gold ingots. As part of his disguise, Dan had taken to wearing leather gloves to hide his deformed hand, with the empty fingers of his left-hand glove padded with scraps of fabric.

As they rode along the creek they saw Bullen Bullen walking toward their direction on the opposite bank. Jack immediately knew something was up.

"Hang back, I'll ride slightly ahead and see what's there. Try and be inconspicuous."

Dan slowed his horse down and veered towards the tree line as Jack rode forward slightly. Beyond the Aboriginal man, Jack saw five approaching police horses. He looked back over his shoulder to see where Dan was — he was out of sight.

As the police came closer, he tried to avoid looking but knew it was hard to find a rational reason not to acknowledge five mounted police and their tracker in the middle of the bush. He felt flushed. He turned to Haigh and tapped the brim of his top hat. Haigh did not even acknowledge his existence. The other police also seemed more concerned with their journey than in the scruffy-looking squatter on the opposite bank.

Following Jack's path, Dan rode in the scrub to avoid detection. Bullen Bullen caught the sounds of the horse in the scrub and realised the rider was trying not to be seen. He gazed across the creek and could see movement in the bush but decided not to raise it with Haigh as it gave him a little glee to realise that Haigh may have just let the exact men he was looking for slip through his fingers because he wasn't paying attention. Besides, it was getting late in the day and his legs were tired.

Almost ten minutes later, Haigh decided that, perhaps, the brother and aunt were in the opposite direction. As he turned, his constables remained motionless.
"Come on, let's get down the creek."
"Sir, I don't think we're going to find anyone down there," said Mainwaring.
"Did I ask for your opinion?"

"He's right though, sir. Billy hasn't seen any tracks since we came out onto the road. Surely, they would have left some traces," Molloy chimed in.

"So, this is how it is? You're all insubordinate? If this has all been the result of a bad lead it's through no fault of mine," Haigh snapped, "It was the nigger that brought us here."

He glared at Bullen Bullen and dismounted.

"You led us up here on purpose just to send us astray, didn't you?"

"No, Boss."

"Don't talk back to me!"

Haigh swung his crop at Bullen Bullen, striking him across the head with the brass pommel.

"I'll teach you a lesson, you black bastard!"

Haigh struck Bullen Bullen again and again. The blows were heavy, and blood began to pour from an open wound on his scalp. The brutality of the blows was ugly, and the constables sat watching, with the exception of Constable Martin, who dismounted and grabbed Haigh by the hand. Martin was not a strong man and Haigh shrugged him off easily. The Senior-Constable then turned his attention on Martin and clouted him across the face with the crop. Haigh was like a wild animal backed into a corner, snarling and lashing out. Martin collapsed, cradling his jaw. His mouth was full of blood, and he spat a broken tooth onto the dirt.

"Head back to the station. They can find their own way back, but they'd be damned fools to come within my sight if they do," Haigh growled at the others as he mounted his horse. The troopers took off at a brisk pace leaving Martin and Bullen Bullen badly injured and bleeding behind them.

***

At the hut a discussion was being held about what to do about the police. By the time Jack and Dan had returned and put their horses in the clearing at the back everyone was on edge.

"If the traps are scouting this area, they know we're about," Owen had stated.

"But they obviously have no idea who they're looking for because we passed right by them without being recognised," Jack replied.

The argument was interrupted by the rumble of hooves passing by. Lillian poked her head out of the door and saw four of the police going past. They did not stop or even slow down.

"It's the traps; they've just gone straight past us. Only there seemed to be one less and the blackfellow wasn't with them," she informed the rest of the group while watching the horsemen ride away.

"You don't suppose they left the tracker and a constable behind to keep looking for us, do you?" Owen asked.

"It's possible," Jack answered, "But I don't want to take a chance. I'm going to scout."

Jack exchanged his velvet frock coat for a weathered sack coat, and his top hat for a low-crowned cabbage-tree hat with a blue band, grabbed a shotgun and headed out.

Following the creek, he traced the hoof marks left by the police, which led him to Constable Martin's horse, which was ripping bark off a tree with its teeth. Jack remained cautious as he continued along the creek. He saw Constable Martin and Bullen Bullen sitting on the ground, dazed and covered in blood. He stuck his hand into his coat and fingered the grip of his pistol as he approached them.

"Who are you? What are you doing here?"

"Condable Mardn," the injured policeman mumbled with his broken teeth and lacerated tongue. Bullen Bullen was unresponsive.

"Why are you here?"
"We... ah hurdd. Neeh a dogg-der."

Jack scrutinised the figures before him. Martin with his mouth covered in blood, Billy bleeding from head wounds and barely conscious. He knew they were in a bad way and considered leaving them to their fate, but part of him felt that there was something to be gained by being the bushranger who helped rescue a policeman and his tracker. In spite of his misgivings, he dismounted and went to their aid.

"Get up, come on."

Jack helped Constable Martin to his feet and managed to pick Bullen Bullen up as well. They made their way to the horse, which was unwilling to cooperate as Jack made a grab for the reins.

"Get out of it, you bastard. Do as you're told," Jack growled. He managed to hold the animal in place as Constable Martin mounted and then assisted Bullen Bullen onto the back of the horse as well.

"Dank-oo."

"Do you realise who I am?" Jack said, revealing his revolver.

"You...?" Martin began.

"If you've any brains left, you'll get yourself to a doctor. If anyone asks, leave me out of it. You never saw Jack Cooper and he certainly didn't help you get on your feet when you were in a bad way. Savvy?"

The policeman gave Jack a confused expression.

"Go on."

With a slap on the flank, the horse took off leaving Jack to ponder the strange turn of events of that afternoon. He knew that the saying was that one good turn deserves another, but he also knew that where the police were concerned one never knew what constituted a "good turn" in their eyes. Either the trooper would keep his mouth shut about who helped him, or he would be forced to state what had happened, thus giving him a bit of good publicity that could serve him well later. He returned to the hut where the others waited expectantly for the all-clear.

***

It was a peculiarity of the squatter class that though they may have all viewed each other as rivals and competitors, a common enemy was grounds to form a sort of "council of war". Indeed, many of the key squatters in the region around Ironbark had come together in the Purple Rose Tavern, with the express purpose of forming an alliance.

The spearhead was Elliot McKenzie, still harbouring rage from his confrontation as if it had occurred mere moments beforehand. Also included were James Churchley and his wife, Wilhelmina, who refused to allow him into town unescorted; Theodore Amery, a local barley farmer; Michael Cornell, owner of *Birrawung*, a large cattle station; Francis Barnard, renowned horse breeder; and Samson P. Samson, who owned a sheep farm and a very profitable oat crop. Each one of them had been affected either by Cooper's gang or by other lawless behaviour that had either deprived them of property or cut into their profits. In Samson's case, he wasn't sure which was more egregious.

After much discussion the squatters agreed to form what they referred to as the Upstanding Citizens League. A manifesto was drafted, detailing how each one would endeavour to protect life, limb, and property against the ravages of criminals, with or without the aid of the authorities. It involved using their social standing to influence magistrates to implement harsher sentences, to influence constables to make more arrests and even to influence politicians to push for harsher laws if possible. Their stance was to eradicate crime by taking anyone that had the potential to commit it out of the equation. Of course, it had taken some convincing to shift McKenzie from his policy of "shoot the bastards" to something less illegal for the time being, but the Scotsman was adamant that they should agitate for protections under the law that allowed them to shoot without question and without consequences. He even presented a small tin box on a leather thong he had been wearing around his neck. Upon opening it, he revealed to his associates the fingers he had blasted off Dan's hand during the bushrangers' escape. He had smoked them in order to mummify them and kept them as a trophy.

"Next time it will be his head," McKenzie swore.

The following day a letter arrived on the desk of the local newspaper editor in an unstamped envelope. It read:

> *We, the members of the Upstanding Citizens League, wish to give fair warning to wrong-doers, miscreants, ne'er-do-wells, harlots, thieves, vagrants and bushrangers of all inclinations that we will no longer tolerate lawlessness in our community. You have, for too long, kept the hardest working and most valuable contributors to this society in a state of dread and it will no longer be tolerated.*
>
> *We will do all within our ability to bring you to heel for your transgressions and to deter any other wayward people from a life of crime and villainy.*
>
> *Your days are numbered, by notice of the undersigned.*

Below the missive were the myriad ornate and illegible signatures of the members of the league. The editor knew he had a scoop and by the time the ink had dried on the newspapers that morning the Upstanding Citizens League had become the proclaimed enemies of the bushrangers.

Eight

With the passing of the stormy weather, it had been decided to create a better enclosure for the horses. Jack and Owen built a new pen using whatever wood they could find and the limited tools they had with them to create the fencing. It was a rudimentary chock-and-log style thing due to their lack of nails and milled wood, but it seemed to be enough to keep the horses contained for the moment. Owen then spent much of the afternoon sitting at the fence playing his flute to the horses while Jack went off with Ellen and a shotgun into the bush to walk along the creek and catch some dinner. Dan was busy napping in the hut near the fireplace.

Lillian sat outside the hut looking down towards the horses listening to Owen's playing and absent-mindedly rubbing her belly. It was in the rare quiet moments like these when she was able to finally feel a connection to the life growing inside her. Her belly was now growing quite round, but she had not noticed any movement inside. She did not know how far along she was since Jim Churchley had refused to allow her to see a doctor or tell anyone of her condition.

Listening to Owen's music began to make Lillian feel melancholy, but at the same time it almost felt like a weight being lifted. Something in the way that Owen played touched her heart and told her that her pain wasn't hers alone to carry. The feeling puzzled her, and she decided to get closer so she could hear better. As she came nearer to the pen, Owen continued to play with his eyes closed, almost as if in a trance.

"Hey," said Lillian. Owen jolted out of his trance and whipped around. Lillian put her hand to her mouth. "I'm sorry, I didn't mean to startle you."

"It's alright," said Owen, "I shouldn't be getting carried away like that."

"What was that song you were playing?"

"Oh, it wasn't anything really. Sometimes I just like to play what I'm feeling."

"It was beautiful," said Lillian, "but it felt so sad."

"Well, sadness and beauty go together more often that you would think. I suppose the beauty makes the sadness easier to bear."

Lillian smiled. She liked the way Owen spoke. He spoke less than the others, but she thought he was more thoughtful in the things he said. She wasn't used to men like that.

"Do the horses like you playing?"

"I like to think so, but they aren't always the best critics."

"Which one is yours?"

Owen pointed to a chestnut mare. "Ruffy over there is mine." He gestured to the black mare, "You know Jack's horse, Pathfinder. The nag is Ellen's — Old Tom."

"What about Dan's?" Lillian asked, gesturing to the flea-bitten grey.

"Well, Dan lost his old horse, Kelpie, at McKenzie's farm when we had to escape quickly. That one is our pack horse. Dan named him Tombstone."

"Tombstone?"

"Because he's grey like a tombstone. Dan's not great with names."

There was a lull before Owen plucked up the courage to ask about Lilly's condition.

"So, you're in the family way?"

"Yes," said Lillian guardedly.

"Must be tough going through all of this and all of that."

"It is."

"Babies are special though. I always wondered what it would be like…"

"What?"

"Being a parent. My father was a bully, especially after mother died. Took all his grievances and frustrations out on me and my sister. He hurt us in many ways I don't wish to describe. I wouldn't be cruel or cowardly like my father."

"That would be a fine thing," Lilly replied.

Owen stood up and looked at her with a kindly expression. "If there's anything I can do to help you, Lillian, you just tell me. I will do it. For you and the little one."

Lilly was taken aback.

"That's not your responsibility."

"It's not about responsibility. It's about looking out for people. I may be a bushranger, but that doesn't mean I have to be selfish and careless all the time."

"You hardly know me," Lilly replied.

"So, tell me about yourself."

Lilly relaxed somewhat and told Owen all about the tribulations she had endured and the few happy memories she could recall. Owen barely said a thing, soaking in every word the young woman spoke. They continued to converse for a considerable time before they were called inside for tea.

Jack had shot a couple of cockatoos and Ellen had plucked and roasted them in an old iron pot with some potatoes. The meal was not tasty, but it was enough to keep everyone going. Ellen apologised for the meagre offering, but the others didn't want to hear it. They appreciated the effort.

"Can I head into town tomorrow to get more supplies?" Lillian asked the group as they ate.

"I suppose," said Jack.

"We need some substantial food and some preserved items to last us a while. If anyone knows how to stock a larder, it's me. We've got money, don't we?"

The others nodded.

"I'll take you," said Owen, "you shouldn't be travelling alone."

"We have enough food here to keep us going for a few days, but that's not an excuse for you to waste any time." Jack said. "We have enough money from the gold to cover the bill, so we shouldn't have any concerns there. You are to head into Sydney Flat, which is the nearest township. It's east of here and should take the better part of the day to get to if you go at a reasonable pace. Owen knows the way. Take Tombstone so you have an animal with you to help carry supplies."

Lillian nodded. Shortly after the conversation everyone turned in, except for Dan who kept watch. Again, everybody slept on the floor, but this time it was much easier to drift off to sleep than it was during the storm.

***

The next morning Owen and Lillian departed for Sydney Flat. Owen was mounted on Ruffy, Lillian on Tombstone.

"I was thinking," said Lillian after a short while, "maybe once we have the supplies, we can have a little fun?"

"Fun?"

"You know — enjoyment, *recreation*? I hope you haven't forgotten how to have a good time."

Owen made a strange expression as if struggling to remember what fun meant, flicking his eyes around as if furtively looking for the answer that was escaping him. Lillian swatted his arm and giggled.

"Don't be silly, it'll be a lark."

"If you say so," Owen replied.

They arrived on the outskirts of the town where Lillian watched a Chinese man walking down the road with a wooden yoke across his shoulders carrying two baskets of vegetables. A short distance up the road was the store where Owen dismounted and hitched the horses to the rail before helping Lillian down.

The store was different to what Lillian had been used to in the days when she had to run errands for the Churchleys. There were far fewer things to choose from for a start. No fresh food to speak of but plenty of flour and sugar, a very limited range of soap and laundry equipment, a few shelves of tinned food — mostly offal and preserves — and a stack of newspapers on the main counter next to a set of scales and jars of sweets. On the shelves on the wall behind the counter were kitchen tools and sewing equipment. Owen remained silent as Lillian perused the shop looking for what she needed. She lingered by the counter examining the five large glass jars proudly displaying brightly coloured confectionary and took particular interest in the acid drops.

Lillian eventually made her way to the counter and laid out a decent spread of preserves, soap, a small bag of flour, sugar, tea, yeast, and an apron.

"I will take all of this as well as a sewing kit and a bread tin."

The woman behind the counter seemed baffled by the sheer quantity of goods as much as Lillian's forthrightness.

"My husband will cover the cost. Won't you, dearest?" Lillian said, winking at Owen.

"Of course..."

Lillian turned to the shopkeeper, "is there a grocer and a butcher nearby?"

"A short stroll down the road and you will find them," the woman replied.

Lillian trotted out of the shop while Owen sorted out payment for the shopping. He packed as many of the goods into the leather saddlebags as he could and everything else he strapped to the saddles.

With their mission accomplished there was time to kill.

"What do you want to do now?" Owen asked Lillian.

"You know where the Chinese village is?"

"What do you want to go there for?"

"I've always wanted to see a gambling den."

Owen was shocked. "A girl shouldn't be going places like that."

"A *bushranger* can."

Owen shushed Lillian and she giggled.

"Alright, we'll go down. Just be careful of what you say. You never know who might be listening."

They rode down the road. The sun was sinking, and they listened for any sounds that might indicate human activity. Owen gestured for Lillian to move with him down a side street, and they soon found themselves on the outskirts of town in the Chinese village, which was really more of a strip of shops with a few tents nearby than a fully formed village.

There was a large tent with red paper lanterns hung outside, from which could be heard men chatting and shouting in Cantonese. The horses were hitched, and Owen led Lillian inside, handing a shilling to a Chinese boy who was attending the entrance. In the centre of the single-room interior was a large table under a lantern, around which a group of men, some young, some old, all of them Chinese, were observing a game of Fan Tan.

In the centre of the table was a square board, within which was an upturned bowl. On the sides of the square some of the men had placed Chinese coins, distinct from British coins by their intricate detailing and the peculiar square hole in the centre. There was a brief hush as a man with a thin bamboo stick lifted the bowl and used the stick to spread a pile of dried beans that had been concealed by the dome across the square. He divided the beans neatly into groups of four until there were only three left. The man whose coins were on the side that correlated with the number three cheered and pumped his hands in the air.

"Can you see?" Owen asked Lillian.

"Not really, but it sounds exciting," she replied.

The pair jostled around to try and see the action but eventually gave up. The mixture of the unyielding wall of Chinese men around the table and the fog of tobacco smoke made for a distinctly unpleasant spectating experience.

By the time they emerged, it was dusk. Lillian complained that she was starving.

"I could go for a feed too. Shall we head to the pub?"

It was only a short walk to the Australian Arms Hotel, which was one of the most refined pubs in the town, of which there were quite a number. They could see that the gold rush, as fleeting as it had been, had really helped the publican earn the funds to build something rather grand. It was a great improvement on what had essentially begun life as a glorified tent.

The horses were stabled at the rear and Owen and Lillian entered the pub, where they were met with the warm glow of kerosene lamps, a roaring fire, walls papered with actual wallpaper sent all the way from Melbourne, and a painting of a nude woman with lily white skin, a soft belly and no sign of body hair, standing in a forest.

"She doesn't leave much to the imagination, does she?" Lillian said with a smirk. Owen blushed.

Owen ordered the pair of them beef steaks with onion and ale before they took up a spot by the fire.

"So, where did all of this money come from that you can afford beef steak and all those goods from the store?" Lillian asked.

"We bailed up a gold escort a little while back."

Lillian was shocked, her eyes wide. She leaned forward and grasped Owen's hand.

"*You* robbed the gold escort?"

"Yes."

"That was *you?*"

"All four of us, actually. We've been slowly melting the gold down into ingots and cashing them in. Bank clerks don't seem to ask a lot of questions."

"I knew you were bushrangers, but I had no idea that it was you lot who did that. I can barely even picture you with a gun."

"What's that supposed to mean?"

Lillian averted her gaze momentarily.

"Well, because you aren't like the others. You're not rough or scary or anything. You're gentle and thoughtful."

Owen pouted. "I can be scary when the situation warrants it."

"I won't believe it until I see it."

"Well," Owen hesitated, "I'm sure you'll see soon enough."

When the meals arrived, it was the first time in a long time either of them had been served a proper beef steak, let alone vegetables. It was eaten eagerly but savoured. The meat had been cooked thoroughly and was bedecked with fried onion rings. Beside the slab of meat on the plate was a blob of relish to be added to each mouthful per the diner's taste. It was pure opulence for people who were getting by on cockatoo stew.

When the ale came out Owen took small sips, but Lillian quaffed like a Viking raider.

"Good Lord, you can really put it away, can't you?" Owen said in astonishment.

"Back when I worked for the Churchleys I used to get into drinking competitions with the stable boy, Ron, and a couple of the rouseabouts. I beat them hands down every time. Why don't you knock yours back?"

"Not a big drinker," Owen explained, "I think Dan does enough drinking for all of us."

"I see."

"I've seen what evil drink does to a man. I do not wish to risk putting myself in a position where I could go down that path. Drinking slowly helps me stay in control."

Lillian noted a sadness in Owen's eyes. He grew quiet.

"So, I suppose another is out of the question, then?"

"I'll get us more, but I think you should go easy on it. You don't want the little one coming out pickled."

Lillian frowned.

"What's that supposed to mean? You think I'm being irresponsible?"

Owen sat up straight and looked her in the eyes.

"Yes, I do..."

Lillian felt like slapping him as the rage bubbled up.

"...But I'm not the one with the baby, so it's not my place to judge. All I can do is share what I think, and you can do with that what you like."

With that Owen stood and went to the bar. Lillian sat confused for a moment, unsure if she should be offended or not.

When Owen returned with more drinks Lillian stared at him, her eyes studied the man before her as if he were a sign in a foreign language.

"What is it?" Owen asked.

"You're so strange. I've never met anyone like you before."

"I wouldn't think so. Maids and bushrangers don't mix terribly often."

"That's not what I mean."

Lillian drank slowly this time, letting the fruity, bitter taste of the ale linger.

"So, Jack tells me that it was your old boss that did you wrong," said Owen.

Lillian nodded.

"I think it would be good to go and pay him a visit and teach him some manners," Owen continued.

"His wife could do with a flogging," said Lillian.

"Nasty old biddy, is she?"

"Mad as a hatter. German. The things I'd love to do to her with a hot poker..."

"I don't suppose your folks are too pleased with the situation."

"Why do you think I'm still with all of you? You know how unwed mothers are treated. My parents would take that sort of persecution to terrible new places."

Owen drank quietly and pondered to himself. "I reckon we ought to board here for the night. It'll be too dark to travel. They only charge a few shillings for a room," he suggested. Lillian nodded. Near the bar, a concertina player was wheezing a melody into life.

The meals settled into Owen and Lillian's bellies and the ale made them somewhat more mellowed. Owen paid for a room and a maid took them upstairs. The accommodation was a tiny space indeed, barely room for the one bed and dresser. The solitary window overlooked the main street and was showing off a sunset that streaked the sky with pink, purple and yellow.

"Only one bed," Lillian pointed out.

"I know."

"Don't you think that's a bit inappropriate?"

"Well, if you're worried about improprieties then you can take the bed and I'll sleep on the floor."

"Good," said Lillian as she wandered into the room. She paused and turned with a big grin.

"I'm joking, you idiot."

Owen nodded awkwardly. He closed the door behind him then went to the window.

"It'll be nice to sleep in a bed for a change," Lillian said after a while. Owen nodded. Lillian looked up at him and tried to figure out what was going on in his head.

"Did I say something wrong?" Lillian asked.

"No. What makes you say that?"

"You're not talking to me. Something must be the matter."

Owen tore himself away from the window and sat next to Lillian on the bed.

"This is probably the worst possible idea, but what would you say to getting married?"

"To whom?"

"To me."

Lillian scrunched her face up at the question.

"Hear me out. It only has to be for the sake of the babe – so he's legitimate, you know. It's what you said about unwed mothers, see. If you're married, then your folks can't send you away and they can't call him a bastard, can they? In their eyes it would all be acceptable."

"You're not the father."

"They don't need to know that though, do they?"

Lillian smiled at Owen and held his hand.

"You're a sweetheart, but I don't think that's going to work. It's not exactly fair on you, for starters. Besides, how would we get married?"

"Shouldn't be hard to find a priest. I reckon the lay reader here would be happy to oblige us. And if not we can convince him."

Lillian stared into Owen's eyes, her brow furrowed, and she shook her head.

"You're really being serious, aren't you? It isn't a joke."

"Of course I am serious. Look, when Jack told me why he brought you to our camp it made me so angry that anyone could do that to a pretty, young woman. To use you for their own satisfaction, then cast you out in your time of need. In our gang we don't turn people out unless they're traitors. We know what it's like to struggle; to be outcasts. I want to help you."

There was a moment of silence as their eyes locked and Owen's words hung in the air like cobwebs fluttering on a draft.

"Is that the only reason you want to marry me?" Lillian asked. Owen blushed and averted his gaze as he struggled to find words.

"No..."

Lillian planted her hand on his cheek and guided his face to hers and they kissed tenderly. Owen was trembling.

"Are you alright?"

Owen nodded. "Yeah, just... I wasn't expecting our shopping trip to turn out like this."

***

There was a rapping on the side door of St Augustine's Church, rousing the Very Reverend from what had been a lovely wine-induced slumber. He staggered to the door and opened it to see Owen and Lillian standing expectantly.

"What is it, children?"

"We want to get married."

"What? What time is it?"

"A little before midnight."

"What on God's green earth are you about?"

"We will pay whatever it costs if you'll do it now and secretly," said Owen.

"If you want to get married, I suggest you come back another day when you've made the appropriate arrangements."

"Let me put it this way, your grace, we can either repay your kindness in gold or your contempt in lead," said Owen brushing aside his coat to reveal his pistol grip poking out of his trousers.

There was an anxious pause.

"Gold will do just fine."

It was a hugely truncated ceremony with the priest zooming through the formalities with comical haste to make the marriage official. Once the ink had dried on the books, money was handed over and the newlyweds returned to their lodgings at the hotel. Owen carried Lillian over the threshold and laid her on the bed as gently as he could manage and then stood awkwardly next to her.

"Well, what now?" Lillian asked.

"I hadn't thought this far ahead. It's a bit strange, isn't it? I thought you were supposed to feel different or something when you were married. It's a big moment, but I feel just the same as I did before."

"Well," Lillian replied, "it wasn't a normal wedding, so I guess that's why it doesn't feel real, you know?"

"What do you suppose your folks will make of it?"

Lillian went to speak but struggled to find words to match the jumble of thoughts tumbling over themselves in her head. Owen gave her a weak smile.

"It's alright, no need to worry about that. I'll lock the door and then we can get to bed. It has been a long day."

Owen closed the door and fastened the latch while Lillian got up and began to undress. As Owen hung his coat from the peg on the back of the door he fetched a paper bag from the pocket.

"Here, I got these for you. I would have given them to you earlier, but I was a bit distracted," he said as he offered the bag to Lillian. She took it and he helped her out of her dress. She looked into the bag and saw it was full of boiled sweets. She turned around and kissed Owen sweetly.

"How did you know acid drops were my favourite?"

"I didn't, but I saw you eye them off and figured they were what you would like."

Now dressed in her undergarments, Lillian sat on a wooden chair opposite the bed and extended her leg.

"Can you help me get these boots off?"

Owen immediately began to loosen the laces of the polished leather boots, then slid them off one by one, giving sweet relief to Lillian's poor, swollen feet. For a moment she relaxed, spreading her legs and resting her hands on her baby belly. The split in her drawers gave her new husband a glimpse of her feminine parts. Suddenly she realised and snapped her knees together.

"I'm sorry," said Owen as he began to remove his outer garments.

"It's not your fault, I just forgot myself for a moment."

"I imagine it would be nice to forget yourself sometimes," said Owen quietly.

"I don't do it often. Only when I feel safe."

"You feel safe now?"

Lillian nodded. Owen gazed at the floor and unbuttoned his shirt.

"I wish I could promise you that it will always feel this safe. We're bad men and the way we live is the price we pay for that. You're an honest woman now, but you don't have to stay with me. I can be whatever you need me to be from afar in order for you to stay respectable — a drover, perhaps. If you decide to ride with us, then you'll be part of everything that comes with that too, do you understand?"

"Of course I do. I wouldn't have agreed to your ridiculous proposal if I didn't understand what accepting it would mean. I have no intentions of going anywhere. Now I get to say whatever I'm doing is with my handsome husband by my side, and I like the sound of that. I like that I get to call myself *Mrs. Owen Brady*." She stroked Owen's arm. "Come on, there's no need to be worried about any of this. I'm happy that we're together. Most of the girls I grew up with got married when they were fifteen. Martha Tabram's father married her off to a fat old Welshman when she was twelve. I'm like an old maid compared to them."

Suddenly, Lillian felt a fluttering in her belly. She paused and waited for the feeling to repeat but it disappeared as soon as it had arrived.

Now divested of their clothes, the pair lay in bed gazing into each other's eyes and processing the strange turn of events of the day. Lillian reached out and stroked Owen's hair gently.

"Shall we consummate the marriage?" Lillian asked.

"What about your condition?"

"What about it?"

Lillian sat up. Her body was still covered in bruises and scratches, but they were healing; her breasts were full with darkened nipples as her body prepared itself for feeding the infant that was growing inside her. Her belly was round and becoming more taut. Her skin was soft and almost luminous. Owen's heart began to race. He had experience in the world of carnal delights, but this moment was so intense it was like experiencing it all for the first time again. Lillian took his hand and placed it on her belly as she reclined on the bed.

"You won't hurt him."

Owen positioned himself between her legs. He hesitated. He had robbed and plundered and seen horrendous things on the goldfields, but much to his own confusion this terrified him.

Lillian looked up into Owen's eyes then let her gaze drift over his willowy body. She reached down and stroked his belly with the tips of her fingers.

"Are you sure this is alright?" Owen asked.

"Yes, it will be nice."

"You're sure?"

"Just shut up and fuck me please. I'm not exactly the virgin Mary, I have done this before, *evidently*," said Lillian gesturing to her belly, "This time, though, it's *my* choice."

***

The following morning, Ellen rose early to attend to the horses in Owen's absence. While she was at work, Owen and Lillian arrived with the supplies. Both were positively beaming as they rode into the pen and dismounted.

"Where have you two been?" Ellen asked.

"We got married," Lillian replied.

It took a moment for Ellen to understand what had just been said. "What?"

"Owen made an honest woman out of me."

"As honest as a bushranger can be," Owen said.

Ellen shook her head in disbelief. "Did you at least get the shopping?"

"We did, and you'll be very interested in what was published in the newspaper," said Owen, withdrawing the paper from the saddlebag and handing it to Ellen as he carried the supplies to the hut.

***

The letter from the Upstanding Citizens League had caused quite a sensation in the press, with the editor of the newspaper using it as an opportunity to wax lyrical about the moral decline of society, the ineffectiveness of the police and the general poor character of the bushrangers. Owen read the article aloud to the rest of the gang as they sat in the hut.

"What does it say about the state of our civilisation that the formation of such a league has become necessary to combat the criminal scourge? And what use the police that are paid from the public purse to pursue these malefactors? Surely there are better uses for public money than paying men to wander fruitlessly through the forest!"

Jack bristled at the imperious tone of the editorial and the open letter from the squatters. He instructed Owen to lay the article out so that he could examine each of the names of the men who had signed the letter.

"If we're up against this so-called *league* I suppose we better know our enemy," Jack said. "A few of these are familiar names, but some are not. I reckon we ought to give them something to really complain about."

"We don't want to make things too hot for ourselves," said Ellen, "we should get some proper disguises, so we aren't recognised."

"Does this mean we have to be on the move again?" Lillian asked.

"Yes, but maybe not just yet," replied Owen.

"Were you getting comfy?" asked Dan.

"One thing I'm learning very quickly with you boys is that getting comfortable is out of the question."

***

It was advantageous to Lillian that she was yet to be associated with the rest of the bushrangers. It meant she could move freely without fear of interference. Fortunately, the use of disguises during the gang's exploits meant that it took longer for the crimes to be pinned on them, but as the police had supplied the press with written descriptions, including their various disguises, to be widely circulated there was always a chance the men and Ellen would be recognised. So, it was decided that they would need entirely new clothes to wear when travelling if they were to go unmolested.

Ellen and Lillian rode to Sydney Flat on Ruffy and Old Tom. They headed to the clothiers and obtained a bundle of men's outer garments and felt hats with wide brims. Lillian also grabbed a handful of peacock eye feathers that were in a vase on the counter, a length of black crepe fabric, and a sewing kit.

"That's quite the haul," said the woman behind the counter as she collected the items and tallied up the cost.

"We're part of a troupe of... travelling players. We needed new outfits for the performers," said Lillian.

"Oh my," said the woman with excitement, "I would love to be a part of that. I always wanted to be a singer or an actress. I just remember being a little girl and going to the theatre and seeing those beautiful ladies up there singing in the most splendid gowns all bedecked in embroidery and jewels. I wished I could be with them but, alas, my father never allowed me. He said that actresses and singers were fallen women and no daughter of his would turn their back on the Lord." She sighed. "The Lord didn't factor in much when he died of a heart attack between the thighs of a girl in the whorehouse, though. Always said the most remarkable thing was that he should die of a heart attack when I was certain sure he had no heart at all. One rule for thee and another for me, that was his motto." She paused and let out another sigh, "Still, how wonderful it must be to travel the country bringing joy to people."

Ellen and Lillian exchanged glances.

"Yes, how wonderful indeed," said Ellen.

***

That evening Ellen and Lillian returned to the hut and laid the clothes out. There was enough for the three men as well as clothes for the women to disguise themselves in male garb. By lantern light, Lillian and Ellen cut the black crepe into strips and converted the pieces into a complete set of eye masks and matching hat bands. They then sewed peacock feathers into the hat bands and added them to the new headwear.

Meanwhile, the men discussed Jack's list of all the members of the Upstanding Citizens League who they hadn't robbed yet. First target was to be the smallest, Francis Barnard. Though he had one of the most successful horse studs in the district, he was miserly and tended to wear clothes until they fell to bits, and the buildings on the farm were all in disrepair because he didn't want to fork out to get them fixed. If he had anything that was worth stealing it was never on show. The obvious value was in the horses he bred.

"Do you reckon we steal some new horses, then?" Dan asked.

"I thought that at first," said Jack, "but buyers know Barnard's brand as well as the kind of stock he's breeding so we'd never be able to shift them if we took them to auction or private sale. I suggest we do a simple raid on the place, maybe nab ourselves some nice gear for our mounts. I reckon he'd have to have some good saddles and bridles there."

"Gonna nab a mount for the little missus?" Dan said to Owen.

"Of course. Probably a good idea to get something strong and fast for yourself, Danny. Tombstone is a fine packhorse, but I don't think there's enough speed in them to get us out of trouble in a hurry."

"I agree," said Dan, "Tombstone is not a patch on Kelpie."

He missed his old horse. Sure, it lost its mind whenever they rode near flowing water and could be stubborn as a brown stain on a pair of Long Johns, but Dan just hadn't bonded with Tombstone the way he wanted to. He needed a fast, reliable horse.

***

Under cover of night, the gang rode to Barnard's Horse Stud. Each member of the gang was dressed in their new outfits complete with hats decorated with peacock feathers and their black masks. Ellen had gone so far as to paint her jaw and lip with black soot to suggest stubble. Lillian, however, was wearing her new dress, topping off the look with the hat and mask, a frock coat and a leather belt around her hips on which was a cartouche filled with ammunition for the shotgun slung across her chest.

The group hitched their mounts to a fence and Owen took Lillian and Dan to the stables. Ellen and Jack armed themselves with revolvers and headed to the homestead.

The trio entered the stables and Lillian began to browse the stalls for a horse that took her fancy. She saw a beautiful blonde horse with a flowing, snow-white mane and immediately fell in love. She gestured to Owen.

"I want this one."

"Palomino? She'll stick out like a sore thumb."

"But, *sweetheart*, this is the one I like!"

"How good a rider are you?"

"I'm an excellent rider, as you should well know."

"I'm not stealing you a thoroughbred palomino unless you know how to ride her properly."

Lillian folded her arms and cocked her head to the side. Owen rolled his eyes and opened the stall. The horse was uncertain at first, shying away and snorting loudly, but it was no time at all before Owen managed to calm her.

"Alright, get me a bridle and saddle."

As Owen and Lillian concerned themselves with the palomino, Dan took a shine to a bay stallion who was getting agitated by the commotion. He went in and got the horse saddled and bridled with the gear that was sitting on the partition. There was a name stamped into the leather bridle that Dan could just make out: *Sancus*. He liked the name, even though he didn't quite know how to pronounce it and didn't know anything about Greek mythology. He muttered it under his breath as he followed the text with his finger, "San-Kuss."

Outside, Ellen noticed movement on the veranda of the homestead.

"Jack," she hissed and gestured to the source of her alarm.

The sound of the riders approaching had caught the attention of the occupants of the house and when nobody had come to the door it had alerted them to the possibility that something was amiss.

"Bugger," Jack said to nobody in particular.

"What should we do?"

"There isn't anything we need in the house," said Jack, "as long as we keep them in our sight, we can stop them interfering with the others in the stables if we need to."

Suddenly, Lillian rushed out of the stables on the mare, followed by Dan on Sancus and Owen carrying as much tack as he could humanly manage.

"So much for a quiet escape," Jack grumbled.

Owen, Jack and Ellen ran back to their horses and mounted, but not before helping Owen load the new stock saddle he had pinched onto Ruffy.

The men on the veranda rushed inside and grabbed guns before charging towards the thieves. Luckily for the bushrangers, they had been able to get moving before the pursuers got within firing range. The men watched impotently as the gang left. They then went to the stables to assess the damage.

"Bloody hell; they've nicked Diana and Sancus!"

The men returned to their boss to inform him that they had only been able to stand and watch as his prized broodmare and stallion took off into the night carrying bushrangers who wore peacock feathers in their hats.

***

"What was that nonsense?" Jack shouted at the others when they returned to the hut, "Did I not tell you to get in and get out quietly?"

"What difference does it make?" Lilly retorted.

"It means we're going to have to get moving; the police will be increasing their searches and staying here is too dangerous now," said

Jack. "Do you reckon there's a chance we'd be able to shelter at your selection again?" he asked Ellen.

"I really doubt it. I imagine the traps will be checking in regularly to see if I've come back. From what Haigh told Lilly when he came sniffing around, they know full well I've chucked my lot in with you boys. It's too risky."

"I have relatives not far from here," said Lillian, "I'm sure they would be able to provide us with shelter for a while. The police would have no idea we would be heading that way."

Jack ran his fingers through his hair and sighed.

"Any other suggestions?"

"Why don't we give Lilly's idea a go?" Owen suggested. Jack shifted uncomfortably.

"Alright. We'll take what we can fit in our saddlebags. I'll load the provisions onto Tombstone. Anything we can afford to leave behind stays here. We travel light, we travel fast. If it doesn't work out, we can hopefully double back and lie low here until I figure out something."

***

Later that night, Ellen and Jack went down to the creek with lanterns. They had decided to indulge themselves in some moonlight bathing before having to hit the road again. Once they reached the bank Ellen disrobed, her nakedness dyed blue in the moonlight. She waded out into the water with soap in hand until she was up to her hips. It was cold and her skin erupted into goosebumps.

"There's a chill in the water. Might need you to warm me up," she said.

Jack responded without a word, casting aside his clothing and taking a moment to brace himself for the cold water.

Ellen scanned her eyes over his body and limbs, muscular but slim and well-defined looking for all the world like Cellini's sculpture of

Narcissus. She guided her gaze to the appendage between his thighs flopping from side to side as he entered the water.

"Jesus Christ, Nellie, this is way too cold," Jack gasped as his balls touched the water and immediately began to retreat into his body. He cupped his genitals snugly in his left hand and continued to move towards Ellen.

"Just give me a hand with the soap and then we can get out," Ellen replied.

Jack scrubbed at Ellen's back and buttocks with the brick of carbolic soap, then she took the brick and rubbed it over her arms, breasts and belly with haste. A quick splash to get the suds off was followed by both of them awkwardly staggering back to dry land.

"That went a lot different to how I expected it to go in my head," said Ellen as she dabbed her legs with a rag.

"I think we're dirtier than before we tried washing," Jack said with a groan as he looked at the slime and mud on his legs.

"I just wanted to try out the creek before we had to go. I'm sorry."

Jack, without further word, grabbed Ellen and pulled her close, kissing her passionately. His hands wandered between her legs.

"Out here?" Ellen whispered.

"Why not?"

"What if they see us?"

"I don't care, I want you now."

Jack laid Ellen down on the bank of the creek and she gasped as her back was covered in mud. She could only let out a shocked, "Oh!"

Jack cackled as he playfully smeared mud on her breast.

"You are a devil, Jack Cooper."

"You don't know the half of it, Nellie."

In the moonlight, by the creek, smothered in muck, Ellen and Jack made love.

***

At dawn the gang mounted and rode out. It proved to be hard going but they pushed themselves and their mounts as best as they could. At about midday they spotted a covered wagon pulled off to the side of the road and a small fire crackled on the far side of the vehicle. Seeing a potential opportunity for a rest and possibly gaining a few supplies, Owen rode up alongside the fire and saw a stocky man with a manicured beard and dressed in a frock coat and Wellington boots poking the fire with a stick.

"Excuse me," said Owen, "I don't suppose you know the way to Bendigo from here?"

"Bendigo?" the man replied, "Yes, you're moving in the right direction but you're still a good half-day's ride from there."

"Thanks."

Owen looked at the wagon and read the writing on the canvas: *Hutchinson's Theatre*. A flicker of realisation lit up his face.

"You're Dick Hutchinson, the actor, aren't you?"

The seated man chuckled.

"It has been a long time since I heard someone say my name with that much enthusiasm."

"I am a great admirer of yours. I was lucky enough to see you perform in Ballarat. You had a whole gang with you."

"A troupe, yes. They have long gone. Alas, the dramatic arts do not yield the interest around here that they once did. The theatre should always be a safe escape into a new world, away from the dreariness of the mundane. It would seem most working men in these days would prefer to spend their money on imbibing liquor until they lose all sense, rather than experiencing the natural thrills of high drama."

Having grown inquisitive, the rest of the gang rode up to see what was taking Owen so long. A brief introduction led to Hutchinson inviting them to sit with him.

For the next few hours he regaled everyone with tales of his adventures as a troubadour and thespian.

"Mr. Hutchinson," said Jack, "it would be disrespectful not to inform you of who we are. We're outlaws. We're wanted by the police for a number of crimes."

Hutchinson looked over the group and nodded. "I suspected that may have been the case. I detected a certain air of desperation. I'm afraid I have nothing of value to give. Anything worth a pound or more was pawned off to keep me going until I could find more employment."

"We don't intend to rob you," said Ellen.

The thespian thought for a moment and an idea struck him.

"I have something for you, if you will humour me. Stay right there," he said as he waddled to his wagon. He rummaged in the back and reappeared with a basket full of theatre costumes.

"My friends, as fugitives you will need to disguise yourselves and what better way than with these..." Hutchinson said as he plucked a mask out and held it up to his face.

"Let me see... Ah, just the thing!"

He drew out an ornate black leather domino mask with a golden lace trim and placed it over Lillian's eyes.

"*Columbina*, the beautiful maid. Witty and clever, never afraid to stand up to her master. She can be sensual and flirtatious, but she can also be sharp with her tongue and ruthless in her machinations."

He drew out another half-mask that was made of black leather and shaped like a plump-cheeked face with a broad nose and a curly moustache. He gave it to Owen.

"*Harlequin* — the captain's trusty servant and lover of Columbina. Though he be fairly down on his luck, he never carries a grudge and always finds a way out of his troubles."

Hutchinson next drew out a black leather mask depicting the face of a sad old man with a large, hooked nose. He placed it over Dan's face and tied the ribbon behind his head with care to secure it.

"*Pulcinella* — the loyal peasant. Though he may be a little too fond of the bottle, he always comes through for his friends in a pinch. He is a rebel and utterly without fear. He will play the fool to throw off his enemies."

Hutchinson paused and looked Jack up and down thoughtfully before selecting a mask depicting an angry man with mighty eyebrows, an enormous moustache and a long pointy nose.

"*Il Capitano* — the noble soldier. His ambition is only matched by his vanity. He is a leader of men, but if he lets his arrogance run wild, he will fall on his own sword. His greatest fear is that others may see that he is not really the strategic genius he portrays himself as."

Finally, he stood before Ellen and drew out a white mask with a pointy nose and a sort of beak where the mouth should be.

"For you, my lady, I present the *bauta*. The ultimate enigma. It is a face that has no name, no sex, no age. It both hides you and allows your true self to emerge. It is the perfect way to externalise your persona and empower yourself. Be who you were always meant to be."

***

It was a strenuous ride peppered with frequent stopping to allow Lillian to take the necessary breaks to relieve her bladder but, in the evening, the gang finally approached the property on the outskirts of Bendigo that they had been aiming for. It was, by the standards of housing in the area, quite grand – brick walls, squared posts holding up the veranda awning, a shingle roof, stone chimney.

"Who is it that lives here again?" Jack asked.

"My aunt and uncle."

"They're pretty flush?"

"Uncle struck it rich on the goldfields early on. Got in before the mining companies."

It struck Dan as odd that there was no smoke from the chimney or other signs of activity in the house.

"How long since you saw them?"

"Not since before I started working for the Churchleys."

They got closer to the house and hitched their mounts to the veranda posts. Lillian knocked on the door but there was no answer. She knocked again and listened. She thought she heard movement inside.

"Uncle Albert? Aunty Mary?"

No answer.

Owen drew his pistol and jiggled the brass doorknob. The door opened and he peered into the gloom. The dust was thick. He gestured for Lillian to stay put as he entered.

He scanned the main room and saw no sign of recent activity. In fact, there was an eeriness to the place that he couldn't quite pin down. There was a thick layer of dust on all the furniture. He moved into the dining and kitchen area where he saw bowls of soup that were furry with mould.

Suddenly there was movement behind him. He turned in time for a large figure to leap upon him, sending him to the floor. It seemed barely human and utterly feral, with hair and beard thick, long, and tangled, obscuring the face. The fingernails were long and yellowed, like ragged claws. The clothes were filthy and tattered, reeking of urine, and other bodily excretions. In one clawed hand the raging feral beast clutched a dirty butcher's knife and Owen struggled to restrain it. He beat his attacker around the head and neck with his revolver, but they were relentless. In desperation he cocked the pistol, pressed the muzzle to his attacker's shoulder and squeezed the trigger. The shot blew a chunk of flesh and bone out of the feral man, who collapsed and gave out a hideous scream. It was enough of a distraction for Owen to flip the feral onto the floor where he pinned his arm with a foot and wrenched the knife from his grip, a move he was unfortunately becoming accustomed to employing.

Alerted by the blast, the others ran in with lanterns and discovered Owen with the knife, standing over what appeared to be a vagrant or some kind of wild man. Lillian scrutinised the figure and recognised her uncle's golden signet ring on the prone figure's left hand.

A quick search of the house uncovered the partly mummified body of Lillian's aunt, propped up in bed as if she had only been unwell and recuperating. A silver tea service sat on the bedside table with a pot of tea and an unfinished cup of brew. Wishing to spare Lillian the shock of seeing the body, Jack and Dan wrapped it up in the bed sheets and carried it outside. A rummage through a tool shed by an overgrown vegetable garden yielded a spade and Jack dug a shallow grave for the unfortunate woman.

Inside, the feral man had been tied to a kitchen chair and was being questioned. He fidgeted and strained against his bonds.
"Uncle Albert, what happened to you and Aunty Mary?"
Albert grunted and gyrated his head.
"She was ill. I took care of her, I did."
"Why was she ill?"
"The snake whispered lies about me. Told her things, it did. Terrible, terrible."
Albert began to buck and gnash his teeth. Owen led Lillian out of the house for fresh air. He could see she was visibly shaken.
"He murdered her."
Owen nodded.
"What for?"
"We can only guess, but maybe he just went mad. I found a jar of arsenic in the kitchen. Looks like maybe it was being used in the food or something..."
Lillian paced along the veranda wringing her hands.
"What do you want to do, Lilly?"
"We shoot him down like the diseased cur he is."
Owen nodded. He held Lillian close.
"Leave him to me and the lads. We will sort him out."

***

In the dead of night there was the clattering of hooves in the street outside the police barracks in Bendigo, a grand sandstone building that also housed the law courts. Constable Lee, in response to the commotion, got up from the duty desk and opened the door to reveal a smelly, ragged figure bound and laying in the dirt with an empty flour sack over his head and bloodstains all over his clothing. He was incoherent when answering questions and upon having his bonds cut attempted to strangle the policeman, earning him an overnight stay in the cells with darbies on and, in the morning, a trip to the hospital whence he was transferred to the new Aradale Asylum. He was registered under the name of "Rat" as all he would say when asked his name was, "I am the rat," though he was really Albert Brook. It was a strange end for a man once considered by his friends to be prime material for a role in local government or as a Justice of the Peace.

***

After Uncle Albert had been dealt with the gang attempted to make the house more suited to their needs. Ironically, in seeking refuge from the fury of the squatters they themselves had become squatters of a different kind. For the first time in many months the oil lamps were lit, and the thick layer of dust cleaned from the furniture. Expired food was discarded and replaced with the gang's rations.

Almost all refused to enter the master bedroom, and none entertained the notion of using the bed with its mattress soaked through with the grease and fluids from the decayed body of Aunt Mary. Lillian allowed herself into the room to look for anything useful, especially clothes and boots.

It was decided, out of respect to the deceased, to confine themselves to the main living area where the fireplace was, and the kitchen — for obvious reasons. Until another, more suitable, stronghold could be found this was to be the gang's centre of operations. Plans were already brewing for their next exploit.

Nine

Lillian and Dan had experienced a fantastic thrill from the success of the raid on Barnard's stud farm, but it was not without consequences. Word reached the other members of the Upstanding Citizens League immediately following the outrage, and the decision was made by the members to arm some of their rouseabouts and stockmen on the stations and keep them employed as guards after work hours. It was a procedure that required paying the men an extra shilling per day, except in the case of Elliott McKenzie who had negotiated it to be a weekly shilling, but it gave the squatters that extra level of assurance to relax at night.

Word reached the press about the daring raid on the stables and the bold bushrangers who did it. It naturally made it into the columns of the *Bendigo Gazette*:

> "The identity of this band of desperadoes remains a mystery, however they wore a uniform of sorts in the form of large felt hats decorated with peacock feathers. Of some fascination was the detail that these daring brigands appear now to be joined by at least one woman in their depredations."

Upon reading the news, Senior-Constable Haigh immediately suspected the culprits were the bushrangers he had been looking for. He could not prove it yet, and the uniform these bandits had adopted was new, but his gut told him this was no random crime, rather an attack directed at the men who had rallied together in opposition to their lawlessness.

Since Haigh's outburst of violence in the bush, the search parties had been put on hold and the police attended to the other duties that had been neglected in the meantime. Haigh appreciated the extra staff on hand to delegate these issues to, especially in light of Constable Martin's sudden resignation that would have otherwise left him short-staffed.

He often wondered why he alone should be so worked up about these bandits when none of the other local law enforcement seemed concerned at all. He hoped calling the search parties off would convince the outlaws to spread their crimes to other districts and lead other police to appreciate the seriousness of this outbreak of lawlessness. After all, *why should he be solely responsible for keeping this menace at bay?*

However, he was not willing to let things lie completely and began venturing out to the shadier places to see if anyone could share information about the gang. He figured that bandits needed places to fence their stolen goods and lie low when they weren't in the bush, and the only people who would harbour such criminals would be the bottom rung of society.

He rode out to Quartz Hill and began questioning the locals. It took no time at all for Dick McFeely's name to come up.

When Haigh approached the dodgy butcher's shop, McFeely saw him coming and hid. Haigh entered the apparently unattended business and began calling out. McFeely, terrified that his operation was about to be exposed, crawled away on his belly to the back door and slithered out surreptitiously before bolting to the back of the blacksmith's shop.

Haigh's excursion wasn't entirely fruitless. He ventured to a tearoom nearby, hoping the staff or the patrons there might help with his enquiries.

He went straight to the counter where Long Liz stood to attention.

"Guid mornin', whit kin ah git ye th'day?" Liz said by way of introduction.

"I'm looking for information," Haigh replied.

"Aye," Liz said.

"I am trying to track down a gang of bushrangers who have been operating around here. Their leader is a man in his twenties, tall, dark-haired, handsome, a colonial, probably flush with money. Have you seen anyone like that here?"

Liz nodded.

"Aye, that soonds lik' a jimmy called Jack Cooper wha enjoyed mah services a while ago. Ye dinnae forgoat someone lik' that aroond 'ere gey quick."

Haigh took a moment to process the woman's thick accent and extract the useful information.

"Jack Cooper, did you say?"

"Aye."

"Was anyone with him? A little blackfellow or a tall, thin man with light coloured hair?"

"Nah, nobody lik' that. Juist him oan his ain."

"Not a woman with him?"

"Nah. If he hud a lassie, ah dinnae think he wid hae wantit mah services."

"Interesting," Haigh said, stroking his chin.

"Is that everything? Wid ye lik' a dram? Fur a shilling ah kin sook yer boaby."

"Suck my... Uh, no. That will be all. Thank you. This has been *enlightening*."

"Suit yersel'," said Liz as Haigh turned to exit. She scratched herself and returned to her chores, grumbling under her breath about the English.

***

Having had time to think about their most recent outings, Jack had decided that in future the smaller scale raids should be undertaken with fewer gang members in order to reduce the chances of members being caught or injured. Two at a time was the new rule.

The first of these was a visit by Jack and Owen to the farm of Samson P. Samson at Eaglehawk, where he grew his lucrative barley, wheat and oat crops. It was here that he had built a grand home for himself that he had called *Albatross*. Nobody knew why he had named a farmhouse on an inland property after a seabird, but few were willing to question the eccentric squatter. Some suspected that the name might have been an obscure reference to *The Rime of the Ancient Mariner*, as Samson was said to have been a seaman in his past life before coming to Australia. It was a broad, whitewashed homestead with corrugated iron roofing, bookended with brick chimneys, and surrounded by lavender bushes and fig trees.

As the two bushrangers approached the property they drew their new theatre masks over their faces and observed the men patrolling the outskirts carrying lanterns and rifles.

"Do you think all the squatters are going to be guarded like this?" Owen asked.

"Maybe. I suppose it's something we will find out soon enough," Jack replied.

Keeping the horses hitched to a tree outside the property, Jack and Owen began to sneak up to the fence line, staying low and keeping behind cover as much as possible. They observed that the guard nearest to them was a young man of around twenty-six and bearing a determined expression.

"I don't think gentle persuasion will work on him," said Owen.

"Time for a more heavy-handed approach, then."

Jack dashed to the fence, vaulted over it and before the young guard could call out, he had been tackled to the ground. Jack held a hand over the young man's mouth and pressed a revolver to his head.

"No talking. No screaming. You stay silent unless I say otherwise. Savvy?"

The man nodded, terrified of the strange figure with huge, furious eyebrows, a curled moustache and threateningly phallic nose.

"Good. How much is the old man paying you to strut around with a gun to protect him every night?"

Jack lifted his fingers from the man's mouth.

"A shilling…"

"Alright, here's the situation: you're going to take us to the storeroom. If you co-operate, I will give you a pound. If not…" Jack raised his pistol in front of the man's face, "I suppose you can guess what might happen."

The man went to speak but Jack half-cocked the revolver and he went quiet.

Owen moved to Jack's side, his merry Harlequin mask distorting his face into terrible shapes in the gloom. They helped their victim to his feet and liberated him of his firearm. Bringing the lantern, they walked to a large shed. They entered and Jack took out his gunny sack and went to work grabbing anything useful – jars of salt, small bags of flour, bottles of gin, a box of shotgun cartridges and more all finding their way into the haul. Owen kept the guard covered with his own rifle.

"Got anything else around worth grabbing?" Jack asked. The man shook his head.

"Alright then. Time to go."

Owen and Jack left the distraught guard behind, unarmed but one pound richer, as they ran back across the property and bounded over the fence. They mounted and took off before any suspicion could be raised. No doubt this would be incredibly embarrassing, if not downright infuriating, for Samson, but it was a small victory for the bushrangers.

***

The gang allowed a few days to pass before they contemplated their next raid. Reports in the newspapers kept them informed of increasing police numbers being sent to the areas around where the robberies had occurred, which were fortunately a comfortable distance away from the hideout in Uncle Albert's house.

Meanwhile Ellen had become stricken with fever, pelvic pain and a burning sensation when answering the call of nature. The men were completely baffled but Lillian believed she understood what to do.

"We need some laudanum to get her through it," Lillian told Jack. "I think I know just the place to get some. Mrs. Churchley was always knocking the stuff back like drinking water. If we go to the Churchley place I know where she keeps it all."

"Alright, but the Churchley place is going to be too dangerous for just two of us to tackle given we've robbed it recently. I think all of us need to go, but we will split so that some of us guard the outside while the others do the dirty work inside," said Jack. The others agreed.

***

In the parlour of their house the Churchleys sat relaxing. James concerned himself with reading a book about India, while Wilhelmina crocheted a scarf. There was a viciousness to the way she crocheted that made the ivory hook seem like it could easily become a weapon. Neither looked at the other or indeed acknowledged the other's presence. It was a very cold, loveless situation.

Outside, the bushrangers reached the boundary on horseback. Ellen lurched forward in the saddle, her face was drained of colour and dewy with sweat, her abdomen wracked with pain. They all drew their masks over their faces, resembling an absurd, dishevelled theatre troupe.

"Lilly, you know where the stuff is. Take Owen and Dan with you and grab it. Try to make it quick, and only take what we need," Jack directed. The others nodded. Lillian, Dan and Owen continued through the gate that the workers usually left open so they could sneak out at night and go to the pub without being noticed by the lady of the house.

They rode to the homestead and hitched the horses at the side of the house as if they were simply making a social visit.

Lillian marched to the door with grim determination, her sleek boots poked out from the raised hem of her baby blue dress with each purposeful step. Her long blonde curls bobbed on her shoulders from under the canopy created by the wide brim of her hat. Her black, ornate Columbina mask gave her a darkly elegant flourish, which only added to the strange menace of the small but heavily-armed figure. She adjusted the satchel slung across her chest and checked her shotgun. It was loaded and ready.

Owen and Dan brought up the rear, adjusting their Harlequin and Pulcinella disguises. Owen watched Lillian carefully. He suspected that she might be more than a little unpredictable given the circumstances.

They stood by the front door. A dull glow filtered through the windows, bathing Dan's face in amber light as he peered in.

"Ready?" Lillian asked the men. They nodded. With the butt of her gun, she bashed on the door. After a moment they heard movement.

There was the clunk of a key turning and the grind of a latch being pulled then the door opened a crack, revealing a heavy set old woman with a large nose and ruddy complexion. Evidently Wilhelmina, not trusting her husband, had replaced Lillian with someone far less attractive.

"Evening," Lillian said and she jabbed her gun's muzzle into the maid's huge bosom and pressed forward.

The bushrangers forced their way inside and Dan kept the maid covered while the others headed off to explore.

Upon entering the parlour, they were set upon by Churchley and his wife. Wilhelmina lunged at Lillian with her hooked needle in hand, while James fired off a shot past Owen's head from his pistol. Lillian was lightning fast and blocked Wilhelmina's attack with the shotgun and pushed her back, causing her to fall. Gripping the gun like a staff, Lillian brought the butt of the gun down on Wilhelmina's chest hard, sending her stumbling. A second blow caused her to drop the needle. Wilhelmina dropped to her knees with the wind knocked out of her and Lillian followed up with a kick to the prone woman's face before kicking the needle out of reach.

Owen crashed into James Churchley and brought him to the ground, knocking over a side-table in the process. He wrenched the squatter's hand viciously and yanked the pistol free from his grip and cast it aside. Although the single shot had been expended, it was still useful as a blunt weapon.

On the other side of the room, Lillian held Wilhelmina at bay, the muzzle of the gun pressed into the German's breast.

"You move and I shoot that black heart right out of your chest."

The prisoners were pushed back into a corner, covered by Dan and Owen, who looked utterly grotesque in their masks, as Lillian made a beeline for her former employer's bedroom upstairs. The case was on the dressing table in Wilhelmina's room, and she opened it to find the drug she needed, but upon seeing the collection of small glass bottles she opted to take the whole thing.

She hesitated before leaving only to grab a jewellery box that she emptied into her satchel. Obviously, Jack had overlooked the item on his previous visit.

She joined the others and handed her loot to Dan, who immediately went outside to mount his horse in preparation to leave.

Even the briefest of gazes at her former employers filled Lillian with a sickening rage that was overwhelming. She ordered Owen to drag them into the centre of the room. He gave her an uncertain look but complied, anticipating she would simply deliver a tongue-lashing and a hollow threat to them before a prompt exit.

Lillian checked her shotgun. The click as it closed made the squatters panic. She addressed Wilhelmina Churchley first of all.

"You are a cruel, vindictive and evil woman. I ought to blow your head off for trying to kill me and my baby. It's no worse than you deserve. But I want you to suffer just as I suffered for years under your tyranny. I haven't the time to flog you and deprive you as you did me for all that time. This will have to do."

Lillian levelled the shotgun at Wilhelmina, who reached out to grab the gun. In a flash Lillian fired, exploding her victim's right hand. She howled sickeningly in agony and terror as she looked down at the gory pulp where her hand should have been.

She turned to James Churchley. He stared up into baleful eyes that glowered at him from behind the black mask. He was at her mercy.

"You ruined my life. You forced yourself on me and stole my virginity like it was a meaningless thing to be used up and discarded. All these years you never protected me from your wife. You just promised me things you never intended to give and now I'm carrying your bastard child. I'm going to make sure you can never do that to another poor girl ever again."

Owen grabbed the gun, "Jesus Christ, what are you doing?"

"Get back," she growled at him. She stared into his eyes with animalistic rage and snatched the gun back.

"No more, please," Owen begged.

"You know what they did. If you care about me the way you say you do, you'll let me have this," said Lillian.

Owen lunged at Lillian as she aimed the shotgun between Churchley's legs and pulled the trigger, his crotch exploding in a burst of gore. Owen's attempt to stop her was a split second too slow.

As Wilhelmina grabbed pathetically at the chunks of what remained of her severed fingers on the floor, blood gushing from the pulped stump on the end of her arm, James lay on the floor in the foetal position and fell unconscious from the shock of his injury.

Lillian turned to the maid.

"Sorry about the mess."

Without stopping to examine her handiwork further, she turned and exited. Owen followed, trembling and white as a sheet. As they left the scene, Wilhelmina's screams piercing the night. As they reached the horses, Owen lurched and heaved out the contents of his stomach.

They rode to the boundary and joined the others.

"What in God's name happened?" Jack asked.

"I did what we came to do. The drugs are in the haversack. That's what matters. Let's get going," said Lillian.

The gang took off, leaving the carnage behind them.

**

At the hideout Ellen was in a blissful stupor after a dose of laudanum and a spoonful of sugar to clean the bitter taste out of her mouth. Meanwhile the other four were in a serious discussion about what had transpired. Jack was beside himself.

"We don't operate that way, Lillian. You start killing and maiming and we're no better than the Clarkes, or Peisley, or Morgan," Jack said. "You look at the Churchleys and see squatters who have caused you misery, but that is not how the papers will spin it. As for the police, they will just see you as someone taking the money out of their pockets. Just you watch. They will all be baying for our blood now. We were not killers, but you have branded all of us that and now we are destined for the gallows if we get caught. Do you understand what you have done?"

"We don't know if the old man has died or not," said Dan.

"Be that as it may, it's not safe to stay here anymore. The traps will be everywhere like flies on carrion. We have no choice but to get out of the colony, then perhaps we need to leave Australia altogether," said Jack.

The gravity of her actions finally began to dawn on Lillian and her cool façade slipped. Suddenly she burst into tears and sobbed.

"Why didn't you two stop her?" Jack asked.

Dan avoided Jack's gaze.

Owen folded his arms and leaned back into his chair. "They got what they deserved."

Jack could not believe what he was hearing. "We need to get our things packed and start moving," he said.

"What about the missus?" Dan asked.

Jack looked over to Ellen who was passed out in an armchair.

"I'll worry about that. You just get your things sorted. You're lucky I don't turn you in myself."

Dan went outside to have a smoke while Owen and Lillian went to the stables to calm down.

"Do you think I've killed the Churchleys?"

"I don't know. They were still alive when we left. I don't suppose you did kill them. Time will tell."

"I'm scared, Owen."

Owen looked down at Lillian, his kind blue eyes reassured her as he stroked her hair. Without further words he held her close to him and kept her there until he was sure that she was calm. He wondered who would soothe him. A thought at the back of his mind began to niggle. It was incoherent and quiet, but it was persistent. Something even bigger and worse was brewing.

***

Under the cover of night, the gang ventured out into the wilderness. Jack did his best to keep his horse neck and neck with Ellen's so he could keep her upright in the saddle. The horses moved slowly, which suited Lillian as her belly was growing at such a rate that she had begun to feel the pressure on her pelvis more acutely while in the saddle in the past few days.

After hours of travel, the sight of a large barn was a promising one and the gang decided to take their chances. They rode up to the fence and entered the property, which was evidently a run belonging to reasonably successful farmers based on the number of well-maintained buildings and green grass that was growing around a large dam on the property.

Owen opened the barn doors, and the gang rode inside. The space was large enough to shelter the horses overnight and for the gang to shelter beside them, so long as they weren't bothered by sleeping on hay and manure. They took the gear and supplies off the horses and allowed them to nibble at the hay on the floor. It was almost pitch black and though the gang had become accustomed to the dark, it was still a strain to see what they were doing.

"Shouldn't someone go and check to see what the natives are like?" Ellen asked, sinking down onto a large deposit of hay in the corner of a stall.

"Natives?" Jack replied.

"The people that live here."

"Dan, Owen, go and do a quick scout. Try not to shoot anyone," Jack ordered.

As the men went about their business, Ellen and Lilly sat together. Neither had spoken during the ride — Ellen due to her poor health, Lillian due to her shame.

"Talk to me," said Ellen.

"What is there to say?" replied Lillian, "I'm a murderer."

"Perhaps you've killed. That's not who you are though," said Ellen, "Soldiers kill scores of people, yet they are given medals for it. The best killers are given higher positions of power. So, what makes them less of a murderer than you?"

"I don't know," Lilly mumbled.

"Your crime is not that you killed. It's that you killed a man in a man's world. If James Churchley had killed you, where would he be right now? Prison? On the gallows?"

"He'd be alive," said Lilly.

"That's right. He would be alive and living well. There's no punishment for men like him under the law. Not in our world."

"But I've put nooses around all of our necks…"

Ellen grabbed Lillian by the arm and looked her in the eye. Though she was on the cusp of delirium from her pain she was still cogent.

"Listen to me. You've done nothing to be ashamed of. Jack had his spat and that's for him to think on. I have your back. We all have your back. We are in this together, whatever happens. Frankly, I can think of a few women who would applaud your actions rather than condemn you."

"Not Mrs. Churchley. She won't be applauding anything with one hand, " said Lilly stifling a grin. Ellen pretended to chide her for such off-colour humour.

It had been Jack's scorn that had hurt Lillian more than anything. It had felt like a betrayal for him to have spoken of his sympathy for her situation only to condemn her for taking her revenge on those who had caused it. Dan and Owen had both stood up for her, and now Ellen, but something in her brain only allowed her to believe Jack's words until now. Ellen had put it all into perspective.

Meanwhile, Dan and Owen headed out and took stock of their surroundings by moonlight. There was a homestead, a cow shed, a latrine, and a paddock where two horses and three goats were kept. The bushrangers went to the homestead to try and look inside. They trod tenderly and cautiously on the veranda, slowly approaching the windows. Owen pressed his nose against the glass and could see a dining table covered in crockery and candlesticks, faintly outlined by moonlight. Dan did the same at the side of the house and fancied he saw a bed in a tiny room. It was too gloomy to tell if it was occupied, or by whom.

Owen moved to the front door and gently touched the handle. It moved. With all the trepidation of a house cat sneaking up on a grass parrot he nudged the door open enough to slip through the gap. Dan followed. With every groan of a hinge or crackle of a floorboard they expected trouble. None came.

They went to the bedroom and put their heads inside and saw the bed. It was a rough wooden-framed bed, the sort that suspended the sleeper on crossed ropes. There was only one occupant of the bed: an old woman who was asleep and snoring like a crosscut saw. At her feet an old cat was curled up asleep.

"Older than Moses," Dan whispered, "let's check the rest of the place out."

Dan and Owen went through the hut and found nothing of note apart from some vegetables and a bottle of sherry. There were no other occupants and no weapons. They left everything as it was and headed back out.

When they returned to the barn Ellen and Lillian were cuddled up together and settling in to sleep under a shared blanket. Jack was waiting by the door with his shotgun. He slung it onto his shoulder and gestured for the others to join him away from the women.

"What did you find?"
"Place seems to be empty apart from an old woman. As long as we're out of here before she's awake then we won't have any complications," replied Owen.
"You two better get some sleep. I'll guard."
"No," said Owen, "I'll take the guard tonight."
"Reckon you can handle it?" asked Jack.
"Just give me the bloody gun," Owen snapped.

Jack handed Owen the shotgun and found a place to settle in. Dan curled up near his horse under a blanket, nursing a bottle of brandy. His maimed hand ached in the cold.

Owen sat by the door and peered outside until sunrise. In his head he continued to replay the horror of the visit to the Churchley farm. The hideous sound of Wilhelmina Churchley screaming echoed in his mind.

He berated himself for not stopping Lillian. It wasn't the first time he had experienced something like this moral paralysis, though. The floodgates opened and long buried memories rushed forward to remind him of the despicable things in his past.

He remembered his last day on the goldfields as a constable.

The Chinaman...

+++

They had been getting complaints about a Chinese miner who had been sneaking around other people's gold claims. Some men claimed things had gone missing from their tents like food and tools. Then came the report that a young schoolteacher, working on the goldfields educating the children in a tent, had been abducted by a Chinese man and defiled. The senior-constable tracked down his suspect. It wasn't hard. He didn't seem to care about hiding.

They already had truncheons in their hands when they approached him, crouching by a creek cupping water to his mouth with his hands.

"Ah Ling?"

The man looked up and nodded. That was enough. The senior-constable swung his truncheon into the side of the man's head. He went down easily and wailed, clutching his skull. A second blow. Then a third, and a fourth.

"You fucking yellow filth!"
"No savvy! No savvy!"

They all took turns beating the man into an insensible and bloodied pulp. Owen, however, stood back and watched. He was paralysed with fear. The senior-constable pointed to their victim with his truncheon and glared at Owen.

"Get in and give him some, boy!"
"I can't…"
"You want him raping more women? Spreading his filthy Mongolian seed among our daughters and sisters?"
"No, it's just…"
"Use the fuckin' Billy club and drum it into him."

Owen stood over Ah Ling, who was flat on his back. All of his front teeth had been knocked out, his nose smashed, the bones in his face broken so that he was unrecognisable. Ah Ling gurgled. Owen closed his eyes and struck the dying man with as much ferocity as he could manage; the man's blood splattering up on his handsome blue uniform with each blow. He hoped he could put the man out of his misery.

"Good job, Brady," the senior-constable said, patting him on the shoulder.

There was not much life left in their victim to snuff out. The senior-constable ordered Owen to shoot him and finish the job off. He did as he was ordered to and considered it a mercy killing.

The next day Owen burned his uniform and fled into the bush. It was almost a year before he could spend a night without the image of the pulped face haunting his dreams. Blood bubbling and gurgling in a toothless mouth as Ah Ling tried to find some kind of way to ask why he was being attacked.

It emerged a few weeks later that the schoolteacher had not been abducted at all. She had eloped with a man that had been courting her who happened to be Chinese. It was not the same Chinese man that the constabulary had killed, but in the eyes of the miners and goldfields police it didn't matter. After all, *they all look the same anyway, don't they?*

+++

Owen had lost count of the times these memories had led him to place the muzzle of his gun under his chin while his finger hovered near the trigger. The survival instinct was too strong, but the thought was always in his mind ready to pop out and tempt him down the path of self-destruction.

As he guarded the gang he contemplated it. Nobody would be able to stop him. He propped the gun up under his jaw and rested his finger near the triggers.

He thought about Lillian and how, as much as he had suggested the marriage for the sake of preserving her honour in the eyes of others, there was more than a little selfish part of him that had simply wanted to make sure he had her all for himself. Her acceptance of the marriage proposal was a most unexpected shock and he had been sceptical about why she had so readily agreed. It became clear to him over the following weeks that it was not merely a marriage of convenience. There were looks she gave him, odd moments where she slipped her hand in his, that were not necessary for an arrangement that was made simply to keep up appearances. Owen had not experienced anything like it before, nor expected it.

An image slipped into his mind of Lillian crying over his remains. It hurt him.

He laid the gun down.

Sunlight seeped through the morning fog and Owen roused the others. With much grumbling they got up.

Jack made a point to approach Owen.

"No trouble last night?"

"No trouble at all," said Owen as he returned the shotgun to Jack, "I suppose wonders never cease, eh?"

The gang prepared their horses and promptly rode away into the bush. By the time the old woman awoke the gang had ridden away.

Ten

The gang were heading north-easterly towards Rochester. Jack used his compass to guide them. Up to this point he had kept fairly close to places he was familiar with, but it was no longer safe. He had never gone as far as New South Wales before, but he knew that heading roughly north was the best bet for getting there. The dense bushland they were pushing through had proven to be especially challenging with Ellen in such poor health, Lillian being pregnant and Dan rarely sober enough to sit up in the saddle half the time.

Two days into the journey, Ellen was struggling to maintain her seat after downing a strong dose of laudanum, which had essentially rendered her insensible. Owen rode beside her to keep her upright. Jack began to grow concerned that she would prove to be a risk to their continued liberty and safety if she continued in such a state. He made the executive decision to find a spot to rest. They finally located a good spot beyond the township of Huntly.

As Ellen slept, the rest of the gang sat around the campfire and discussed their options.

"How well do you know this area?" Jack asked Owen.

"Well, without a map it's hard to get a precise bearing on where we actually are. I think if we keep heading east, we should reach the Campaspe River. Then we should be able to just follow it up towards the border and cross at Echuca."

Jack thought for a moment. *A map would be a very useful thing to have.* He filed the thought away in his mind to be accessed later when they reached a town.

"Barnadown should be near here. Do you want a couple of us to see if we can find it?" Owen asked.

"You and I will go," said Jack.

"Why not just go into town here?" Lillian asked.

"My concern is that if we get spotted and recognised then they'll send traps out looking for a camp, and Ellen is in no shape to have it on her toes right now," Jack replied.

With Dan and Lillian keeping watch over Ellen, Jack and Owen rode out. A few hours later they wandered onto the main drag of Barnadown. They made a beeline for the post office and general store.

"Good afternoon, gentlemen," said the shopkeeper, a burly man with a large moustache and whiskers.

"Good afternoon," replied Jack. "I wonder if you might be able to help us out?"

"Always happy to help."

"Well, first I would like some help with an issue my, uh, wife is having," said Jack.

"Women's problems, is it? What are the symptoms?"

"She has a fever and suffers greatly from pain in her belly and her back. She hasn't been eating much."

"Ah, yep. I know that one," said the shopkeeper. "Have you given her anything for the pain?"

"Laudanum."

"I suspect she's off with the fairies then, is she?"

"Very much so."

"Well, my wife, God rest her soul, would suffer much the same. What worked for her was bed rest and tea — and as much of both as she could manage. She was a real trooper; her health was always precarious."

Jack leaned on the counter. "How did she pass, if you don't mind my asking?"

"She got kicked in the head by a horse. It was over so quick she never felt a thing. My wife on the other hand..." the shopkeeper laughed. Jack couldn't find the humour but felt relieved.

"Thanks for the advice, I'll get a box of tea. There is one other thing, do you have any maps?"

The shopkeeper scratched his chin.

"Map o' where?"

"Victoria. We're aiming to head off for a new gold claim up north and need to know where we're going. Figured a map would help us plot the journey."

"Well, my friend, you are in luck. I happen to have the old map from the police station in the back. It is a little outdated but should still give you a good sense of direction. You can have it for a shilling."

After much meandering conversation, the men left the store with a small wooden chest of tea, a new Billy can, a magnifying glass, the latest newspapers and a lithograph of an out-of-date map of the colony. They mounted up and headed back to camp.

***

That evening the gang remained in camp. Dan occupied himself with reading the newspaper, the women rested in a tent, and Jack and Owen studied the map carefully with a magnifying glass to plot the next steps of the journey. They couldn't find Barnadown on the map and estimated they must have been somewhere between the railway and the Campaspe River near Huntly. They marked the approximate spot with a pencil then tried to plot a route towards Echuca.

"We can head towards Runnymede, near Cooper's Lake, in the morning. I suppose it will take us about a day to get there at the rate we've been going, and we will have to cross the Campaspe River, but if we don't, we will be too close to the railway. Then we continue to make our way north, following the river. Next stop after that will be Rochester where we should be able to replenish our supplies. What d'you reckon?" said Jack.

"Sounds like a good plan. We just need to be mindful of the locomotives as we come upon the tracks. How do we get across the river?"

"If we can't find a bridge, we will have to just push the horses through."

***

At dawn the gang packed up camp and began their journey. They emerged from the bush into a clearing and then rode their horses along the train tracks towards the north.

"Why don't we simply follow the rails all the way? Wouldn't that be easier than crossing the river and trying to find a path up north through the bush?" asked Dan.

"We don't want to be spotted, do we?" said Jack. "Trains are always full of potential witnesses, and the area along the rails is too open to hide whenever a train comes past."

"But we're in view of the trains now."

"Only briefly. Besides, the lake looks a decent size on the map so it should be ideal as a camp site. We might even be able to stay there a few days to rest if all goes well."

After a few hours of travel, they paused and rested alongside the track. Jack's ears pricked up. He thought he could hear the rumble of a distant train approaching. He dismounted and gazed down the line, but he saw nothing. Then, gazing back up the line, he began to notice the grey plume from a train bringing passengers down from Echuca billowing over the tree line. He motioned for everyone to move back from the tracks and vaulted into his saddle.

As anticipated, a B Class locomotive from the Phoenix Foundry came chugging along the line. It was a small engine with six wheels, a funnel-shaped smokestack, a glistening brass dome over the boiler and only a few carriages trailing behind. In the cab a fireman shovelled coal into the firebox while the engineer poked his head out to check for obstructions on the track. Noticing the riders ahead, he sounded the whistle. The gang's horses were spooked by the eerie sound, but the riders kept them under control.

The gang watched from the relative seclusion of a nearby copse of trees. The train seemed to glide along the polished rails with great noise from the locomotive. The passengers closest to the windows gazed out absent-mindedly as they went. None seemed to notice the bushrangers.

Once the chugging and clacking of the train had dissipated and the vehicle vanished into the distance, the bushrangers re-emerged and continued their ride.

"That is why we need to keep away from the tracks when we find a good spot to cross," said Owen.

"They're a lot bigger up close," said Dan.

***

When the gang finally arrived on the bank at a narrow portion of the Campaspe River, the water was surprisingly low. Still, some degree of coaxing was necessary to get the horses across the water, which was deftly managed by the men, who had much experience with such a chore. Ellen and Lillian's horses required a little extra help from Jack and Owen to get them across.

Further travel took them through Runnymede where there was nothing much to note apart from a few farms with some good wheat, barley and tobacco crops. There was a considerable amount of forest still in the area, mostly comprised of she-oak and gumtrees. However, as the gang moved further inland the surroundings became drier and much more sparse, with few farms to note.

Finally, they reached Lake Cooper, a normally huge expanse of water that was surrounded by boggy ground where the water level had receded. As the gang approached the water, they noticed many bones from ill-fated cattle and sheep that had not succeeded in getting enough water from the lake during the drought or got irretrievably stuck in the slop.

The gang set up camp and Dan attempted to fetch some water from the lake but found himself struggling in the gloopy mud.

Ellen was given a kangaroo skin to recline on as they rested. Jack brewed up some tea and implored Ellen to drink. Despite her body telling her not to, she partook of drinking the tea. Anything was worth a shot, and it had not harmed her yet.

"I'm really not suited to this life at all, am I?" Ellen said to Jack as he poured the steaming brew into a pannikin.

"We will reach Rochester tomorrow and find a doctor. Are you feeling any better?"

Ellen sat up and accepted the drink. "A little less feverish I think, but there's still a lot of pain."

"Have you ever felt like this before?" Lillian asked, reaching out to touch Ellen's shoulder tenderly.

"Yes, actually. It was when I was pregnant with my Susie. Wallace fetched a doctor, and the verdict was that I had an infection. Something to do with the water going bad, Wallace thought. It was not long after the Black Thursday, and our water supply was low due to the heat and the water had been pretty unclean. From then on, I was only to bathe and drink with water that had been boiled first. A fuss, to be sure, but until now I've been free of anything like this."

Lillian paused in thought for a moment. "Do you suppose that it had something to do with the creek near the hut?"

"I suppose it could have. You're fine though."

"Well, I wasn't exactly bathing in that creek. No higher than my knees at any rate," said Lillian. "Besides, I've always had a difficult constitution to break. I was the only one in my family that never seemed to catch a cold. There were times my brother was stricken with stomach complaints from eating meat that was on the turn, but I was fine. Maybe I'm just lucky?"

"Well," Jack responded, "regardless, I think this idea of boiling water before using it might be a good idea for both of you. We can't afford to be slowed down. You're not going to be very good bushrangers if you're laid up all the time."

Ellen glared at Jack. "You've no idea what it's like being a woman, Jack Cooper," she snapped, "We're tougher than you think. Our bodies put us through all kinds of hardships you can only imagine. Don't you dare condescend to us about being 'laid up' or I'll give you a taste of the kind of pain that we put up with regularly by introducing your family jewels to a nutcracker."

Jack did not respond. Instead, he slunk away and sat silently for the next ten minutes, stewing about the dressing down.

**

The next morning, everyone was up early to get going, including Ellen. To suppress her pain, she dosed herself up with laudanum, but she had found that the pain had been starting to subside even without the drug. She was relieved that she seemed to be past the worst of it.

Jack was glad to be leaving the lake behind. With such open country all around it was hard to keep a low profile. Furthermore, the lack of resources and farms put him on edge despite them having plentiful rations to get them to the next township. If they continued west, he surmised, they would be at risk of getting stranded without proper access to food and water. Luckily that's not where they were going.

They headed north-west, which took them through the bush. It was a mercifully brief trek that saw them approaching the township of Rochester before midday.

There was nothing especially remarkable about the place compared to other towns they had been, except that it seemed to be somewhat busier.

The first stop was at a small shop advertising itself as a tearoom.

"Here we are," said Jack, "we can have some tucker."

"It will be nice to have tea from a pot instead of a can," said Ellen.

The gang went inside and were seated away from the window. The building was a simply decorated place with printed wallpaper and lace curtains. It was a stark juxtaposition against the rough, grubby bushrangers that had drifted in.

A waitress approached the table and asked what the strange visitors wanted.

"A decent pot of tea and five cups would be a good start," said Dan with a wink. The waitress struggled to hide her distaste.

"Do you do scones?" Jack asked.

"We have scones with jam and cream," the waitress replied.

"We will have a round of those too."

Once the young woman had left, the gang leaned in conspiratorially.

"What do we do next?" Dan asked.

"Ellen and I will pay a visit to the local doctor. You lot, see if you can get a good feel for the town; identify the shops and any potential for running into traps while we're here."

"Right," Dan replied, the others nodded.

The waitress returned a short time later with a plate full of scones, a pot of cream and a pot of strawberry jam. The gang wasted no time tucking in. They clutched at the scones like starving beggars and slathered them with condiments before wolfing them down. Only Ellen struggled with her diminished appetite from the lingering pain in her pelvis and kidneys.

They did not notice the staff staring at them from across the room with disgust.

Once the scones and tea were dealt with Jack went to the front counter and pressed £20 into the woman's hand.

"Don't worry about the change."

Suddenly her demeanour completely changed, and she perked up.

"Thank you, sir!"

The gang all filed past with Dan bringing up the rear. He paused for a moment and caught the woman's eye.

"For future reference, love, you might want to work a bit harder on hiding your judgement. Jacky there usually drops about a hundred pounds on the maids he likes. Looks like he didn't think much of you hovering around looking daggers at us."

The woman couldn't help but stare aghast, realising she had just cheated herself out of a much bigger payout.

"As for me," Dan continued, "I liked the look of you when we came in. I might have given you £150." Dan reached into his coat and produced a fat stack of bank notes. "Ah, well, this cash is burning a hole in my pocket. I had best go and find somewhere to lighten the load."

As Dan left the tearooms fanning himself with cash he looked the waitress up and down with sass. The wait staff covered their mouths in disbelief.

***

After a short journey through the town, Jack and Ellen located the surgery of Doctor Samuel Wren. It was a small shopfront next to a saddlery and across the street from a hotel. They entered and were greeted by a woman of early middle age with mousy hair and sad eyes.
"Yes?"
"We would like to see the doctor," said Jack.
"Which of you is unwell?" asked the woman.
"I am," said Ellen, stepping forward.
"Wait here."

The woman disappeared into the office and muffled talking could be heard on the other side of the closed door. A moment later the woman reappeared with a short, silver-haired man wearing *pince nez* spectacles.

"Come in," said Dr. Wren. Ellen and Jack moved towards the office, but the doctor held up his hand to stop Jack's approach. "The lady only."
Jack nodded and begrudgingly took a seat.

***

Elsewhere, Owen, Lillian and Dan were walking along the main street looking for a good place to get supplies.
Dan had been bringing up the rear, but he got closer to Owen and Lillian, who were holding hands, and planted his hands on their shoulders.

"Listen, now that I have you both alone, I need to talk to you," said Dan.

"About what?" Lillian asked.

"Come down this alley where we can speak quietly."

The trio turned down a narrow passage between two buildings. Dan looked uncomfortable.

"What's the matter?" Owen asked.

"I was reading the paper. I found a report on our little visit to the Churchley farm. I would have said something earlier, but I just wanted it to be between us…"

"Spit it out, man," said Lillian impatiently.

"The old man is dead. There was an inquest, and they reckon he bled to death after he was shot."

The colour drained from Lillian's face.

"What of the woman?" Owen asked.

"She's alive but they're making a big fuss about her losing a hand."

Owen and Lillian were dumbfounded for a moment as Dan plucked up the courage to continue.

"That league Jack has been griping about has written to the parliament asking them to bring a law in that will make it easier for them to shoot us on site, like the one they have over the border. The maid spoke to the police. The three of us are wanted for murder, but only you were named, Lilly. The old woman must have recognised you."

There was a moment of silence to let the news sink in. Tears welled up in Lillian's eyes. Owen rubbed the back of his neck nervously as he began to pace up and down.

"Another thing," said Dan, "the papers have given us a name. They're calling us the Peacock Gang. They've also identified Jack as our leader and named Ellen as his accomplice. I guess you and I need to work a bit harder to get out names in the papers, Owen."

Dan attempted to crack a smile, but his mood was too heavy.

"We need to tell the others," Owen said.

"Of course, but let's wait until the sawbones has had a look at Ellen first," Dan replied.

***

Meanwhile, in Dr. Wren's office, Ellen had stripped down to her undergarments and was being examined.

"Now, how long have you had the pain while passing water?"

"Almost a week."

"And the pain in your back and abdomen began around the same time?"

"They did."

The doctor gently pressed around Ellen's kidneys, and she groaned. He then pressed her belly near her groin and got the same response.

"Have you noticed any change in the number of times you need to relieve yourself?"

"It happens a lot more, which is not very helpful when we're travelling so much."

"Hmm. Lie down on my table here," said Dr. Wren pointing to a bench against the far wall. Ellen complied. The doctor asked her to part her legs, which she did, and he examined her through the split in her drawers.

"Well, it's definitely an infection. Though I would say it is internal, my dear. Unfortunately, there's nothing much we can do. The best I can suggest is bed rest and keeping your fluids up. Have you been doing anything for the pain?"

Ellen sat up and adjusted herself before putting her dress back on.

"I've been using laudanum."

Dr. Wren sat at his desk and leaned back in his chair.

"Well, that will do it. Just be careful you don't overdo it. I've seen too many women meet their maker after becoming dependent on laudanum. An infection like this will usually last a week or so. You are extremely lucky. I've known more than a few people that have died from infections of this nature."

Ellen paused for a moment. It had not occurred to her how dangerous the illness had been.

"What could have caused it?"

"You say you've been travelling a lot?"

"Yes."

"I don't suppose you've had much access to clean water to wash up?"

"I thought you might bring that up."

"There is a lot of evidence that unclean water can make people unwell, it's not such a radical idea. You just need to make sure that you are not using fouled water for bathing, especially on your intimate areas. Definitely don't drink dirty water either."

"I know," said Ellen. She wondered why she had bothered coming to sell a doctor only to be told what she already knew.

"Clean, dry clothes will help too. I can tell yours are in desperate need of a wash."

Ellen took a seat opposite the doctor. He leaned forward and made eye contact with his patient.

"Mrs. McReady, I want you to be honest with me. That man out there is not your husband, is he?"

"No. My husband is dead. I'm a widow."

"And all this travel is not normal for you, is it?"

"No. It's new for me."

"There are a number of cuts on your body that I have noticed. Should I be concerned at all?"

"Oh, those are just from when I fell off my horse."

Dr. Wren narrowed his eyes.

"You would be surprised how many women I see who 'fell off their horse', 'walked into a door' or 'slipped when doing chores'..."

Ellen took a moment to let the subtext sink in.

"Doctor, Jack is not hurting me. I fell off my horse in the bush while I was being chased. That's all."

"Chased?"

"A constable was chasing me. They killed my dog... I... I really shouldn't be talking about it." Ellen shifted uncomfortably in her seat.

Dr. Wren stroked his chin thoughtfully.

"You're a fugitive, then?"

Ellen gazed at the floor.

"Well, that explains a lot. I won't ask any more questions. I just need to understand my patients so that I can give them the care they need. When you've worked around the goldfields you learn to turn a blind eye to certain things."

A few moments later doctor and patient emerged from the office. Dr. Wren gestured for Jack to join them.

"A little way down the street you will find the Royal Mail Hotel. I want you to go there for the next few days to rest. The publican is a man named Thomas O'Bryan. He won't ask any questions you don't want to answer. He's trustworthy. Let him know I sent you and he'll take care of everything."

As Ellen and Jack moved towards the door, Ellen turned to face the doctor.

"One of our companions is a young woman. May I bring her in so that you can check up on her? She's expecting but has never seen anyone about it."

"Of course, Mrs. McReady."

***

Ellen and Jack caught up with the others a short time later and expressed their plan to stay in the hotel for a few days. There was no argument from anyone else.

The Royal Mail Hotel was two levels with accommodation up top and a public bar underneath. When Ellen had introduced herself to O'Bryan that evening with a note from Dr. Wren, he immediately knew what rooms to put them up in. It was decided to put the women in one room and the men in a second so that Ellen and Lillian could rest while the men plotted their next moves.

***

The following day was spent by the women relaxing in bed. The beds in question were rather classy brass affairs with ornate ends. Neither woman had experienced such luxury before.

"How is the mother-to-be this morning?" Ellen had said when they awoke.

"Well, everything aches, and what doesn't ache feels itchy no matter how much I scratch. I haven't felt sick for quite a while, which is a small blessing, but now I'm hungry all the time, which is driving me mad because we don't have the food to be eating that much. Beyond that, I'm more exhausted than I could ever imagine being. I can't think straight a lot of the time..."

Ellen took note of the anguished expression on Lillian's face.

"What's troubling you?"

"My fears were true. Jim Churchley is dead."

"What do you mean?'

"He died because I shot him. His wife is still alive."

Ellen remained quiet and allowed her friend to unpack everything.

"I never meant to kill him, I just wanted to stop him doing to anyone else what he did to me. I don't understand what happened to me in that moment, it was as if something had taken control of my body, and I couldn't stop myself. I just wanted revenge so much…"

"That's what happens to us sometimes. If we let our feelings in the heat of the moment dictate our actions, we will do something we regret," said Ellen.

"Wasn't it your feelings for Jack that got you like this?"

Ellen paused. She had never considered her situation from that angle before.

"Yes, I suppose so," she said. "I know that there has to be a balance between the heart and mind, but I also know how hard that can be to control."

"I doubt you would have killed a man."

"You were violated, assaulted and cast aside. I would have had half a mind to do it myself that night if I had been able."

As Lillian lay on her back staring at the ceiling, tears welled in her eyes and rolled down her cheeks.

"I don't want to die, Ellen…"

"Don't talk like that," said Ellen, "We will get you over the border and then the police won't be able to get to you."

"Do you think Owen will come?" Lillian asked.

"Of course. There's nothing to worry about. Jack reckons in a few days we will be able to get moving and then it should only be a day or so until we reach the border. It will be alright."

Lillian nodded and wiped her tears away.

***

That afternoon Ellen and Lillian walked leisurely down to Dr. Wren's office where they were promptly received.

"This is my friend, Lilly. You said you would be able to check up on her," said Ellen.

"Of course. Come in, Lilly. Come in."

The examination was fairly brief, but Lillian came out of the consultation with the knowledge that she was about half-way into the pregnancy and that the weird bubbly feeling she had been getting was probably the baby moving inside her belly. She conveyed the information to Ellen and the glimmer of brightness in such a dark time led to tears shed by both women.

For Lillian it was the first time it had all seemed really real. This was a *person* she had growing inside of her, and, in a few months, she would be holding them in her arms. It was surreal but at the same time made her feel more grounded and determined to get herself over the border to safety.

For Ellen it was a way to make up for not being able to be there with her own daughter, Susie, when she had fallen pregnant. The tyranny of distance had robbed her of being a grandparent but now she had this young woman to take under her wing to teach the ways of motherhood like she had hoped one day to do with her own flesh and blood children.

***

It was a balmy evening when Jack made his way into the pub under their accommodation. He went to the bar and ordered ale, then watched carefully as the barmaid clutched the large, phallic tap handle and golden ale poured from a spout shaped like a swan's neck into a pewter tankard.

The tankard had seen much action as evidenced by the dings and dents and the misshapen aperture. He sipped. The ale was passable. After a few more he might even start to enjoy it.

It had only been two days since they had taken up residency in the hotel, but he had found himself growing jealous of Lillian spending so much time with Ellen — or to be more accurate, Ellen spending time away from him.

Another drink.

This jealousy was only made the worse by the fact he could sense Dan and Owen were hiding something from him.
Dan had always been a heavy drinker, but since the McKenzie incident and the Churchley shooting he had been drunk more often than sober. Jack fancied that Dan had been giving him dirty looks and having one too many whispered conversations with Owen. *Could he be trusted?*

Another drink.

He had begun to seriously doubt Owen's loyalty. It seemed like he was always questioning his leadership or somehow undermining it. The Churchley situation had been evidence enough of that. He could have stopped the girl, but he didn't. He had made a point of keeping him close to keep an eye on him, but the doubts grew ever louder in his mind. He had never doubted Owen's fidelity before, but he seemed to have lost his brain by the way he had been behaving ever since Lillian came to the camp. His sudden marriage, his inability to keep her under control at the Churchley house and the horse stud, these were all signs of an alarming shift in his behaviour. *Was he a liability now?*

Another drink.

And what of Ellen? Was she still true to him? What had she told that wretched doctor? Was that teenage harlot filing her head with notions? After all, it had been Lillian who suggested the laudanum in the first place — that flimsy excuse to go back to her old employers and cause mayhem! All that the drug had done was slow them down, make it harder to keep the woman straight in the saddle. *They should be crossing the New South Wales border by now!*

Jack was now hurtling down the rabbit warren of doubt and loathing with great speed thanks to his lubricant of choice. He decided to go for something harder, requesting neat whiskey. He winced at the burn as he drank.

It was at this time that he heard two men in discussion behind him.

"I heard about the Churchley woman yesterday. Apparently, some fancy doctor went to see her with a false arm."

"False arm?"

"Yeah. They say some madwoman broke into the house and blew her arm off with a gun," the first man said.

"Her husband died, didn't he?"

"Yeah, that same madwoman. Apparently the word on the grapevine is that she cut his cock off and took it as a trophy."

"Anyone that knew Jim Churchley would know that wouldn't have been a very big trophy," the second man guffawed into his ale.

"Well, at least he's dead. If some mad bitch cut my cock off I would probably get a gun and finish the job myself."

"What difference would it make, Sam, you ain't using it much these days."

"I use it plenty, old mate. I use it plenty. Maybe I'll pop around and give old Mrs. Churchley some of what she's missing…"

Jack had heard enough. He knocked back the rest of his drink and went upstairs.

He found his room and burst in on Dan and Owen playing cards.

"You wretches," Jack slurred, "you bloody wretches. When were you going to tell me what really happened to the Churchleys?"

Dan rolled his eyes.

"Simmer down, old man. You knew there was a good chance they were dead. Or don't you remember that dressing down you gave poor Lilly?"

"Poor Lilly? Poor Lilly! She's been nothing but trouble since the moment I laid eyes on her. I'm not hanging for a crime committed by that... that... *whore.*"

Owen stood up and crossed the room to where Jack stood, swaying slightly. He gazed directly into his eyes with the intensity of a blast furnace.

"I will give you one opportunity to retract that remark."

"Which one? That the girl is a *whooore?*" Jack smirked, "I bet it drives you mad that she's already got a bun in the oven. I'm surprised it wasn't you that pulled the trigger on Churchley — but not too surprised. You always were a coward in the end."

At that moment Owen struck Jack across the face with the back of his hand. It stung, but in his state of intoxication Jack barely felt it.

"Did you fuck her on your wedding night, Brady? Or were you worried the little bastard would grab your prick when you were inside her?" Jack laughed mockingly.

Owen grabbed Jack around the throat and squeezed until he could see him going red in the face.

"You just don't know when to shut your fucking mouth, do you? I don't care that you're soused. You want to know why we hid the fact that Churchley was dead from you? It's because we know that you can't handle anything being out of your control. Yet you're incapable of making a good decision without us there to point you in the right direction. Nobody elected you leader; you just can't help making everything about yourself."

Jack tried to speak but Owen's grip was too tight. Owen relaxed his hold and Jack freed himself. "You bastards would be *dead* without me."

"I was almost dead *because* of you, you cretin," said Dan. "Look at this," he said raising his mangled left hand, "this is because of you."

"You told me you were fine…"

"I told you what you wanted to hear. That's how it always is with you, Cooper. I'm the cripple, but I have to make sure you don't feel guilty about it or we get nonsense like this."

"So, this is how it is? You're both turning on me? Well, let's see how far you get without me around."

With that Jack stormed off and headed to the stables. Owen and Dan looked at each other with bemusement.

"Been a while since we had to put up with that," said Dan.

"He's lucky I held back."

"Held back? You nearly squeezed his bloody head off!"

A moment later Ellen knocked on the door. The men opened up and let her in.

"What was all that commotion?"

"Jack got drunk and lost his mind. He does that once in a while," replied Dan.

"Where is he now?"

"My guess is he went to the stables. That's what he does to make us scared he'll run off. It usually means he'll spend the night there. In the morning he'll get a bucket of water dunked over him," said Owen.

Ellen began to panic and headed out to the stables, but Jack and Pathfinder were nowhere to be seen. There was a cold, lumpy feeling in her gut. She returned to the men's room.

"He's gone. He must have gone out on Pathfinder. Where would he be going?" Ellen said.

"I suppose he could be trying to head up to Echuca without us, but he left all of his supplies behind, so I imagine he just went off to clear his head," said Owen.

"Or to make us feel guilty," said Dan.

Ellen wrung her hands anxiously, "I wish I shared your optimism. If he's not back in the morning, we should go and look for him."

***

Morning came, but no sign of Jack came with it. Ellen looked for him in the stables again but there was nothing.

"I think we need to go and find Jack," said Ellen upon returning to her room. Owen and Dan were already there discussing the situation with Lillian, who was distinctly unimpressed.

"Why should we go looking for Jack if he's taken off in a huff? Maybe he needs some time on his own to learn to appreciate that this situation we're in is not all about him?" Lillian said.

"Like it or not, we have an obligation to make sure everyone is safe, even if they've brought trouble on their own head," replied Ellen, "there's a few things I could say about that right now, but I will hold my tongue."

"That's clearly not what Jack would do," Lillian said.

"What?" said Ellen.

"Owen told me about how Dan almost lost his hand. It was because Jack made the decision to stick up a station where they were outnumbered and he made Dan guard everyone on his own, even when he told Jack it was a bad idea. He wasn't looking out for Dan then, was he? He was lucky Dan wasn't killed."

Ellen was speechless. She wanted to bark back a retort, but Lillian was, unfortunately, correct.

"And what about this whole situation?" Lillian continued, "You're still unwell and now you're worried about him, even though from where I stand it's pretty clear he is the one who chose to abandon us over an argument that he started. Each one of us has had a part to play in everything from planning our jobs to actually doing them, and it's Jack that bosses us around even though he does the least."

"That's enough!" Ellen had a look of fury on her face and a pinch in her voice that told Lillian she was perilously close to stepping over a line she wouldn't be able to step back over. "I understand what you are saying. Jack's far from perfect but that doesn't change what we have to do as his friends. The moment we all came together we agreed to this."

Lillian sighed. Owen decided to add his piece to the conversation.

"At least wait a little while longer. It may be that he's making his way back now that there's daylight and he'll be here before you know it. No point worrying until there's something to worry about."

***

Jack had ridden throughout the night after purchasing a bottle of rum and another of Irish whiskey to take with him. The bartender had been unsure if it was a good idea, but money was money, and Jack didn't look to be the kind of customer who would take well to refusal of service. He pushed Pathfinder hard to cover as much ground as possible while he swigged from the bottles. The horse had been mostly uncooperative, but Jack dug his spurs in hard enough to get her going.

By the time he had almost finished the whiskey, his spurs were covered in blood from Pathfinder's flanks, and he was approaching a small hut.

The hut was like a great many miner's huts — tiny, with bark slabs for the walls and roof, bark chimney, one room interior and logs stacked against the exterior wall waiting to be fed to the fire. Inside was illuminated by the fireplace and a figure could be seen moving inside through the open window.

Jack dismounted, slipping gracelessly from his mount and falling flat on his back. With difficulty he stood up and staggered to the hut. He slumped against the wall near the door and knocked.

"Open! Openupp!"

The door opened slowly, and a young man was visible on the other side, skinny and beardless.

"What is it?"

"D'ya haff anything to drink?"

The young man winced at the stench of booze on his breath. "I suspect you've had plenty already, sir."

Jack growled and forced his way in and searched for something, *anything*, that could be drunk. He located a clay jug of rum and helped himself.

"Why are you here?"

"I said, I wannud a drink."

"Are you robbing me?"

"I can pay ya for the rum. S'not good qualiddy, but I spect is what you can afford — ya scamp! Will ya drink wi' me?"

The young man was perplexed. "It is a little before five in the morning, I don't think it's the right time to be intemperate. I need to be right to work."

"Fuck work," Jack shouted, "is all fa naught. Y'work 'n' work 'n' try t'play by th' rules but all it gets ya is another day closer to th'grave and barely nuff silver in ya pocket to keep ya from starving."

He swigged from the jug and sat by the fireplace.

"Wazz ya name, son?"

"Michael."

"Microol. Let me tell ya somethin' important, Microol. *Yooou* are better off alone! Frens — bah — will only getcha inna trouble and let ya down when you trust'em. Thezz only one person y' can trust in this world..."

Michael had now shifted from confusion to annoyance. This intrusion was inconvenient, and Jack's drunken rambling was irritating. He said nothing as Jack continued to rant and ramble about the pitfalls of relationships. He realised Jack had no real awareness of if he was even there and wondered if he could slip out to get help.

"D'ya know who I am, Microol?"

"No. I have no idea."

"I am the notorious Jack Cooper, so I am. Bushranger. *Thiefff*. I had a gang, but I left them. They were murderers. Killers! Not me. No. Never... I am the Robin Hood of 'straya. Help th' poor. Robbin' squatters. Thass me."

At that instant Michael knew he had to fetch the police. He was not certain if he was in danger, but he wasn't willing to take the risk.

He waited a bit longer, noticing that Jack began to grow sleepier. When Jack finally slumped over, asleep, Michael ran outside and went to the paddock where his horse was waiting. He quickly threw on the saddle and bridle and took off towards a nearby farm that was well-known to the locals.

This farm was a large one and had many paddocks full of grazing sheep. It was owned by the local Justice of the Peace, Harold Henley. Michael rode to the homestead and knocked on the door in a frenzy. A servant answered.

"Can I help you?"

"Please, you must fetch Mr. Henley. There is a bushranger in my home, his name is Cooper. I need help to arrest him."

"Wait here, please."

There were a few moments of nervous anticipation as the servant disappeared into the house. She returned with a short, pot-bellied man of middle age. He had long features and blue-grey eyes that seemed to hover somewhere between intimidating and jovial. A silvery beard hid his long chin. This looked every bit a man who was past his prime but still sharp as a whip.

"You've got some brigand in your house, is it?"

"Yes, sir."

"Good man, good man. I'll come with you, and we can sort him out."

As both men rode through the dawn back to Michael's hut, the younger man filled the elder in on the situation. When they arrived, they found Jack was still inside, apparently asleep.

They quietly entered and Henley took a pair of handcuffs from his belt. He crept up to Jack and grabbed his wrist, but doing so roused the bushranger and he instinctively went for his sidearm. He brought a double action Beaumont-Adams revolver up and squeezed the trigger, shooting Henley in the chest. The Justice of the Peace stumbled backwards with a groan and sunk to the ground. In a daze, Jack stood up and aimed at Michael.

"Try to sell me, eh? You want blood money, eh?" Jack began to mumble incoherently as he staggered. Michael stood dumbfounded and paralysed by fear. After a moment Jack seemed to give up and lowered the revolver. He shuffled outside past Michael and wandered into the scrub to find Pathfinder.

After a few minutes of drunken scrambling and crashing through the scrub, Jack found Pathfinder and mounted clumsily. He took off back towards Rochester, though at a much slower pace than desired due to his previous maltreatment of the horse leaving the animal in poor condition.

***

Hours passed and as the daylight settled in over the town Ellen, Lillian, Dan and Owen sat in the hotel and discussed their next move to figure out where Jack had gotten to.

"This isn't the first time he's done this," said Owen dismissively, "every once in a while he gets the vapours about something and takes off. He's usually back in a day or so once he realises he needs us. I'm not concerned."

"I'm not going after him," said Lillian, "he made a choice to take off and leave us here. I say we plan our own way to the border."

"That's very disloyal of you," said Ellen.

"So is abandoning your friends."

"Jack is tempestuous and fickle and driven by a need to get one over on others, and I'm getting tired of it," said Owen, "I agree with Lillian that we should find our own way to New South Wales. We still have supplies and plenty of money left from the gold robbery that I made sure was divided up evenly before Jack had his tantrum. I say we get a closed wagon and travel with a low profile. No robberies, nothing. We have nothing to prove, we just need to get out of Victoria."

"What if he comes back while we're gone? How would we know if he is alright?" asked Ellen.

"It's a good point, Brady. Jack Cooper may be arrogant, fickle and stupid, but he's our mate when it all comes down to the quick. We should at least make sure he's safe," said Dan.

Owen frowned. "Fine. How long do we wait to see if he will come back? The longer we stay here the more danger there is of us being caught."

"If we won't go out and look for him, at least give it one more day before we pack up and leave, that's all I ask," Ellen implored.

Reluctantly, the others agreed to remain in town for another day.

***

As the gang were in discussion, Jack Cooper was at that moment pushing his exhausted mare as hard as he could through the bush. The distressed animal was awash with foam and throwing her head around, straining at the bit. Despite his condition, Jack stuck to her like glue, crouching into the saddle as branches struck at him without mercy, slashing and whipping as he barrelled through.

Suddenly, Pathfinder went flying as she snagged her hoof on a root. The horse whinnied with terror as Jack was thrown to the ground. The force immediately knocked him out for a few seconds.

He came around slowly, his vision was blurred and a feeling of everything spinning around him led to a violent expulsion of the contents of his stomach.

He staggered to his feet and stumbled around trying to figure out what had happened. He remembered being on his horse, but he couldn't remember why he was on the ground. He touched his head and felt blood. *Not good...*

He couldn't see Pathfinder, but a cursory examination of the area allowed him to follow a trail of destruction to where the horse was resting. He could tell straight away that she seemed to be lame in her right forelimb. He knew this was a bad sign and had to make an executive decision — take the horse back with him or let her go free.

He had possessed Pathfinder for years and built a strong bond with her, but he knew that she would not be able to keep up the pace he needed. He also remembered enough of what led to the accident to feel some level of guilt that it was his own maltreatment of her that had caused the injury.

He removed the saddle and bridle, stroked her neck and took his leave.

He continued walking until he found a road. He began to question the logic of carrying his gear when he had no horse, and his supplies were all back in town with the rest of the gang. He dumped the saddle and bridle, slung the saddlebags over his shoulders and began walking down the road.

After a half hour of walking, he encountered a mounted trooper. The rider was dressed in his uniform of white skin-tight jodhpurs, leather shako, and blue jacket.

"Morning," said the trooper.

"Yeah. Morning."

"Feeling alright, friend? Looks like you've taken a nasty blow to your head."

Jack stared wordlessly at the trooper for a moment and raised his fingers to his scalp, remembering he had been bleeding. Suddenly he grabbed his revolver from his belt.

"I need your horse. Get down."

The trooper chuckled.

"You must have had a bad knock. Do you really think you can take my horse and get away with it?"

"I don't. But I intend to keep at least a few yards ahead of the consequences, so the horse, if you would be so kind."

The trooper responded by drawing a revolver and levelling it at Jack. It was a more powerful looking piece than Jack's, a mighty Colt Navy with an octagonal muzzle and walnut grip. It was a marvellous weapon, and, in that moment, Jack eyed it with a mix of envy and fear.

"Drop the pistol before I have to drop you," said the trooper.

Jack hesitated and simultaneously the two men fired at each other. There was a pregnant pause as gun smoke cleared and Jack processed the fact he had not been shot. The same could not be said for the mounted trooper whose horse tried to buck its wounded rider off. The trooper was sporting a fresh bullet hole in his throat, at which he clutched with great panic. Finally, the mount succeeded in throwing its rider to the ground where he lost consciousness.

Jack was quick in picking up the dropped revolver and searched the trooper's body, taking his belt and sabre from his waist, as well as the belt and cartouche from across his chest. He then approached the horse, a jittery old nag, and calmed it before mounting. His gaze lingered on the dead man.

I wonder what his name is... Was... Seems like I should know the name of a man I've killed.

He did not dwell on his thoughts and spurred the horse on to Rochester.

Eleven

It was late in the evening when Ellen was roused by a rapping on the door to the room she shared with Lillian. She answered it and was relieved to see Jack on the other side. He looked worse for wear with his clothes torn and bloodstained, his sleek black hair tousled untidily and somewhat matted by dried blood. There was a haunted look in his eyes that told her he was not in a good way. Quietly she slipped out of the room and closed the door behind her.

"What is it?" she asked.

"There was trouble while I was out. There was bloodshed. We have to get going."

"Bloodshed?"

"A trooper... Another fellow with darbies... I can't remember. Pathfinder is gone. I shot those men, Nellie. I know for sure the trooper is dead, I saw him die."

Ellen was speechless. She couldn't quite process what she was being told.

"How?"

"He tried to shoot me. What was I supposed to do, just lie down so he could kill me on the spot?"

"Where were you?"

"I don't know. Somewhere north of here. We need to go before the whole place is swarming with traps."

Ellen's head began to spin. Her concern gave way to anger.

"After you abandoned us, supposedly because you were so aggrieved by what Lillian did, you have the temerity to come back here having done worse and *we* have to run away because of it? What has gotten into you Jack?"

"Nothing has gotten into me. It's them that kept the murder a secret from me. They lied. You do you realise that Lillian murdered that man, Churchley, don't you?"

"Of course. I don't condone it, but she had her reasons for wanting to get revenge and I know that killing him wasn't her intention, but it's what happened. I don't know if I could say the same about you. If we're a gang, we need to look after each other even if we don't agree with the choices they have made — and that includes you."

Jack stood seething.

"They didn't tell me what they knew! Why did they hide things from me? They're up to something, Nellie."

Ellen grew irritated by Jack's petulance.

"Don't you 'Nellie' me. Maybe they didn't feel safe to tell you. I suppose they were right to be worried about how you would respond. We're tired of you making us all uproot and move every time you've been spooked by your own shadow, Jack. Frankly, after this little affair I have found myself growing tired of your decisions too. Did you even stop for a second to think about how worried I was?"

"My decisions have kept us alive!"

"Have they? Look at where your decisions got poor Danny. You almost got him killed. Not to mention that I could have died from the infection I picked up by living like an animal just to be with you — not that you seemed to care much beyond it slowing you down. Your decisions are all about you looking out for yourself, and now they've made you a double-dyed murderer! You only have yourself to blame for that."

Jack's face screwed up with rage and he heard a ringing in his ears. Without a thought he swung his hand and slapped Ellen across the face. Ellen barely moved. She merely clenched her jaw and hardened her gaze at Jack. She heard her father's voice echoing in her mind — *never back down...*

+++

As a child, Ellen had been bullied by a local boy and his friends. She always remembered the ringleader, Tommy, a slim and effeminate-looking boy of twelve years, with straight, pale blonde hair that he wore long. He would call her names and throw things at her either as a remedy for his own boredom or to gain some dubious form of respect from his underlings. Ellen never really recalled much about his followers. They were almost one multi-headed beast in her memories, always hanging back to laugh and jeer at her expense and too cowardly to step forward and take ownership of their role in her misery.

Day after day they pelted her with rotten food then beat her up and spat on her. When she ran home from school bawling one day, her father took her to the back of the butcher's shop where the carcasses were hung up and directed her to the pigs.

"Ellen, I want you to hit this swine with all yer might."
Ellen, all of seven years old, struck with an open palm and barely make the body jiggle. Her father then took her hand and curled the fingers into her palm and closed her thumb around them.
"This is yer fist. God gave you this weapon to carry always. We throw it at our foes."
"How can I throw it if it's part of my arm?"
"Like so..."
Ellen stood back and watched her father make a fist with his mighty, meaty paw, draw his arm back and lunge forward as if hurling a shot. The fist collided with the carcass and made it swing on the hook.

"You stand yer ground against those boys. Never back down. If they hit you, hit 'em back twice as hard. They'll soon learn."

As time went on and Ellen practised her fighting in the back of her father's shop, she grew more confident. Finally came the day that she knew she would get her own back.

It was autumn and the leaves on the wild service trees had turned a deep, rusty red. She spotted the boys under a rowan tree throwing stones at a missel thrush that had come to pick at the blood-red berries growing on the branches bedecked with golden leaves.

There were four boys. She immediately recognised Tommy by his hair, and his usual offsider, Derek, who was a squat boy of twelve years with thick, curly brown hair and a wide nose who always smelled slightly oniony. The other two boys she did not know well, but she knew that they were brothers, and their father was the local miller, a wealthy man named Mr. Scott. The elder brother was named Stephen, although Tommy referred to him as "Hen", and he was eleven years old. The younger brother, Robert, was the same age as Ellen, and had the dangerous trait of being a born follower.

Tommy threw a stone at the bird and just missed, causing it to fly away. The other boys jeered at the animal as it departed.

"Leave that bird alone," Ellen shouted.

The boys turned to her, and she saw young Tommy's face break out into a sly grin.

"That's alright," said Tommy, "we've a better bird to target now."

At that he hurled a stone at Ellen, striking her in the head. She remembered her father's words, *never back down*. The pain from the blow made her want to break out in tears, but instead she shoved the pain deep down and continued to walk towards the group.

The boys took much amusement from this and all of them threw stones and sticks at her. Each one of them hurt, but Ellen merely clenched her jaw and held her arm up to protect her eyes.

"The bitch doesn't know when she's licked," said Derek.

Ellen went straight to Derek and stared in his eyes with as much fury as she could muster.

"What did you call me?"

"I called you a bitch. Like a dog."

"You shouldn't have done that."

Without another word, Ellen threw a fist at Derek's jaw. The blow landed heavily, and he spun around. The Scott brothers laughed heartily at his expense. Immediately Derek ran and hid, whimpering. Ellen turned and glared at the brothers.

"Give her a smack, lads, teach her a thing or two," Tommy yelled at his mates. The Scott brothers stopped laughing.

"But she's a girl, Tommy," said Stephen.

"Are you a girl too, Hen? Hit the bitch!"

Ellen could see the doubt on Stephen's face as he tried to decide on what to do.

"Fine. I'll do it myself," said Tommy and he strode across to Ellen and struck her across the face with the back of his hand.

Ellen swung a fist at Tommy.

The boy was quick, though, dodging the blow and striking Ellen around the ear. She turned and lunged at Tommy, grabbing his shirt to hold him in place. She brought her knee up into his crotch and when he crumpled, she punched him in the chest. She became so enraged that she heard a ringing in her ears and for what felt like only a second she blacked out. When she came around Tommy was on the ground and she was on top of him squeezing his throat until he struggled to breathe, her rage giving her strength beyond her size.

The Scott brothers had her by the shoulders, trying to get her off Tommy with little success. Tommy merely lay still in shock, his pretty, butter-wouldn't-melt face was red and bruised, his left eye already swelling from a hefty blow Ellen had landed. As Ellen regained her awareness, she got up of her own accord and spat at Tommy.

She turned sharply to face the Scott brothers and was a frightful sight. Her face was covered in lacerations from being struck with sticks and stones, her hair was wild, and her clothes were filthy and torn.

"You ought to know better," she said sternly, "what would your father say if he knew what you got up to?"

Bobby Scott began to cry, "I'm sorry, Ellen," he sobbed.

"I'm sorry too," said Stephen with a downcast expression.

"You ought to be," said Ellen.

It would have been satisfying for that to have been the end of the issues, but Ellen continued to experience Tommy's wrath for a few more years. The Scott brothers continued to hang around with him, but they never bothered Ellen again. Derek ended up in gaol after Tommy convinced him to try picking the pocket of the local police magistrate for a laugh.

As for Tommy, he enlisted in the British Army and was killed at Dinghai during the First Opium War.

+++

Ellen no longer saw Jack in front of her, she saw Tommy. She balled her hand into a fist and let it fly. Time seemed to slow down as her knuckles drove into Jack's cheek. The blow knocked him sideways, and he slammed into the wall. He stared up in confusion. He was both terrified and furious.

"Don't you *ever* raise a hand to me, Jack Cooper," said Ellen, "I made them all wait here for you. They were ready to take off, but I was foolish enough to think loyalty meant something to you. What a damned fool I've been. You can ride with us over the border, but as soon as we're in the clear you can go to Hell as far as I'm concerned. Get out of my sight."

With that, Ellen turned and went back into her room. Jack stood outside dumbfounded, massaging his face.

**

The next morning Jack updated the gang on what had happened. The response was not what he had hoped for.

"I move that we elect a new leader," said Owen, "it has become clear that the current leadership is unstable and unreliable."

"I think you should do it," said Lillian.

"Hang about," said Dan, "why not me?"

"Do you want to be the leader?" Ellen asked.

"No," Dan replied, "but it would be nice to be considered."

After much discussion, which Jack elected not to engage in, the gang decided to follow Owen and Ellen as joint leaders. Given the news that Jack had effectively cut off their escape route by murdering people near where they were heading, Owen suggested heading south and laying low for a few days to throw the law off their trail before heading back towards the Murray River.

"Admittedly," said Owen, "this will take much longer, but it may be the only option we have to avoid capture given how many troopers will be looking for us up here."

**

That afternoon they set off, Owen and Ellen leading the group and Jack bringing up the rear. He had barely spoken since the decision to oust him from the leadership, even when he had desired to shout down the new plan. He refused to allow the others to see how much his pride had been hurt. He was especially hurt by Owen being the one to not only oust him but to have suggested it in the first place. He had always seen Owen as a follower, a loyal one at that. He now began to suspect that this had been his ambition for a long time.

What Jack did not know is that Owen was absolutely petrified by his newfound responsibility. It was his insistence that the leadership be shared with Ellen, who he felt was more deserving of the rank.

"Are you feeling alright?" Ellen asked, noticing Owen's visible discomfort.

"There has been a lot of change in a very short period," Owen replied.

"My dear, that is a tremendous understatement."

***

It was evening when the gang stopped to set up a camp near Runnymede. A simple campfire was established, and dinner comprised of salt pork and bread, the loaf having been procured from the bakery just prior to departing. Tents were put up and, for the first time, Jack and Ellen slept separately. Instead, Ellen and Lillian shared a tent, as did Dan and Owen, with Jack being put on guard duty overnight as a sort of punishment.

Jack spent the duration of his watch stewing in his self-pity. He could not accept that everyone had turned their back on him after all he had done for them. After all, he reasoned, when he found Lillian, she had just been fired and he took her in to stop her having to explain her pregnancy and unemployment to her family.

When he met Ellen, she was a lonely widow past her prime and he gave her a sense of identity and enthusiasm for life again.

When he found Owen, he was a sundowner dressed in rags, and it was his guidance that allowed him to gain money and a decent living.

When he found Dan, he was drifting from town to town picking pockets and fighting drunks for money. He had given him a sense of purpose and schooled him in the art of highway robbery.

He resented that none of them seemed to acknowledge what he had done, in his estimation, to raise them up from the aimless, pathetic nobodies they were. Without him they were nothing, and he wanted them to know it. Now, he decided, he would teach them a lesson.

For the next few hours, he plotted in his own mind how he would get the others to see the truth. Should he abandon them? Would they understand why he was so angry if he was not there to explain? In the end he found himself thinking in circles and increasingly frustrated. He decided to leave it and let the others come undone by their own hands. Their own incompetence would teach them the lesson far more effectively.

***

In the morning Lillian was the first to emerge from the tent, her bladder in need of relief. She squatted in the bushes and saw Jack near the fire. He was dressed in only his trousers, boots and undershirt. There were still bloodstains on the clothes from his injured head. He held a shotgun in one hand and gazed into the dying embers. The vision that was presented to her through the branches of the bushes was pathetic and portrayed a man whose bad choices had finally caught up to him, but he was desperately trying to deny the reality of his situation.

Once finished, Lillian approached him cautiously.
"You alright, Jack?"

"Good as gold," he replied with a sneer.

"Anything happen overnight?"

"No. If anyone had been onto us the snoring would have given us away. At least *you* got a good night's sleep."

Lillian had not, in fact, had a good night's sleep and resented the implication that she was somehow ungrateful or oblivious to the risk she put others in by simply sleeping.

"You know, for someone who wants to be seen as some kind of gentleman who is chivalrous and clever, you have a tendency to be nothing short of stupid and cruel."

Jack glared at Lillian.

"You'd know all about stupid and cruel, wouldn't you?"

"I do when I'm looking at it sulking in its underwear. What is it you want from us?" Lillian asked.

"A little appreciation for what I have done for you wouldn't go astray."

"And what would be sufficient to show our appreciation? Do you want me to lay on my back with my legs apart for you?"

"Don't be so vulgar."

"Then what do you want?"

Jack stood and loomed over Lillian.

"Everything was fine until I made the mistake of bringing you in. You're nothing but trouble and you've turned everyone against me. I wish I had just gone straight past you that day. Or even better, put a bullet in you after that business at the Churchley farm. I could have stopped a lot more bloodshed and misery."

Lillian tried to even the height difference, although she was still a few inches shorter than Jack even on tip-toes.

"You want me dead?"

"No point in that now; it'll happen soon, though. We're stuck with you for now. But once we get to New South Wales I never want to see your face again."

"You think I ruined your life, hey? I never would have been dismissed if not for you robbing the Churchleys in the first place. I was almost killed by Mrs. Churchley because of you robbing her. You owed me."

"If it was all my fault then why did you shoot them?" Jack asked smugly.

"Why did you shoot the trooper and the old man?"

"My life was in danger, yours wasn't. There's a difference. If you're too stupid to understand that, it isn't up to me to explain it."

"You threatened me. Maybe I should have shot you? You know I have it in me to do it, so I would be *really* damned careful about the next thing that comes out of that stinking mouth of yours."

The pair glared at each other, neither willing to be the first to back down. It was Ellen who intervened, having heard the commotion from inside the tent.

"Enough," she said, "things are hard enough without you two getting at each other's throats."

Lillian backed down and returned to the tent. Jack remained in place.

"Ellen," Jack said, "I'm sorry about what happened."

"You mean when you hit me or when you convinced me to throw away my life to follow you around like a lost puppy?"

"I shouldn't have hit you."

Ellen scowled. "No, you shouldn't have. You shouldn't have abandoned us either. Nor should you have murdered people, forcing us to go back the other way when we were barely a day from making our escape over the border. Yet, that's what you did. Am I meant to pretend that all didn't happen?"

Jack shifted uncomfortably.

"It was self-defence, Ellen."

"I don't care if you thought you were protecting yourself. That's not the point," Ellen sighed.

"Then what is the point?"

"The point is that you're a hypocrite and your selfishness has put us all at much greater risk and you're too much of a child to accept responsibility."

Jack felt like he was cornered and desperate for a way out.

"What do you want me to do?"

"It's simple," said Ellen, "hold yourself to the same standards you hold everyone else to. They all would have taken bullets for you, Jack, but you showed them that you wouldn't do the same for them. Loyalty and respect can take years to build, but seconds to destroy."

Jack sat by the glowing embers of the dying fire and held his head in his hands and sighed.

"Alright."

Ellen was unmoved.

"A leopard never changes its spots," said Ellen, "but I would love you to prove me wrong."

***

The gang proceeded along the Campaspe River for the next few days, only stopping to camp overnight. Having no horse of his own, Jack was forced to ride Tombstone. They found themselves on the edge of the McIvor goldfields near the foot of Mount Ida. They looked up at the vast dome one and a half thousand feet up, covered in bushy green trees as they approached the township of Heathcote, through which they intended to pass.

Though the miners had mostly gone, there had already been much investment in establishing a township based on the prospect of large gold yields and there were numerous features in the town demonstrating the anticipated importance of this spot including a grand hospital with white pillars framing the doors, numerous shops, police barracks, gardens, churches and a powder magazine. Domiciles dotted the landscape, which was flat and otherwise bare in between the slopes and gullies.

They passed a large racecourse and cattle yards as they moved deeper into the town. Heading east through the allotments took them towards the hospital and the courthouse. The latter was a huge white stone building that seemed altogether too grand for the quiet village around it. The gang tried to be inconspicuous as they rode past.

As they approached the Heathcote Hotel, Jack spotted a foot constable emerging from the building and walking to the roadside. He gazed up as the group passed and eyed them suspiciously, particularly Jack who he seemed to recognise. He then noted the blood on Jack's clothing, and the peacock feathers in their hatbands.

"You there, hold up," the constable shouted.

Immediately Jack drew the Colt revolver he had purloined from the slain trooper and aimed it at the policeman. Owen saw this and immediately rode alongside Jack and struck Tombstone on the flank. It took off down the street at a gallop, Jack roaring in frustration as he tried to control the beast.

Owen turned to the rest of the gang, "Go!"

They all set off as fast as their mounts could go. The constable stood dumbfounded with his heart racing by the road. He was regretting his decision not to take his revolver with him when he popped in to visit the staff at the hotel, but thankful for the impulsive bushranger that had just saved his life.

The gang rode hard until they were outside of the town limits. When they finally drew to a halt Jack dismounted and stormed over to Owen.

"You idiot! The gun wasn't even loaded. Look," Jack thrust the Colt into Owen's hand. He half-cocked it and spun the barrel. He cocked it fully and pulled the trigger — it clicked impotently.

"There was no need to pull the damned thing out," said Owen.

"I was getting the drop on him to keep him covered while you lot got away."

"Given your track record, can you blame me for doubting?" Owen replied.

"Get back on your horses," Ellen snapped, "we don't have time for this nonsense."

As they bid farewell to Heathcote, Ellen saw a large gum tree covered in posters. She paused upon seeing a fresh calico poster bearing the word REWARD in bold block letters. Underneath she could read her name, Lillian's and Jack's along with descriptions of Dan and Owen in a long passage under the words ROBBERY AND MURDER, and a price — £2000. She snatched it off the bark and hurried to catch up with the others.

"Everyone," Ellen announced, "I have news."

She presented the wanted poster to the group. Dan leaned in close to read the poster.

"£2000 reward," he exclaimed.

"This is it," said Owen, "there's nothing here for us now."

Ellen let the words sink in. *Nothing here for us now.* She realised that for the past few months, ever since Jack and the boys had forced their way into her life, this was what she had been running away from. She realised that there was nothing keeping her in this wretched colony. Her husband was dead. One daughter was over the border, one was in another country, her son had vanished into thin air. Even her dog was dead. Even if she had wanted to return to the selection she was only biding time until she was evicted anyway.

"Well, boss," said Jack to Ellen, "where do we go from here?"

"This changes nothing," she replied, "we cross that border and we burn the fucking bridge if we have to. Are we in this together?"

She looked around at the determined faces that surrounded her. Each member of the gang nodded, even Jack. Ellen wondered if there was hope for him yet.

This was her new family — even Jack, who all her instincts were telling her was bad news. She owed them nothing, but she couldn't even contemplate abandoning them now. Whatever was on the other side of that horizon, for better or for worse, they would all confront it together.

To be continued...

About the Author

Aidan Phelan is an independent writer and is the writer and historian for *A Guide to Australian Bushranging*, a website that has been bringing Australia's outlaw heritage to a worldwide audience since 2017. Since 2020 he has released two editions of his novel *Glenrowan*, *Aaron Sherritt: Persona non Grata*, *Bushranging Tales: Volume One*, and his edit of William Westwood's autobiography, published as *William Westwood: In His Own Words*. He is also a member of the Australian Crime Writers Association and has edited and illustrated books for other authors including Georgina Stones and Judy Lawson.

Also by this author

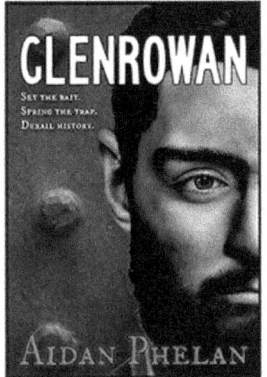

The Kelly Gang have been on the run for months and are the most wanted men in the British Empire. No expense has been spared in the hunt to bring them to justice. With the introduction of highly specialised trackers to hunt them and rumours of treachery amongst their supporters, the outlaws are desperate. Soon their leader, Ned Kelly, will hatch a plan that will not only bring an end to the pursuit, but will leave an indelible mark on the history of Australia. *Glenrowan* is the story of how one man's burning obsession can have far reaching consequences, and how a tiny town between towns became as iconic as Gettysburg or Waterloo.

Bushranging Tales: Volume One depicts real cases of Australian bushranging through a series of short stories, biographies, original illustrations and archival material. Discover thrilling and horrifying true stories of robbery, prison escape and murder, featuring events from the lives of Michael Howe, Matthew Brady, Martin Cash, Daniel Morgan, Johnny Gilbert, Harry Power, Captain Thunderbolt, Captain Moonlite and Ned Kelly.

Aaron Sherritt: Persona non Grata explores a perspective of the hunt for the Kelly Gang, and Sherritt's role in it, that has been rarely examined. You will learn how internal politics led to Aaron Sherritt's tragic demise. In popular perception he has been portrayed as a traitor, a double-agent, or a victim of false accusations through over 140 years of slander, myths and misinformation.

Did Aaron Sherritt really betray his friends for money?
Were there others who were more deserving of such scorn and suspicion?
How did Aaron Sherritt go from everyone's mate to *persona non grata*?